凱信企管

用對的方法充實自己，
讓人生變得更美好！

凱信企管

用對的方法充實自己，
讓人生變得更美好！

訂了機票，就出發！
旅行不能忘記帶的英語百寶袋

Survival English for Travelers

User's Guide
使用說明

英文不合文法也沒關係～～
輕鬆說出口 ╳ 老外聽得懂，就是旅人必備英文！
113 個旅遊狀況、逾 3000 個旅遊常用句，你需要的通通有！

01

迷你句＋完整句隨你說，
輕鬆 ╳ 正式場合都OK！
　　出國旅遊≠英文考試，迷你句教你輕鬆
表達，就算不合句型＆文法，只要對方聽得
懂，就是100分的旅遊英語！文法正確的完
整句一起學，正式場合也能輕鬆應對！

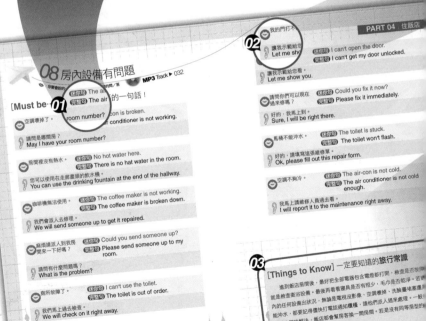

PART 04 住飯店

02
我的門打不開。
讓我示範給您看。 Let me sho
迷你句 I can't open the door.
完整句 I can't get my door unlocked.

請讓我示範給您。
Let me show you.

01
[Must be... 的一句話！

🗨 空調壞掉了。
room number?
迷你句 The air
完整句 ...on is broken.
...conditioner is not working.

👂 請問是哪間房？
May I have your room number?

🗨 房間裡沒有熱水。 迷你句 No hot water here.
完整句 There is no hot water in the room.

👂 您可以使用在走廊盡頭的飲水機。
You can use the drinking fountain at the end of the hallway.

🗨 咖啡機無法使用。 迷你句 The coffee maker is not working.
完整句 The coffee maker is broken down.

👂 我們會派人去修理。
We will send someone up to get it repaired.

🗨 麻煩請派人到我房間來一下好嗎？ 迷你句 Could you send someone up?
完整句 Please send someone up to my room.

👂 請問有什麼問題嗎？
What is the problem?

🗨 廁所故障了。 迷你句 I can't use the toilet.
完整句 The toilet is out of order.

👂 我們馬上過去檢查。
We will check on it right away.

🗨 請問你們可以現在過來修嗎？ 迷你句 Could you fix it now?
完整句 Please fix it immediately.

👂 好的，我馬上到。
Sure, I will be right there.

🗨 馬桶不能沖水。 迷你句 The toilet is stuck.
完整句 The toilet won't flash.

👂 好的，請填寫這張維修單。
Ok, please fill out this repair form.

🗨 空調不夠冷。 迷你句 The air-con is not cold.
完整句 The air conditioner is not cold enough.

👂 我馬上請維修人員過來看。
I will report it to the maintenance right away.

08 房內設備有問題
MP3 Track ▶ 032

03
[Things to Know] 一定要知道的旅行常識

進到飯店房間後，最好把全部電器包含電燈都打開，檢查是否故障，
就是檢查衛浴設備，最後再看看器具是否有短少，毛巾是否乾淨。若使
內的任何設備出狀況，無論是電視沒影像、空調壞掉、洗臉臺垃圾還
能沖水，都要記得儘快打電話通知櫃檯，請他們派人過來處理。一般
無辦法即時解決，飯店都會幫房客換一間房間。若是沒有同等房型的
時候免費升等恐怕是必要的。

108

○ 我的門打不~

◊ 讓我示範給您看
Let me show

請問你們

02 老外應答絕對聽懂，
能聽 ╳ 會說 = 玩得盡興！

只會「說英文」還不夠，問路／殺價／
搭訕都要聽得懂，才會最開心！每個情境句
下方，舉出老外會回應的句子，雞同鴨講掰
掰，要你真正能聽又會說！

03 旅遊更便利～加碼附上旅遊
常用句型／生字速查／文化常識！

依各情境狀況交替補充三種不同元素：1. 旅遊常
用句型，套入馬上用！2. 使用頻率高的
旅遊生字速看！3. 旅遊文化常識訊息報你知！最完整
的資訊都給你，不用東查西找，省時間玩更多！

[Vocabulary] 生字**不用另外查字典！**

01 （登機）報到 check-in

02 登機櫃檯 counter

04 靠窗 by window

06 登機證 boarding pa

seat

機票 ticket

[Things to Know] 一定要知道的**旅行常識**

進到飯店房間後，最好把全部電器包含電燈都打開，檢查是否故障
就是檢查衛浴設備。最後再看看寢具是否有短少，毛巾是否乾淨。若遇到
狀況，無論是電視沒影像、空調壞掉、洗臉臺堵塞還是
櫃檯，請他們派人過來處理。一般如

[Words to Use] 替換字放空格，**一句多用!!**

• _____故障了。
The _____ is out of order.

01 廁所 toilet

02 空調 air conditione

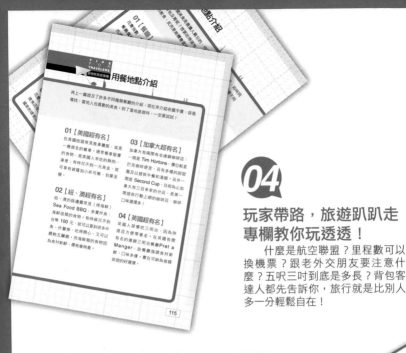

TIPS FOR TRAVELERS

各地用餐地點介紹 **用餐地點介紹**

再上一篇就及了許多不同種類餐廳的介紹，現在來介紹各國平價、容易尋找、當地人也喜歡的美食。到了當地旅遊時，一定要試試！

01【美國超有名】
在美國街頭常見推車攤販，或是一應俱全的餐車，通常賣著販賣的食物，是美國人常吃的熱狗、漢堡，有時花不到一元美金，就可享有披薩或加小林可樂，划算至極。

02【紐、澳超有名】
紐、澳的路邊攤常見！Sea Food BBQ、多實炸魚、海鮮這類的食物，有時候花不到台幣 100 元，就可以買到很多炸魚、炸薯條，吃得開心，又可以攝取五臟廟。而海鮮新鮮的食物因為食材新鮮，價格會銷售。

03【加拿大超有名】
加拿大有兩間有名連鎖咖啡店：一間是 Tim Hortons，價位較平實的咖啡研究，另有多樣的甜甜圈及可提供午餐和湯類。另外一間是 Second Cup，目前為止加拿大有三百多家的分店，是實一間賣供行動上網的咖啡店，咖啡口味選擇多！

04【英國超有名】
英國人習慣吃三明治，因為快速且方便帶著走。在英國有間有名的連鎖三明治餐廳Pret a Manger。話多嚴選調食材新鮮、口味多樣，實在可以納為省錢旅遊的好選擇。

115

04

玩家帶路，旅遊趴趴走
專欄教你玩透透！

什麼是航空聯盟？里程數可以換機票？跟老外交朋友要注意什麼？五呎三吋到底是多長？背包客達人都先告訴你，旅行就是比別人多一分輕鬆自在！

增訂版全新收錄
學一句可以用好幾次！
旅遊情境句型+超多替換字，
任你隨心所欲應用。

每個PART精選6個旅遊超好用的情境必備句型，搭配可替換語彙，想怎麼講都可以，舉一反三就是這麼簡單！

旅遊常用句型＋超多替換字，套入馬上用！

PART 02 飛機上

兌換時去兌換嗎　付費講
● 你打算接受　　　　？
Do you take　　　?
國 美金 US dollars
國 人民幣 Renminbi (RMB)
國 日幣 Japanese yens
國 新台幣 New Taiwan dollars
國 信用卡 credit cards

旅遊常用句型＋超多替換字，套入馬上用！

PART 03 抵達入境

入境過海關 (1)
● 我是來過遊　　　的。
I'm here　　.
國 看 for sightseeing
國 洽商 on business
國 探親友 to visit a friend
國 度假 on vacation
國 轉機 transit

入境過海關 (2)
● 拜訪期間我會住在　　　。
I will be staying　　during my visit.
國 親友家 at my friend's place
國 溫泉飯店 in the Grand Hotel
國 學校宿舍 in the school dormitory
國 青年旅舍 at my auntie's
國 青年旅館 in a youth hostel
國 員工宿舍 in the staff dorm

轉機
● 我想是在轉機中停去　　　。

行李不見了　沒有出現在行李轉送帶上。
● 我的　　didn't show up on the luggage carousel.
My　　luggage
國 行李箱 suitcase
國 託運行李 checked luggage
國 背包 bag
國 旅行袋 travel bag
國 後背包 backpack

在新世紀結樓點
● 可以請您告訴我怎麼去　　　嗎？
Can you tell me how to get to　　?
國 第一航廈 International Terminal 1
國 出境大廳 the departure lounge
國 三十二號登機門 Gate 32
國 入境大廳 the arrival...

旅遊常用句型，套入馬上用！

櫃台報到劃位
● 我比較喜歡　　。
I prefer a/an
國 靠窗位 window
國 緊急出口位 emergency...
國 最前排 bulkhead

來逛免稅商店
● 免稅商店裡的　　　實在很便宜。
　　in the duty-free shop are a ste...
國 巧克力 Chocolates
國 酒類 Liquors
國 香水 Perfumes
國 香煙 Cigarette
國 化妝品 Cosm...
國 設計師名牌精品 D...

托運行李
過　　　也可以託運嗎？
an I check in this
國 (長) 紙箱 cardboard box
國 畫作 painting
國 嬰兒車 baby trolley

護照、簽證有問題
● 我沒注意到我的　　過期了。
I didn't notice that my　　has ex...
國 護照 passport
國 簽證 visa
國 學生簽證 student visa
國 香港 visa
國 觀光英語 tour...

　　旅外多年，我卻不曾覺得離台灣很遙遠，因為我在加拿大的家，是台灣親友來旅遊時的第一站，所以接待台灣來的親朋好友，也是我平時的任務之一。飛越了一個太平洋，身心俱疲的親朋好友，往往都想要先休息一下，因為旅遊的興致暫時都被舟車勞頓給消磨了。他們最常告訴我：搭飛機已經很累了，還要用英文吃力地說話、用力聽懂對方說什麼，讓他們在一開始就被出國旅遊嚇到了，說英文、弄懂情況，真的好辛苦，出國旅遊根本就不好玩！還有很多英文程度不差的朋友，也被旅遊英文弄得頭痛，因為他們說英文時考慮太多，認為文法、句型絕對不能出錯，結果弄得自己很緊張，老外在一旁也替他們捏一把冷汗。為了語言、搞懂情況而弄得頭昏腦脹，實在太辛苦，也浪費了旅行可以帶給我們的養分。

　　這一次，很高興可以再次跟凱信出版社合作，可以根據自己和親友互動的經驗，重新整理出 113 個最常遇到的旅遊情境，並且替每個常用句，找出當地人可能會說的回應，希望每個出國旅行的朋友，能夠不必再為英文煩惱，輕鬆與老外對談，對所有旅遊狀況都能從容應對，好好享受得來不易的假期。這次凱信出版社的編輯，還找了踏遍世界五大洲的背包客達人志暉一起合作，提供每個旅行者都需要的旅遊常識，讓大家不再對轉機、飛機里程，甚至是國外單位重量……等旅行的眉角一頭霧水。語言是用來溝通的，本來就沒有這麼可怕，是考試制度讓語言學習之路，變得艱困難行。希望本書能替大家的旅行增色，不再為語言隔閡煩惱，能夠開始享受與當地人、新朋友閒聊的放鬆感，好好享受假期！

黃文姝

Preface

　　雖然非英文本科系出身，英文程度也只是像一般人一樣普通，但是我還是很喜歡四處旅遊，英文對我來說並不是一個阻礙。會有這樣的理念，是因為在非洲甘比亞的外交替代役生活，我才真正發現語言的用處：語言並非只是用來考試的，應該是用來與人溝通，也應該是用來生活的。我開始了解到，並沒有所謂的「破英文」，只有不敢說、不知道怎麼說的心態。後來至美國賓州讀研究所、工作，我發現即使是美國人，也常常使用文法不正確的句子，因為就和我們說中文一樣，只是用來與人來往、交談、溝通。語言的確博大精深，也有它的美感和研究價值，但若要用來放鬆旅遊或生活，就的確不需要著墨在太微小的文法概念上。來到美國後，因為沒有升學考試的壓力，我就這樣每天說著不是 100% 正確的英文，聽力、口說卻也進步了不少。我不是在鼓吹錯誤的英文用法，只是認為在生活和旅遊的領域當中，語言應該是幫助我們認識世界的工具，而非只是一門高高在上的學理。

　　這次與凱信出版社的編輯合作，我特別補充了一些大家需要知道的旅遊常識，讓大家出門在外旅遊，不用太費神蒐集資訊，只需要好好地運用時間、享受假期、體驗當地文化。希望每位讀者，都能先忘掉「學英文就是為了考試得高分」的觀念，把英文當成可以幫你輕鬆旅行的工具，而不是一個讓你不敢開口的旅行絆腳石。祝福每位旅行者，都用美麗的心看見美麗的人、事、物，好好品味旅行帶來的禮物。

溫志暉

CONTENTS
目錄

出發前～一定要知道的基本會話！

PART 01 到機場

PART 02 飛機上

PART 03 抵達機場

PART 04 住飯店

PART 05 吃四方

PART 06 交通工具

PART 07 到處玩

PART 08 到處買

PART 09 交朋友

PART 10 通訊聯繫

PART 11 緊急狀況

附錄～不可不看的旅遊資訊！

出發前～
一定要知道的
基本會話！

✪打招呼

◉ 最常這樣說

01	嗨！	Hi!
02	你好嗎？	How are you?
03	哈囉！	Hello!
04	你好！	Good day!

◉ 對話演練

A：你好嗎？	How are you?
B：我很好。	I'm good.

✪早安／晚安

◉ 最常這樣說

01	早安！	Good morning!
02	早！	Morning.
03	（傍晚、晚餐時間）晚安！	Good evening.
04	（深夜、晚餐之後）晚安！	Good night.

◉ 對話演練

A：早安！	Good Morning!
B：早啊。	Morning.

✪ 很高興認識你／見到你

◉ 最常這樣說

01	很高興認識你。	Nice to meet you.
02	認識你很榮幸。	Pleasure to meet you.
03	沒想到會遇到你！	What a surprise!
04	好久不見。	It's been a while.

◉ 對話演練

A：很高興認識你。	Nice to meet you.
B：我也是。	Me, too.

✪ 最近好嗎？

◉ 最常這樣說

01	最近好嗎？	What's up?
02	最近怎麼樣？	How is it going?
03	你好嗎？	How are you?
04	過得好嗎？	How have you been?

◉ 對話演練

A：最近怎麼樣？	How is it going?
B：很好。	Pretty good.

☆謝謝

◉ 最常這樣說

01	非常謝謝你。	Thank you so much.
02	謝謝。	Thanks.
03	很謝謝你。	Thanks a lot.
04	十分感謝。	Thanks a million.

◉ 對話演練

| A：很謝謝你。 | Thanks a lot. |
| B：不客氣啦。 | Don't mention it. |

☆對不起／不好意思

◉ 最常這樣說

01	對不起。	I'm sorry.
02	我道歉。	I apologize.
03	不好意思。	Excuse me.
04	是我的錯。	It's my fault.

◉ 對話演練

| A：對不起。 | I'm sorry. |
| B：沒關係。 | Never mind. |

03 是／不是怎麼說

☆是的

◉ 最常這樣説

01	你可以這樣做。	Yes, you can.
02	沒錯，這是我的。	Yes, it's mine.
03	是的，我喜歡。	Yes, I like it.
04	好的。	Okay.

◉ 對話演練

A：請出示護照。	Could you show me your passport?
B：好的。	Okay.

☆不是

◉ 最常這樣説

01	你不可以這樣做。	No, you can't.
02	這不是我的。	No, It's not mine.
03	我不喜歡。	No, I don't like it.
04	不用，謝謝。	No, thanks.

◉ 對話演練

A：要參加我們的行程嗎？	Do you want to join the tour?
B：不要，謝謝。	No, thanks.

04 不太明白時怎麼説

☯我不知道/我不明白

◉ 最常這樣説

01	我不知道。	I don't know.
02	我不確定。	I'm not sure.
03	我不明白。	I don't understand.
04	我有點搞混了。	I'm confused.

◉ 對話演練

A：你有聽懂嗎？	Are you following?
B：我不明白。	I don't understand.

☯我不會説英文

◉ 最常這樣説

01	你會説中文嗎？	Do you speak Chinese?
02	我不會説英文。	I don't speak English.
03	我會説中文。	I speak Chinese.
04	我會説日文。	I speak Japanese.

◉ 對話演練

A：你會説英文嗎？	Do you speak English?
B：我説中文。	I speak Chinese.

05 各種疑問怎麼說

✪如何？

◉ 最常這樣說

01	健行之旅如何？	How was the hiking?
02	感覺怎麼樣？	How are you feeling?
03	你喜歡這個嗎？	How do you like it?
04	台灣怎麼樣？	How is Taiwan?

◉ 對話演練

A：健行之旅如何？	How was the hiking?
B：還不錯。	It was quite nice.

✪在哪裡？

◉ 最常這樣說

01	廁所在哪裡？	Where is the restroom?
02	你的包包放在哪裡了？	Where do you put your bag?
03	那家酒館在哪裡？	Where's that bar?
04	公車站在哪裡？	Where's the bus station?

◉ 對話演練

A：廁所在哪裡？	Where is the restroom?
B：在轉角那裡。	It's around the corner.

✪什麼？

◉ 最常這樣説

01	你叫什麼名字？	What's your name?
02	你帶了什麼？	What are you bringing with?
03	你是做什麼工作的？	What do you do for a living?
04	地板上那個是什麼？	What's that on the floor?

◉ 對話演練

A：你叫什麼名字？	What's your name?
B：我的名字是彼得·潘。	My name is Peter Pan.

✪為什麼？

◉ 最常這樣説

01	你為什麼遲到了？	Why are you late?
02	為什麼不去歐洲旅行？	Why don't you go travel around Europe?
03	為什麼那麼貴？	Why is the price so high?
04	你為什麼要那樣説？	Why did you say that?

◉ 對話演練

A：你為什麼遲到了？	Why are you late?
B：路上塞車了。	There is traffic jam on the way.

✪誰？

◉ 最常這樣說

01	那個女孩是誰？	Who is that girl?
02	你打算和誰一起去？	Who are you going with?
03	昨晚你跟誰在一起？	Who are you with last night?
04	誰要去看電影？	Who is going to the movies?

◉ 對話演練

A：那個女孩是誰？	Who is that girl?
B：是我同學。	She is my classmate.

✪什麼時候？

◉ 最常這樣說

01	什麼時候出發去上海？	When are you leaving for Shanghai?
02	你什麼時候會在愛丁堡？	When will you be in Edinburgh?
03	你什麼時候離開的？	When did you left?
04	公車什麼時候會來？	When will the bus come?

◉ 對話演練

A：你什麼時候會在愛丁堡？	When will you be in Edinburgh?
B：下個月就會到。	I 'll be there next month.

☺受傷／遇到搶劫

◉ 最常這樣說

01	我受傷了！	I'm hurt!
02	叫救護車！	Call the ambulance!
03	有人搶劫！	Somebody robbed me!
04	抓住他！	Get that guy for me!

◉ 對話演練

| A：有人昏倒了！ | Someone passed out! |
| B：叫救護車！ | Call the ambulance! |

☺車禍／事故

◉ 最常這樣說

01	救命！	Help!
02	失火了！	Fire!
03	快打119！	Call 911!
04	我在這裡！快來救我！	I'm here! Come save me!

◉ 對話演練

| A：十字路口發生車禍了！ | There's a car accident at the crossroads! |
| B：快叫警察！ | Call 911! |

07 數字／時間怎麼說

✪ 數字

◉ 數字怎麼說

1	one	15	fifteen
2	two	19	nineteen
3	three	20	twenty
4	four	23	twenty-three
5	five	34	thirty-four
6	six	45	forty-five
7	seven	56	fifty-six
8	eight	67	sixty-seven
9	nine	78	seventy-eight
10	ten	89	eighty-nine
11	eleven	91	ninty-one
12	twelve	370	three hundred and seventy
13	thirteen	1300	one thousand three hundred
14	fourteen	22000	twenty-two thousand

◉ 大單位怎麼看

百	100	hundred
千	1,000	thousand
百萬	1,000,000	million
十億	1,000,000,000	billion

✪ 數字

◉ 最常這樣説

01	我 23 歲。	I'm twenty-three years old.
02	一份餐點美金 6 塊錢。	A meal costs six dollars.
03	我會在這裡待三個禮拜。	I will be here for three weeks.
04	我們買了兩瓶啤酒。	We bought two cans of beers.

◉ 對話演練

A：一份餐點多少錢？	What's the price of this meal?
B：一份美金 6 塊錢。	A meal costs six dollars.

✪ 時間

◉ 最常這樣説

01	下午 3 點了。	It's three o'clock p.m.
02	早上 5 點 15 分要到機場。	We have to be at the airport at five fifteen in the morning.
03	最後一班火車是晚上 11 點。	The latest train is at eleven at night.
04	我們今天早上 7 點半就起床了。	We woke up at seven thirty this morning.

◉ 對話演練

A：現在幾點了？	What time is it now?
B：下午 3 點了。	It's three o'clock p.m.

08 月分／日期怎麼說

✪月分

◉ 月分怎麼說

一月	**January**	七月	**July**
二月	**February**	八月	**August**
三月	**March**	九月	**September**
四月	**April**	十月	**October**
五月	**May**	十一月	**November**
六月	**June**	十二月	**December**

✪日期的說法

◉ 最常這樣說

01	我的生日是 1980 年 10 月 8 日。	**I was born in October the eighth, nineteen eighty.**
02	今天是2011年12月24號。	**It's December twenty-forth, two thousand eleven.**
03	我九月分出生的。	**I was born in September.**
04	澳洲的八月是冬天。	**In Australia, it's winter in August.**

◉ 對話演練

A：今天幾號？	**What's the date today?**
B：2011年12月24日。	**It's December twenty-forth, two thousand eleven.**

✿星期

◉ 星期怎麼説

星期一	**Monday**	星期五	**Friday**
星期二	**Tuesday**	星期六	**Saturday**
星期三	**Wednesday**	星期日	**Sunday**
星期四	**Thursday**		

◉ 最常這樣説

01	今天星期五。	It's Friday.
02	蘇菲亞下週日結婚。	Sophia's wedding is on next Sunday.
03	博物館星期一休館。	The museum are closed on Monday.
04	歡送派對在星期五下午舉行。	The farewell party is on Friday afternoon.

◉ 對話演練

A：今天星期幾？	What's the day today?
B：今天星期五。	It's Friday.

✿日期的寫法

◉ 2016年9月15日

01	9/15/2016（美式）	Sep. the 15th, 2016
02	15/9/2016 （英式）	15th September, 2016

PART 01
到機場

01 櫃台報到劃位

👄 : 你要會說的一句話　　 👂 : 你會聽到的問／答

MP3 Track ▶ 001

[Must be...] 這個時候最需要的一句話！

👄 請問登記櫃檯在哪裡？
迷你句 Where to check-in?
完整句 Where is the check-in counter?

👂 登記櫃台就在前方。
The check-in counter is over there.

👄 我想要坐靠窗的位置。
迷你句 A seat by the window, please.
完整句 I want a window seat, please.

👂 沒問題，讓我幫您查一下。
Ok, let me check if there are seats available.

👄 我要辦理我的登機證。
迷你句 My boarding pass, please.
完整句 May I have my boarding pass now?

👂 好的，請給我您的護照和機票。
Ok, please give me your passport and ticket.

👄 我的手續已經辦好了嗎？
迷你句 Am I ready to go?
完整句 Am I done with all the procedures?

👂 確認您的文件無誤就沒問題了。
If the information is correct, then you are all set.

👄 我想要更改班機。
迷你句 Change the flight, please.
完整句 I'd like to change my flight, please.

👂 沒問題，請給我您的護照。
Ok, please give me your passport.

😙 請問往法國的班機會準時起飛嗎？

迷你句 How is the flight to France?

完整句 Will the flight to France be on time?

😌 是的，往法國的班機會準時起飛。
Yes, the flight will be on time.

😙 請問這班飛機是全面禁菸的嗎？

迷你句 Non-smoking flight?

完整句 Is this a non-smoking flight?

😌 是的，這班飛機全面禁菸。
Yes, this is a non-smoking flight.

😙 請問什麼時候開始登機？

迷你句 When will boarding start?

完整句 When is the time for boarding?

😌 請在飛機起飛前半個小時登機。
Boarding time is 30 minutes before departure.

😙 請問588班機的登機門是幾號？

迷你句 Gate number for flight 588?

完整句 What is the gate number for 588 flight?

😌 588班機的登機門是69號。
The gate number for flight 588 is No.69.

[Vocabulary] 生字不用另外查字典！

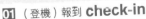

01 （登機）報到 check-in

02 登機櫃檯 counter

03 座位 seat

04 靠窗 by window

05 靠走道 by aisle

06 登機證 boarding pass

07 護照 passport

08 機票 ticket

09 班機 flight

10 準時 on time

11 登機門 gate

12 登機 boarding

031

[Must be...] 這個時候最需要的一句話！

👄 我想托運這兩件行李。

迷你句 Two pieces, please.

完整句 I need to check in these two pieces of luggage, please.

👂 好的，請填寫一下表格。
Ok, fill out this form, please.

👄 我沒有任何托運行李，只有隨身的。

迷你句 I have only a carry-on with me.

完整句 I don't have any luggage to check in, just carry-on.

👂 好的，請讓我確認一下隨身行李的大小。
Ok, let me check the size of your carry-on.

👄 請問可以優先放我的行李嗎？

迷你句 Priority tag?

完整句 Can you put my luggage as priority, please?

👂 好的，讓我註明一下。
Ok, let me make a note.

👄 行李超重要收費多少？

迷你句 How much for overweight luggage?

完整句 How much money do you charge if it's overweight?

👂 每多一公斤要加收 10 元美金。
It costs 10 dollars per kilogram.

👄 請問我應該在哪個櫃台辦理行李托運？

迷你句 Where to check in my luggage?

完整句 Which counter should I go to have my luggage checked in?

👂 請在10號櫃台辦理行李托運。
Please check in your luggage at counter No.10.

我的行李裡有貴重的物品，可以請你們特別小心嗎？

（迷你句）Some precious things are inside.

（完整句）I have some precious things inside it, could you take care of it?

好的，我會貼上『易碎物品』的標籤。
Sure, I'll put a "fragile" sticker on it.

請問一件行李限重多少？

（迷你句）How many kilograms are ok?

（完整句）How many kilograms are available for one luggage?

免費行李托運量是20公斤。
The free baggage allowance is 20 kilograms.

請問我可以托運幾件行李？

（迷你句）How many pieces of luggage are ok?

（完整句）How many pieces of luggage can I check in?

每位乘客可以托運兩件行李。
Each passenger is allowed to check in two pieces of luggage.

我的行李超重了。

（迷你句）It is overweight.

（完整句）My luggage is overweight.

很抱歉，那您必須加付額外的費用。
I am sorry. Then you have to pay extra.

[Vocabulary] 生字不用另外查字典！

01 行李 **luggage**

02 表格 **form**

03 隨身行李 **carry-on**

04 大小 **size**

05 優先 **priority**

06 超重的 **overweight**

07 辦理 **check in**

08 貴重物品 **precious things**

09 易碎物品 **fragile**

10 標籤 **sticker**

11 乘客 **passenger**

12 額外費用 **extra money**

03 候機室在哪裡？

💬：你要會說的一句話　🔊：你會聽到的問／答

[Must be...] 這個時候最需要的一句話！

💬 請問候機室在哪裡？
迷你句 Is there a lounge?
完整句 Where is the airport lounge?

🔊 候機室就在那邊。
The airport lounge is over there.

💬 請問使用這裡的設施是否免費？
迷你句 Is it all free?
完整句 Is it free to use the facilities?

🔊 是的，全部免費。
Yes, you can use all of them for free.

💬 請問有提供網路服務嗎？
迷你句 Is Internet available?
完整句 Do you have Internet service?

🔊 是的，我們有提供網路服務。
Yes, we have wi-fi in the lounge.

💬 我是你們航空公司的會員。
迷你句 I am a member.
完整句 I am a member of your airline.

🔊 會員可以免費使用這裡的設施。
Members are free to use the facilities here.

💬 請問有提供什麼服務嗎？
迷你句 Any service?
完整句 What kinds of service do you have?

🔊 我們提供飲料、熱食、電話以及網路連線。
We offer drinks, hot food, phone and Internet access here.

👄 請問非會員使用休息室要多少錢？

迷你句 How much for non-members?

完整句 How much does it cost if for non-members to use the lounge?

👂 非會員使用休息室需要收費五十美元。
We charge $50 for non-members to use the lounge.

👄 我想要使用ABC航空的候機室。

迷你句 ABC Air member's lounge?

完整句 I want to use the ABC Air member's lounge.

👂 請問你是ABC航空的會員嗎？
Are you a member of ABC Air?

👄 請問我可以在候機室裡抽菸嗎？

迷你句 Can I smoke here?

完整句 Could I smoke in the lounge?

👂 抱歉，候機室是禁菸場所。
I am sorry, the lounge is a non-smoking area.

👄 請問候機室有提供酒嗎？

迷你句 Any alcoholic drinks in the lounge?

完整句 Is there any alcohol service in the lounge?

👂 是的，我們有提供白酒。
Yes, we provide white wine in the lounge.

[Vocabulary] 生字不用另外查字典！

01 候機室 lounge

02 免費 for free

03 設施 facility

04 網路服務 Internet service

05 會員 member

06 飲料 drinks

07 熱食 hot food

08 電話 phone

09 網路連線 Internet access

10 禁菸場所 non-smoking area

11 酒 alcohol

12 收費 charge

04 來逛免稅商店

：你要會說的一句話　：你會聽到的問／答　**MP3** Track ▶ 004

[Must be...] 這個時候最需要的一句話！

我得去免稅商店挑一些禮物。
迷你句 I need to do some duty free shopping.
完整句 I need to pick up some gifts in the duty free shop.

免稅商店就在候機室旁。
The duty free shop is next to the lounge.

請問有免稅商品的目錄嗎？
迷你句 Is there a catalogue?
完整句 Do you have duty free product catalogue?

有的，在這裡。
Yes, here you are.

請問這兩種牌子的香菸價錢一樣嗎？
迷你句 Same price?
完整句 Are these two brands of cigarette the same price?

是的，價錢是一樣的。
Yes, the prices are the same.

請問我買這三瓶酒有什麼贈品嗎？
迷你句 Any free gifts for three bottles of wine?
完整句 Will there be any free gifts if I buy three bottles of this wine?

沒有，但是可以享有八折優惠。
No, but you can have a 20% discount.

請問我可以刷卡嗎？
迷你句 Credit card, ok?
完整句 Can I pay with my credit card?

當然，請給我您的信用卡。
Sure, please give me your credit card.

我要這兩瓶乳液。　　**迷你句** Two lotions, please.

完整句 I want these two lotions, please.

好的，請問是要付現嗎？
Ok, would you like to pay in cash?

可以幫我包裝起來嗎？　　**迷你句** Wrap it up, please.

完整句 Could you please wrap it up?

沒問題，這是您的東西。
Sure. Here you are.

這瓶香水多少錢？　　**迷你句** How much?

完整句 How much is this perfume?

一瓶60美元。
It costs $60.

請問我可以使用折價券嗎？　　**迷你句** Can I use a coupon?

完整句 Is this free coupon available here?

當然可以，您現在要使用嗎？
Of course, do you want to use it now?

[Words to Use] 替換字放空格，一句多用!!

● _____多少錢？
How much is the _____?

01 戒指 **ring**

02 香菸 **cigarette**

03 這瓶酒 **bottle of wine**

04 乳液 **lotion**

05 香水 **perfume**

06 巧克力 **chocolate**

05 登機囉

😊：你要會說的一句話　🔊：你會聽到的問／答

[Must be...] 這個時候最需要的一句話！

😊 請問我們幾點登機？
迷你句 The boarding time?
完整句 What time do we board?

🔊 7:30 p.m. 開始登機。
The boarding time is at 7:30 p.m.

😊 請問登機時間到了嗎？
迷你句 Can we board now?
完整句 Is it time to board yet?

🔊 是的，可以開始登機了。
Yes, boarding has started.

😊 請問這是 874 班機的登機門嗎？
迷你句 Is this 874?
完整句 Is this the gate for flight 874?

🔊 是的，這裡是 874 班機的登機門。
Yes, this is the boarding gate for flight 874.

😊 我要去 55 號登機門，請問要怎麼走呢？
迷你句 Where is gate No.55?
完整句 I want to go to boarding gate No.55. How do I get there?

🔊 直走右轉就會看到了。
Go straight and turn to the right then you will find it.

😊 請問我必須搭乘機場巴士才能到 2 號登機門嗎？
迷你句 Should I take the bus to boarding gate No.2?
完整句 Do I have to take airport shuttle bus to gate No.2?

🔊 不，您可以徒步走到 2 號登機門。
No, you can go to boarding gate No.2 on foot.

我可以在這裡拿登機證嗎？
迷你句 Boarding pass?
完整句 Can you issue my boarding pass here?

好的，這是您的登機證。
Ok, here you are.

請問登機時需要帶什麼？
迷你句 What do I need to board?
完整句 What should I offer when I go aboard?

您要帶好登機證和護照。
Please have your boarding pass and passport ready.

請問我可以優先上飛機嗎？
迷你句 Can we board first?
完整句 Can we board in priority?

沒問題，有小孩的乘客能夠優先登機。
Sure, passengers with young children will be boarded first.

經濟艙可以登機了嗎？
迷你句 Can economy class start boarding?
完整句 Is this time for economy class to board?

是的，經濟艙的乘客可以開始登機了。
Yes, the passengers in economy class can start boarding.

[Vocabulary] 生字**不用另外查字典**！

01 登機時間 **boarding time**
02 登機 **boarding**
03 登機門 **gate**
04 直走 **go straight**
05 右轉 **turn to the right**
06 機場巴士 **airport shuttle bus**
07 徒步走 **on foot**
08 登機證 **boarding pass**
09 護照 **passport**
10 乘客 **passenger**
11 經濟艙 **economy class**
12 優先登機 **board in priority**

06 現場買票、候補

😊 :你要會説的一句話　🔈 :你會聽到的問／答　**MP3** Track ▶ 006

[Must be...] **這個時候**最需要的一句話！

😊 請問 101 號班機仍然客滿嗎？
迷你句 Is flight 101 full?
完整句 Is flight 101 still fully booked?

🔈 是的，我可以把您放在 101 班機的候補名單上。
Yes, I can put you on the waiting list for flight 101.

😊 請問我何時知道能不能上飛機？
迷你句 When can I know?
完整句 When will I know if I can be on this flight?

🔈 有機位時我們會盡快跟您連絡。
We will contact you as soon as the seat is available.

😊 請問我可以在這裡買票嗎？
迷你句 Can I pay for the ticket?
完整句 Can I purchase my ticket here?

🔈 是的，您可以在這裡買票。
Yes, you can purchase your ticket here.

😊 請幫我安排候補。
迷你句 I want to be on the waiting list.
完整句 Please put me on the waiting list.

🔈 我們現在有一個機位，您可以上這班飛機。
One seat is open now. You can be on it now.

😊 我想要買一張台北到紐約的來回機票。
迷你句 One return ticket from Taipei to New York.
完整句 I want to buy a round-trip ticket from Taipei to New York.

🔈 好的，您要商務艙還是經濟艙？
Ok, do you prefer business class or economy class?

請問我的訂位代號是多少？

迷你句 My reservation number?

完整句 What is my reservation number?

您的訂位代號是SK3104。
Your reservation number is SK3104.

起飛前三天需要再重新確認機位嗎？

迷你句 Do I need to check my ticket again?

完整句 Do I need to reconfirm my flight three days before departure?

是的，您可以從網路上查詢。
Yes, you can check your flight on the Internet.

請問我可以享有優惠嗎？

迷你句 Any discount?

完整句 Can I have any discount?

學生買機票可以享有八折的優惠。
Students can get a 20% discount on plane tickets.

現在似乎很難訂到特價機票。

迷你句 It is difficult to get a budget fare.

完整句 It seems very difficult to book a budget fare now.

您如果提前幾個星期買機票會更便宜。
It is cheaper if you buy the ticket a few weeks in advance.

[Things to Know] 一定要知道的**旅行常識**

在電影上常看到，在機場櫃台帥氣地賣一張機票就出國的場景，在台灣不太可能發生。由於台灣不是轉機樞紐，現場購票的票價，通常比網路上訂票高出 3~10 倍。在旅遊旺季，機位一位難求；若有急事出國，可以向櫃檯誠實說明自己的難處，也有排到候補的機會。

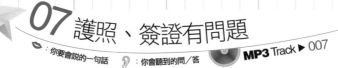

👄：你要會說的一句話　👂：你會聽到的問/答　MP3 Track ▶ 007

[Must be...] 這個時候最需要的一句話！

👄 我的護照掉了。　**迷你句** My passport is missing.
　　　　　　　　　完整句 I lost my passport.

👂 請到服務台詢問。
Please go to the Information desk.

👄 我可以在這裡待多久？　**迷你句** What is the validity?
　　　　　　　　　　完整句 How long can I stay here?

👂 觀光簽證最多可以待到三個月。
You can stay up to three months with this visitor visa.

👄 我可以在美國工作嗎？　**迷你句** Can I work here?
　　　　　　　　　　完整句 Am I allowed to work in the US?

👂 持觀光簽證是不准在美國工作的。
You are not allowed to work in the US with a visitor's visa.

👄 我的護照過期了。　**迷你句** It's expired.
　　　　　　　　　完整句 My passport is expired.

👂 您需要辦理新的護照。
You need to have a new passport.

👄 我是來觀光的。　**迷你句** I am a visitor.
　　　　　　　　完整句 I am here for sightseeing.

👂 好的，請出示您的回程機票。
Can you show me your return ticket?

簽證逾期的罰金多少錢？

迷你句 How much is the fine?

完整句 How much is the fine for the expired visa?

簽證逾期一天的罰金是 250 元美金。
The fine for an expired visa is \$250 per day.

我可以在機場延長簽證時間嗎？

迷你句 Can I extend my visa here?

完整句 Could I get a visa extension at the airport?

很抱歉，要去移民署辦理。
I'm sorry, you'll have to do it at the immigration bureau.

現在該怎麼辦？

迷你句 What can I do now?

完整句 What am I supposed to do now?

我們會有專人來幫您。
The officials will help you out with this.

簽證過期一天，我還可以上飛機嗎？

迷你句 Can I still get aboard?

完整句 Am I allowed to go aboard with my visa expired for a day?

很抱歉，我們只讓有可用簽證的旅客上飛機。
We only take passengers with a valid visa.

[Things to Know] 一定要知道的**旅行常識**

　　如果簽證、護照過期了，在國內的櫃檯 check in 時，就會無法登機。如果在國外要搭飛機返國時，發現護照、簽證有問題，可以在離境幾天前趕快去當地的移民局詢問補救措施，通常會罰款，並要求重新申請簽證。如果在機場登機時才被海關發現，不僅會被罰款，還會留下違法的紀錄，在幾年內都無法入境該國，須特別注意。

08 行李超重

[Must be...] 這個時候最需要的一句話！

😊 請問行李超重如何收費？
迷你句 How much is it for overweight luggage?
完整句 How much do you charge for overweight luggage?

🔊 行李超重要收費75美金。
There will be a $75 charge for overweight luggage.

😊 我可以重新將行李打包成兩件。
迷你句 I will make it into two.
完整句 I will re-pack them into two luggage cases.

🔊 是的，你可以試著重新打包或把一些東西拿出來。
Yes, you can re-pack them or take something out.

😊 我會拿出一些東西。
迷你句 Some items can be taken out.
完整句 I will just take some items out.

🔊 好的，這樣就沒問題了。
Ok, that will be fine.

😊 請問這裡有店讓我買個行李箱嗎？
迷你句 Any suitcase shops here?
完整句 Is there any shop here for me to buy a suitcase?

🔊 那邊轉角有家行李店。
There is a luggage shop at the corner.

😊 請問再加上這件行李會超重嗎？
迷你句 Can I include this bag?
完整句 Will I overload my baggage if I include this bag?

🔊 是的，這樣會超重。
Yes, that will be overweight.

因為我買了一些書比較重，能否通融一下呢？

迷你句 Could you make an exception?

完整句 It is overweight because of these heavy books, could you make an exception?

很抱歉，但是您的行李已經超過限重了。
I am sorry, but this luggage is over the limited weight.

請問我的行李超重了該怎麼辦呢？

迷你句 What can I do now?

完整句 My luggage is overweight, what should I do?

或許您能夠將這件較小的行李拿上飛機。
Maybe you can take this small one onto the plane.

我不確定我的行李到底有沒有超重。

迷你句 Is it overweight?

完整句 I am not sure if it is overweight.

好的，請把您的行李放在秤上。
Ok, please put your luggage on the scale.

我會付超重的錢。

迷你句 I will pay for it.

完整句 I will just pay for the extra money.

您要用現金付費還是信用卡？
You want to pay with plastic or cash?

[Things to Know] 一定要知道的**旅行常識**

因油價上漲，若是行李超過航空公司限定重量，旅客會被多收飛機燃油費。跨洋的航班，行李限重較高；短程航班則落在單件行李 23kg 左右的限制。若要託運的行李超重，可與同行的朋友商討分攤重量，或是將超重的部分直接帶進機艙，當作隨身行李。

👄：你要會說的一句話　　🗨：你會聽到的問/答　　**MP3** Track ▶ 009

[Must be...] 這個時候最需要的一句話!

👄 我的班機被取消了，請問是真的嗎?

迷你句 My flight was canceled. Really?

完整句 Is it true that my flight was canceled?

👂 是的，很抱歉給您造成不便。
Yes, we are sorry for the inconvenience.

👄 請問這班飛機會延遲多久?

迷你句 Delayed for how long?

完整句 How long will the flight be delayed?

👂 很抱歉，我們會盡快通知您。
Sorry, we will contact you as soon as possible.

👄 請問為什麼班機被延後?

迷你句 Why is it delayed?

完整句 Why is the flight delayed?

👂 我們會盡快公布原因。
We will announce the reason shortly.

👄 請問會有其他的班機嗎?

迷你句 Will there be another flight?

完整句 Is there going to be another plane?

👂 很抱歉，我們還不確定。
Sorry, we are not sure yet.

👄 可以讓我們搭另一班往首爾的飛機嗎?

迷你句 Can you put us on another flight to Seoul?

完整句 Is it possible that we can get on another flight to Seoul?

👂 很抱歉，另一班飛機已經客滿了。
I am sorry, the other flight is full.

請問有地方可以邊等邊休息嗎？

迷你句 Where can we rest?

完整句 Is there any place for we to rest while waiting?

您可以在候機室等候。
You can rest in the lounge.

為什麼這麼晚才到？

迷你句 Why was it late?

完整句 What the reason cause the flight delayed?

天氣狀況讓我們晚了兩個小時。
We are behind schedule due to the weather conditions.

我必須轉機到達拉斯，請問會不會有問題？

迷你句 But I need to transfer to Dallas.

完整句 I need to transfer to Dallas, will that be ok?

您大約還有一個小時的時間可以轉機。
You still have one hour for transferring.

請問我搭乘的班機會延誤嗎？

迷你句 Will it be delayed?

完整句 Will the flight I take be delayed?

是的，看來延誤似乎是無法避免的。
Yes, the delay seems to be unavoidable.

[Things to Know] 一定要知道的**旅行常識**

　　因天候不佳、航班太多導致空中塞車、或是技術問題，都有可能導致班機誤點。出發前應先打電話向航空公司確認。若是搭同一公司的飛機轉機時，因上一班飛機延誤，導致沒搭上飛機，可向櫃檯說明，請航空公司解決。但在訂購機票時，就需特別注意。

[Must be...] 這個時候最需要的一句話！

💋 我們剛好錯過了往阿姆斯特丹的飛機。

(迷你句) We missed our flight.

(完整句) We just missed the flight to Amsterdam.

🕙 你們可以搭下一班，下一班往阿姆斯特丹的飛機三小時後出發。
You can take the next one. The next flight to Amsterdam departs in three hours.

💋 請問下一班往柏斯的飛機是什麼時候？

(迷你句) When is the next plane to Perth?

(完整句) When does the next plane to Peth leave?

🕙 今天下午三點半。
It will leave at 3 p.m. today.

💋 請問我得重新買一張機票嗎？

(迷你句) Do I need to get a new ticket?

(完整句) Is it necessary for me to buy a new ticket?

🕙 恐怕是的。
I am afraid so.

💋 請問355班機已經起飛了嗎？

(迷你句) Did flight 355 already leave?

(完整句) Excuse me, has the flight 355 taken off yet?

🕙 是的，您已經錯過了。
Yes, you have missed it.

💋 我需要跟來接機的朋友連絡一下。

(迷你句) My friend is meeting me. I need to call him.

(完整句) I need to contact my friend who is coming to pick up.

🕙 候機室有提供電話可以使用。
We offer phone service in the lounge.

我們本來想搭 212 班機的。
迷你句 It is our flight.
完整句 We are supposed to be on flight 212.

很抱歉，您恐怕得重買一張機票。
Sorry, I am afraid you have to buy a new ticket.

請問有其他班機嗎？
迷你句 Alternatives?
完整句 Is there any alternative?

讓我幫您查一下。
Let me check for you.

我要搭 666 班機。
迷你句 Where is flight 666?
完整句 I need to take flight 666.

很抱歉，您的飛機十分鐘前已經起飛。
I am sorry, your flight has just departed 10 minutes ago.

那我現在應該怎麼辦？
迷你句 What can I do now?
完整句 What should I do now?

您可以試試荷蘭皇家航空，他們傍晚有一架往愛丁堡的飛機。
Maybe you can try KLM. They have a flight to Edinburgh this evening.

[Things to Know] 一定要知道的**旅行常識**

錯過班機時，請先向航空公司櫃台說明。如果是因為轉機誤點，航空公司通常會負責；如果是自己的關係，航空公司有權利拒絕乘客上飛機。但是大多數的航空公司，都會幫乘客安排下一般還有空位的飛機，只是旺季時很可能候補不到位置。

旅遊常用句型 + 超多替換字，套入馬上用！

櫃台報到劃位

● 我比較喜歡 ＿＿＿＿ 座位。謝謝你。
I prefer a/an ＿＿＿＿＿ seat. Thank you.

01 靠窗 window
02 靠走道 aisle
03 緊急出口旁的 emergency exit
04 出口排 exit row
05 靠艙板 bulkhead
06 後排 back row

托運行李

● 這 ＿＿＿＿ 也可以託運嗎？
Can I check in this ＿＿＿＿ as well?

01 （個）紙箱 cardboard box
02 （把）吉他 guitar
03 （幅）畫 painting
04 （個）折疊式腳踏車 folding bike
05 嬰兒推車 baby trolley
06 （個）電器用品 electric appliance

使用候機室

● 我希望候機室會有 ＿＿＿＿。
I hope I can find a/an ＿＿＿＿＿ at the departure lounge.

01 投幣式按摩椅 coin operated massage chair
02 廁所 restroom
03 冷飲販賣機 cold beverage machine
04 賣吃的店 food store
05 點心販賣機 snack vending machine
06 充電站 charging station

來逛免稅商店

● 免稅商店裡的 ＿＿＿＿ 實在很便宜。

＿＿＿＿ in the duty-free shop are a steal.

01 巧克力 **Chocolates**　　02 香煙 **Cigarettes**

03 酒 **Liquors**　　04 化妝品 **Cosmetics**

05 香水 **Perfumes**　　06 設計師名牌商品 **Designer items**

護照、簽證有問題

● 我沒注意到我的 ＿＿＿＿ 過期了。

I didn't notice that my ＿＿＿＿ has expired.

01 護照 **passport**　　02 簽證 **visa**

03 學生簽證 **student visa**　　04 觀光簽證 **tourist visa**

05 工作簽證 **employment visa**　　06 商務簽證 **business visa**

班機延誤了

● ＿＿＿＿ 使我們的班機延誤了。

The ＿＿＿＿ has delayed our flight.

01 暴風雨 **storm**　　02 颱風 **typhoon**

03 濃霧 **thick fog**　　04 惡劣天候 **bad weather**

05 維修 **maintenance**　　06 跑道關閉 **runway closure**

登機門代碼字母簡稱

登機門的代碼多為一個英文字母 + 數字，如 C9、A7、G2...等。空服員在飛機上、機場裡廣播時，未免發生英文字母聽不清楚的狀況，都會把英文字母擴大成一個單字，好明確指出到底是哪個字母。如 C9 則會唸成 Charlie 9。

以下是各個字母與單字對應表。

英文字母	對應單字（中文翻譯）
A	Alfa （蘆葦草）
B	Bravo （喝彩）
C	Charlie （查理）
D	Delta （幾何符號）
E	Echo （回音）
F	Florida （佛羅里達）
G	Golf （高爾夫）
H	Hotel （旅館）
I	India （印度）
J	Juliet （茱麗葉）
K	Kilo （一千克）
L	Lima （利馬）

M	Mike （麥可）
N	November （十一月）
O	Oscar （奧斯卡）
P	Papa （教宗）
Q	Quebec （魁北克）
R	Romeo （羅密歐）
S	Sierra （山脊）
T	Tango （探戈舞）
U	Uniform （制服）
V	Victor （勝利）
W	Whisky （威士忌）
X	Xray （X光）
Y	Yankee （美國北方人）
Z	Zulu （祖魯人）

PART 02
飛機上

[Must be...] **這個時候**最需要的一句話！

👄 請問我的位子在哪裡？

迷你句 Where is my seat?

完整句 Could you tell me where is my seat?

🗩 您的坐位是 19A。
You seat is 19A.

👄 請問 33B 在哪裡？

迷你句 Where is 33B?

完整句 Where can I find 33B?

🗩 33B 就在這個走道。
33B is in this aisle.

👄 不好意思，我想這是我的位子。

迷你句 Sorry, this is my seat.

完整句 Excuse me, I think this is my seat.

🗩 噢，對不起。
Oh, I am sorry.

👄 我可以移到那裡的空位嗎？

迷你句 Can I move to there?

完整句 Could I move to an empty seat over there?

🗩 請在起飛以後再移動，謝謝。
You will have to wait until we take off, thank you.

👄 我可以坐在這裡嗎？

迷你句 May I?

完整句 Can I sit here?

🗩 很抱歉，這裡已經有人坐了。
Sorry, it is already taken.

😮 抱歉，我找不到位子。

迷你句 Where do I sit?

完整句 Sorry, I can't find my seat.

👂 我可以帶您到位子上。
I can take you to your seat.

😮 請問這個位子是靠窗還是靠走道？

迷你句 Aisle or window?

完整句 Is it a window seat or an aisle seat?

👂 是靠走道的位子。
Your seat is an aisle seat.

😮 請問我可以跟您交換位子嗎？

迷你句 Can we change seats?

完整句 Can I change the seat with you?

👂 當然，沒問題。你的位置在哪裡？
Sure, no problem. Where's your seat?

😮 我們的位子被分開了。

迷你句 We are separated.

完整句 Our seats are separated.

👂 後面還有一些空位子。你們可以移到後面。
There are some empty seats in the back. You can move to there.

[Things to Know] 一定要知道的**旅行常識**

國際航線的飛機座位通常都有三、四百個之多。例如波音 747 有三大排，左右兩大排分別有三個座位，中間那一大排則有四個座位相連。座位號碼通常包含數字（排）和英文字母（座位代號），座位代號為面對駕駛艙的左側按照字母順序由 A 排到 J。

: 你要會說的一句話　　: 你會聽到的問/答　　**MP3** Track ▶ 012

[Must be...] 這個時候最需要的一句話！

請問洗手間在哪裡？

迷你句 Lavatory?

完整句 Could you tell me where the restroom is?

就在走道的盡頭。
It is at the end of this aisle.

請問有中文雜誌嗎？

迷你句 Chinese magazines?

完整句 Do you have any Chinese magazines?

有的，在這裡。
Yes, here you are.

請幫我把包包放到上面好嗎？

迷你句 I want to put this up there.

完整句 Could you put this bag up there, please?

沒問題。只有一件嗎？
No problem. You have only one bag?

請給我一條毯子。

迷你句 A blanket, please.

完整句 May I have a blanket?

好的，我去為您拿。
Ok, I will go get you one.

我可以把袋子拿開一下放我的行李嗎？

迷你句 Do you mind if I move this around?

完整句 Can I move this bag to make some room for my luggage?

當然。
Not at all.

可以幫我找個地方放行李嗎？

迷你句 Other place for this?

完整句 Can you find me a place to put my luggage?

我可以幫您放到頭頂置物箱裡。
Let me help you to put this in the overhead bins.

這個頭頂置物箱滿了。

迷你句 It is full.

完整句 This overhead bins is full.

那麼請將袋子放到位子底下。
Then you can put this bag under your seat.

我不知道這行李要放哪裡？

迷你句 Where can I put this bag?

完整句 Is there any place I can put my bag?

我會幫您找個位子。
I will find a place for you.

我可以抽菸嗎？

迷你句 Can I smoke?

完整句 May I smoke here?

抱歉，飛機上是禁菸區。
Sorry, this is a non-smoking flight.

[Words to Use] 替換字放空格，一句多用!!

● 抱歉，我找不到我的_____。
  Sorry, I can't find my _____.

01 座位 seat

02 護照 passport

03 表格 form

04 行李 luggage

05 錢包 purse

06 登機證 boarding pass

機艙內座位周邊設施介紹

在飛行中，旅行者將會在同一個座位上坐著 3 ～ 16 小時，因此飛機的座位雖然小小的，但是周圍也有許多設施。好好運用每一個設施，讓你也能好好地閱讀、吃飯、玩遊戲，也能好好地睡上一覺。

【常見生字】

座位	seat	服務鈴	call button
扶手	armrest	頭頂置物箱	overhead bins
安全帶	seatbelt	閱讀燈	reading light
桌子	tray table	氧氣罩	oxygen mask
遮陽板	sun shading board	緊急手電筒	emergency flashlight

【最常用的旅行句】

01 這個位子有人坐了。

This seat is taken.

02 你佔到我的扶手了。

Please move your arm off my armrest.

03 起飛時請繫上安全帶。

Please fasten your seatbelt while taking off.

04 我要開閱讀燈，卻按到服務鈴了。

I accidentally pushed the call button as I wanted to switch on the reading light.

飛機內設備介紹

終於，一連串的手續告一段落，現在你可以坐在屬於你的位子上享受空姐、空少完善的服務。另外，為了確保飛航安全，上飛機之後請關掉您隨身的電子產品，直到廣播可以使用為止。

【常見生字】

餐車	dining car	洗手間	lavatory
乘客手冊	passenger safety manual	影音設備	entertainment equipment
嬰兒安全帶	infant seat belt	應急艙門	emergency hatch
救生艇	lifeboat	救生衣	life vest
水滅火器	water fire extinguisher	保溫箱	thermal insulation box
應急藥箱	emergency medical box		

【最常用的旅行句】

01 我的影音播放設備壞掉了。

The entertainment equipment is not working.

02 洗手間有人在使用。

The lavatory is occupied.

：你要會說的一句話　：你會聽到的問／答　**MP3** Track ▶ 013

[Must be...] 這個時候最需要的一句話！

請問你們有什麼飲料？
迷你句 Any drinks?
完整句 What kind of drinks do you have?

我們幾乎什麼都有。
We have almost everything.

請問有可樂嗎？
迷你句 Coke?
完整句 Do you have coke?

有的，這是您的可樂。
Yes, here you are.

能給我一杯啤酒嗎？
迷你句 Beer, please.
完整句 Can I have a beer?

您想要哪一種啤酒？
What kind of beer do you want?

我要一杯加了奶精的咖啡。
迷你句 Coffee with cream.
完整句 Can I have a cup of coffee with cream, please.

好的，需要糖嗎？
Ok, need any sugar?

我用完餐點了。
迷你句 I am done with my meal.
完整句 Excuse me, I am finished with my meal.

好的，那麼我要把餐盤收走了。
Ok, then I will take this tray.

請問你們晚餐供應什麼？
(迷你句) What do you have for dinner?
(完整句) What are you serving for dinner?

我們提供雞肉和豬肉。
We offer chicken with rice and pork steak.

我吃素。
(迷你句) I'm a vegetarian.
(完整句) I am a vegetarian.

好的，我們提供您素食餐。
Ok, we could offer you a vegetarian meal.

我想要喝飲料。
(迷你句) Drinks, please.
(完整句) Can I get something to drink?

請問您要咖啡還是紅茶。
Do you want some coffee or black tea?

我還沒吃完。
(迷你句) I am not done yet.
(完整句) I haven't finished my meal yet.

好的，我待會兒再來。
Ok, I will come back later.

[Words to Use] 替換字放空格，一句多用!!

● 能給我_____嗎？
Can I have _____, please.

01 可樂 **coke**

02 水 **some water**

03 熱茶 **hot tea**

04 果汁 **orange juice**

05 咖啡加奶精 **coffee with cream**

06 啤酒 **beer**

04 飛機上免稅購物

👄：你要會説的一句話　　🗨️：你會聽到的問／答

[Must be...] 這個時候最需要的一句話！

👄 我想要一條這樣的口紅。
迷你句 Can I have this one?
完整句 I would like to have this kind of lipstick.

🗨️ 好的，請問要付現嗎？
Ok, do you want to pay in cash?

👄 我要買免税商品。
迷你句 I want some duty free products.
完整句 I would like to have some duty free products.

🗨️ 好的，我們即將要開始販售免税商品了。
Yes, we will start selling duty free products shortly.

👄 請問你們有什麼樣的商品？
迷你句 What kinds of things do you sell?
完整句 What kinds of duty free product do you have?

🗨️ 目錄上有列的商品幾乎都有貨。
Most of the items in the catalogue are available.

👄 我要刷卡。
迷你句 On credit.
完整句 I am going to pay by credit card.

🗨️ 沒問題，請給我您的信用卡。
Sure, please give me your credit card.

👄 我要收據。
迷你句 A receipt, please.
完整句 I need a receipt for my purchase.

🗨️ 給您。
Here you are.

請問這支錶有打折嗎？
迷你句 Is this on sale?
完整句 Is this watch on sale?

不，這支手錶並沒有打折。
No, it isn't on sale.

請問有任何的折扣嗎？
迷你句 Any discount?
完整句 Can I have some discounts?

如果用網路預購，就能夠享有 75 折的優惠。
You can have a 25% discount if you make an online order first.

我可以看這條項鍊嗎？
迷你句 Can I see this necklace?
完整句 Can I take a look at this necklace?

當然，給您。
Sure, here.

目錄上的商品全部都有販賣嗎？
迷你句 Do you have everything in this book?
完整句 Are all the items on the catalogue available?

抱歉，有一部分的商品已售完。
Sorry, some of the items are sold out.

[Vocabulary] 生字不用另外查字典！

01 口紅 **lipstick**
02 免稅商品 **duty free product**
03 商品 **item**
04 目錄 **catalogue**
05 收據 **receipt**
06 手錶 **watch**
07 打折 **on sale**
08 折扣 **discount**
09 網路預購 **online order**
10 售完的 **sold out**
11 項鍊 **necklace**
12 刷卡 **on credit**

😊：你要會說的一句話　🗨：你會聽到的問／答　　🎧 **MP3** Track ▶ 015

[**Must be...**] 這個時候最需要的一句話！

😊 請問這是入境表格嗎？
迷你句 Immigration form?
完整句 Is this the immigration form?

🗨 是的，您知道該怎麼填寫嗎？
Yes, do you know how to fill it out?

😊 請問這個表格要怎麼填？
迷你句 How do I fill out this form?
完整句 Could you tell me how to fill out this form?

🗨 讓我來幫您。
Let me help you.

😊 我不知道這裡要填什麼。
迷你句 I have no idea.
完整句 I don't know what to write here.

🗨 這裡空下來就可以了。
Just leave it blank.

😊 請問這班飛機會準時到達洛杉磯嗎？
迷你句 Will it arrive in LA on time?
完整句 Will the flight arrive as it is scheduled to?

🗨 是的，飛機會準時到達。
Yes, it will be on time.

😊 請問紐約當地時間是幾點？
迷你句 What time is it in New York now?
完整句 What is the local time in New York?

🗨 現在是早上六點半。
It is 6:30 in the morning.

我們快要到目的地了嗎？
迷你句 Are we nearly there?
完整句 Are we reaching the destination?

是的，請將座椅立起、托盤收起。
Yes, please straight on up your seats and have your tray put away.

請問還要多久才會降落？
迷你句 When do we land?
完整句 How long will it take to land?

15 分鐘內就要開始降落了。
We will start to land in 15 minutes.

我需要入境申請表。
迷你句 Immigration form, please.
完整句 I need the immigration form, please.

在這裡，需要幫忙請告訴我。
Here, let me know if you need any help.

請問每個人都要填一張嗎？
迷你句 One form per person?
完整句 Does everyone have to write one immigration form?

全家人只需填寫一張表格。
You only need to fill out one form for the whole family.

[Vocabulary] 生字不用另外查字典！

01 入境表格 immigration form
02 準時 on time
03 到達 arrive
04 當地時間 local time
05 目的地 destination
06 降落 land
07 座椅 seat
08 托盤 tray
09 立起 straight up
10 開始降落 start to descend
11 填寫 fill up
12 全家人 whole family

065

：你要會說的一句話　：你會聽到的問／答　**MP3** Track ▶ 016

[Must be...] 這個時候最需要的一句話！

請問椅子要怎麼斜躺？

迷你句 How does this work?

完整句 Can you show me how to recline the seat?

好的，讓我幫您。
Ok, let me help you.

請幫我看一下安全帶有沒有繫好。

迷你句 Is my seatbelt correct?

完整句 Please check if my seatbelt is working properly.

您的安全帶沒有問題。
It is perfect.

我的遙控器壞掉了。

迷你句 It is broken.

完整句 There is something wrong with my remote.

我幫您檢查一下。
Let me check.

這是服務燈的按鈕嗎？

迷你句 Is this the call light?

完整句 Is this the button for call light?

是的，有任何問題請按下去。
Yes, press it if you need any help.

請問亂流燈亮時我可以去上廁所嗎？

迷你句 Is it ok to use the bathroom now?

完整句 Can I use the bathroom when the turbulence light is on?

很抱歉，你必須待在坐位上。
Sorry, you have to stay in your seat.

廁所沒有衛生紙了。
迷你句 There is no toilet paper.
完整句 The toilet paper was used up.

抱歉，衛生紙在這裡。
Sorry, here you are.

我需要換一條毯子。
迷你句 A new blanket, please.
完整句 I need a new blanket, please.

好的，我幫您換一條。
Ok, I will replace it for you.

我的電視無法使用。
迷你句 It doesn't work.
完整句 My TV screen is damaged.

您可以換一個座位。
You can change seats.

我找不到我的耳機。
迷你句 Where are my headphones?
完整句 I can't find my headphones anywhere.

耳機就在你的座位前面。
They are in front of your seat.

[Words to Use] 替換字放空格，一句多用!!

- 我需要一個_____。
  I need _____, please.

01 毯子 a blanket

02 遙控器 a remote

03 耳機 a headphone

04 拖鞋 airline slippers

05 入境表格 an entry form

06 枕頭 a pillow

😛：你要會說的一句話　　👂：你會聽到的問／答　　**MP3** Track ▶ 017

[Must be...] 這個時候最需要的一句話！

😛 我覺得不舒服。　**迷你句** I am a little sick.
完整句 I am not feeling very well.

👂 需要喝杯水嗎？
Do you need some water?

😛 我的頭很痛。　**迷你句** My head hurts.
完整句 I have a very bad headache.

👂 您有帶藥來嗎？
Do you have any medication with you?

😛 我有點呼吸困難。　**迷你句** I am feeling out of breath.
完整句 I am having some trouble breathing.

👂 我馬上找人來幫您。
I will have someone help you right away.

😛 請問你有止痛藥嗎？　**迷你句** I need a pain killer.
完整句 Do you have any pain killers?

👂 好的，我去幫您拿來。
Yes, I will go get you some.

😛 請問有暈機藥嗎？　**迷你句** I need some medicine for airsickness.
完整句 Do you have any medicine for airsickness?

👂 有，我幫您拿一些。
Yes, I will bring you some.

👄 我有些頭暈。　　**迷你句** I am dizzy.

完整句 I am feeling a little bit dizzy.

👂 您需要躺下來嗎？
Do you need to lie down?

👄 我肚子不舒服。　　**迷你句** I don't feel well.

完整句 I have a stomachache.

👂 你需要去廁所嗎？
Do you need to use the bathroom?

👄 我想我要吐了。　　**迷你句** I want to throw up.

完整句 I think I am going to vomit.

👂 您可以使用嘔吐袋。
You can use the airsickness bag.

👄 我發燒了。　　**迷你句** I have a fever.

完整句 I am running a fever.

👂 您需要杯熱水嗎？
Do you need a glass of hot water?

[Words to Use] 替換字放空格，一句多用!!

● 請問有治_____的藥嗎？
Do you have any medicine for _____?

01 暈機藥 **airsickness**

02 疼痛 **pain**

03 頭痛 **headache**

04 胃痛 **stomachache**

05 腹瀉 **diarrhoea**

06 嘔吐 **nausea**

旅遊常用句型 + 超多替換字，套入馬上用！

機上換座位

● 我可以把我的座位換到 _____ 的位置嗎？
Is it okay if I change my seat _____?

01 空位旁邊 next to an empty seat   **02** 前面一點 to the front

03 靠近緊急出口 close to the emergency exit   **04** 後面一點 to the back

05 洗手間附近 near to the lavatory   **06** 遠離廁所 away from the lavatory

請空服員協助

● 可以請你幫我 _____？
Could you help me _____?

01 找座位 find my seat   **02** 換座位 change my seat

03 讓座椅向後仰 recline my seat

04 把托盤桌放下來 put down the tray table

05 把袋子放進上方行李艙 put my bag in the overhead bin

06 在我去洗手間時看著孩子 look after my child when I go to the restroom

飛機餐點

● 我在訂機票時的確有要求一份 _____。
I did request a/an _____ when I booked my flight.

01 兒童餐 children's meal   **02** 嬰兒餐 infant and baby meal

03 低脂餐 low-fat meal   **04** 糖尿病餐 diabetic meal

05 素食餐 vegetarian meal   **06** 低鹽餐 low-salt meal

飛機上免稅購物

● 你們接受 _____ 付費嗎？
Do you take _____?

01 美金 **US dollars**
02 日幣 **Japanese yens**
03 歐元 **Euro dollars**
04 新台幣 **New Taiwan dollars**
05 人民幣 **Renminbi (RMB)**
06 信用卡 **credit cards**

飛機上設施有問題

● **我的 _____ 好像不能用。**
It seems that my _____ doesn't work.

01 頭頂閱讀燈 **overhead reading light**
02 耳機插孔 **headphone jack**
03 觸控螢幕面板 **touch-screen tablet**
04 座椅調節裝置 **seat adjuster**
05 遙控器 **remote controller**
06 耳機 **earphone**

飛機上身體不適

● **我覺得 _____。**
I feel _____.

01 頭暈 **dizzy**
02 想吐 **nauseous**
03 喘不過氣 **short of breath**
04 頭昏 **light-headed**
05 虛弱無力 **weak**
06 暈機 **airsick**

飛航規範、里程、航空聯盟介紹

搭乘飛機旅行已經是現代人不可或缺的交通工具,尤其是如台灣的島國,想要出國就一定得搭飛機。搭乘飛機有許多異於地面交通工具的規範,為確保安全,有危險物品、100ml 以上液體禁止隨身帶上機。搭機全程禁止使用行動電話,飛機起降時也禁用任何電子產品等等。聽起來很複雜?別擔心,全程都會有服務人員提醒你所有規範。

01【累積里程的好處】

現今航空產業競爭激烈,各家航空公司紛紛推出許多會員方案如里程常客計劃,以增加會員搭機的忠誠度。利用所搭乘該航空公司航段的距離累積里程數,來換取獎勵,就如同信用卡紅利點數一樣。當累積里程到一定標準,便可讓下次機票艙等升級,兌換免費機票,或是許多的飯店住宿券、電子產品等等。

但航空公司這麼多,總不可能一直都只搭乘一家航空公司對吧?所以現在許多航空公司紛紛結盟,以獲取更大市場與利益。而我們也可以善用這樣的結盟,讓里程累積更加彈性。

02【航空聯盟介紹】

目前國際上有三大聯盟:星空聯盟(Star Alliance)、寰宇一家(oneworld),以及天合聯盟(SkyTeam)是三個最大型的聯盟。以中華航空為例,華航屬於天合聯盟,因此搭乘同樣屬於天合聯盟的達美航空,就可以累積至華航里程帳戶。而我們也可以用華航里程來兌換同樣是天合聯盟的韓國航空的免費機票。

PART 03
抵達機場

[Must be...] 這個時候最需要的一句話！

👄 這是我的護照和簽證。
迷你句 My paperwork.
完整句 Here is my passport and VISA.

👂 好的，請問你會待上多久？
Ok, how long are you going to stay?

👄 我會在這裡待上兩周。
迷你句 For two weeks.
完整句 I will stay here for two weeks.

👂 您是來這裡觀光的嗎？
Are you here as a tourist?

👄 這是我第五次來到這個國家。
迷你句 This if my fifth visit.
完整句 This is the fifth time I have visit this country.

👂 您一定相當喜愛我們的國家。
You must love our county very much.

👄 我是來參加國際電腦展的。
迷你句 For the Computex.
完整句 I am coming here for an international Computex.

👂 您來這裡的原因為何？
May I know the purpose of your visit?

👄 我會住在君悅飯店。
迷你句 At the Grand Hyatt Taipei.
完整句 I am staying in Grand Hyatt Taipei.

👂 您已經預訂房間了嗎？
Have you made a reservation?

😊 我帶了一萬塊美金。

迷你句 I have 10,000 U.S. dollars.

完整句 I have brought 10,000 U.S. dollar with me.

👂 請問是現金嗎？
Do you mean $10,000 in cash?

😊 這是我的入境表格。

迷你句 My immigration form.

完整句 Here is my immigration form.

👂 請給我您的護照，謝謝。
May I have your passport?

😊 我還需要填寫其他的文件嗎？

迷你句 Need more forms?

完整句 Do I need to fill out other information form?

👂 不用了，這樣就可以了。
No, all your procedures are correct.

😊 需要我的來回機票嗎？

迷你句 Return ticket?

完整句 Do you need to check my return ticket?

👂 不用，但我需要看一下您的護照。
No, but may I see your passport?

[Vocabulary] 生字不用另外查字典！

01 護照 passport

02 簽證 VISA

03 觀光客 tourist

04 目的 purpose

05 君悅飯店 Grand Hyatt Taipei

06 預訂 make a reservation

07 現金 cash

08 旅遊指南 tour guide

09 入境表格 immigration form

10 表格 form

11 回程機票 return ticket

12 參考 refer

💬：你要會說的一句話　　🎧：你會聽到的問／答　　**MP3** Track ▶ 019

[Must be...] 這個時候最需要的一句話！

👄 請問哪裡可以領取行李？

迷你句 Where is my luggage?

完整句 Where do I pick up my luggage?

🎧 你可以去行李認領區。
You can go to the baggage claim area.

👄 請問 JE811 班機的行李轉盤在哪裡？

迷你句 Carousel for flight JE811?

完整句 Where is the baggage carousel for flight JE811?

🎧 左手邊第二個就是。
It is the second carousel from the left.

👄 請問哪裡有行李搬運人員？

迷你句 Where are the skycaps?

完整句 Where can I find a skycap to carry my luggage?

🎧 那個穿著棕色工作服的男人就是了。
The man in brown work clothes is a skycap.

👄 我們的袋子在那裡。

迷你句 There it is.

完整句 Our bag is over there.

🎧 您需要幫忙嗎？
Do you need any help?

👄 不好意思，可以幫我拿一下袋子嗎？

迷你句 Could you help me with the bag?

完整句 Excuse me, can you help me to carry this bag out?

🎧 當然沒問題。
Of course I can.

請問我們要怎麼知道行李在哪裡？

迷你句 How do I know where my luggage is?

完整句 How do I know where to get my luggage?

您可以參考行李轉盤上的指示牌。
You can check the flight display board on each carousel.

放行李的推車在哪裡？

迷你句 Where are carts for luggage?

完整句 Where can I get the carts for luggage?

推車就在轉角處。
The carts are in the corner over there.

請問在幾樓領取行李？

迷你句 Which floor to get my luggage?

完整句 At which floor can I get my luggage?

領行李的地方在樓下。
Baggage claim is located on the lower level.

請問哪裡有行李的推車？

迷你句 I need a cart.

完整句 Where can I find a cart for luggage?

就在櫃檯旁邊。
The carts are right next to the check-in counter.

[Things to Know] 一定要知道的**旅行常識**

入境審查完畢之後，就可以循著指標，到提領行李處的大轉盤等候行李。由於行李是按照頭等艙、商務艙、經濟艙的順序出來的，所以坐經濟艙的一般旅客，就要稍等一會兒。另外，行李如果遺失或延遲，可以向航空公司索賠，通常金額不低，但是未免麻煩，還是把重要行李帶上飛機才好。

03 過境／轉機

👄：你要會說的一句話　🦻：你會聽到的問／答

 **MP3** Track ▶ 020

[Must be...] 這個時候最需要的一句話！

👄 請問這班飛機是直飛巴黎嗎？

迷你句 Is this a direct flight?
完整句 Do we fly directly to Paris?

🦻 這不是直飛班機。
It is not a direct flight.

👄 請問我需要過境簽證嗎？

迷你句 Is a transfer VISA required?
完整句 Do I need a transfer VISA?

🦻 是的，您需要過境簽證。
Yes, you will need a transfer VISA.

👄 請問再登機的時間是什麼時候？

迷你句 When will we re-board?
完整句 When is the re-boarding time?

🦻 在三十分鐘內可以再登機。
In 30 minutes.

👄 請問過境時我們需要下飛機嗎？

迷你句 Can we stay on the aircraft?
完整句 Can we remain on board during the stopover?

🦻 是的，您不需要下飛機。
Yes, you don't have to get off the plane.

👄 這麼長的停靠時間我們得找個地方休息。

迷你句 Let's find somewhere to relax.
完整句 We need to find a place to rest for the long halt.

🦻 是啊，我們去喝杯咖啡吧。
Yes, how about getting some coffee?

我必須要等上八個小時才能轉機。

迷你句 I have an eight-hour layover.

完整句 There is an eight hour wait for my connecting flight.

如果您需要休息的話，可以到過境旅館。
You can try the airport hotel if you need a place to rest.

我們必須再一次通過安檢嗎？

迷你句 Do we need to go through security again?

完整句 Do we need to enter security again?

不需要，我們的地勤人員會帶您們到登機口。
No, our ground crew will take you to the gate.

請問轉機櫃檯在哪裡？

迷你句 I need to find the transfer counter.

完整句 Can you tell me where transfer counter is?

在您的右手邊。
It is on your right hand side.

請問我們要在哪裡等候？

迷你句 Where should we wait?

完整句 Were should we wait for our next plane?

您可以在候機室等候。
You can wait in the lounge.

[Things to Know] 一定要知道的**旅行常識**

當你所搭乘的飛機不是「直飛航班」的時候，就會在途中某些地方或城市降落暫時停留，以補充油料、更換機組人員，而機上乘客也必須一起在當地短暫停留，這樣的情況叫做「過境」。你不必換機，也不用再辦登機手續。轉機，顧名思義，就是要轉搭其他飛機，需先弄清楚在哪裡轉搭、搭哪一班飛機或其它手續。

👄：你要會說的一句話　🕪：你會聽到的問/答　**MP3** Track ▶ 021

[Must be...] 這個時候最需要的一句話！

👄 我在找可以兌換貨幣的地方。

迷你句 I need to exchange some money.

完整句 I am looking for a money exchange counter.

🕪 您可以去大廳的銀行看看。
You can try the bank in the lobby.

👄 請問要收取服務費嗎？

迷你句 Is there a service fee?

完整句 Does it change for service fee?

🕪 不需收取服務費。
No charge.

👄 請問銀行有收美金嗎？

迷你句 Are US dollars ok?

完整句 Does the bank take US dollars?

🕪 用美金換錢的話，銀行會收手續費。
The bank takes US dollars with a service fee.

👄 機場的銀行現在還開著嗎？

迷你句 Is the bank at the airport still open?

完整句 I was wondering if the bank at the airport is still open.

🕪 銀行的機場從早上九點開到晚上十點。
The bank is open from 9a.m.-10p.m.

👄 請問匯率是多少？

迷你句 What is the exchange rate?

完整句 I would like to know the exchange rate.

🕪 30 塊台幣兌 1 塊美金。
It is a NT$30 to one dollar.

我想要換成大鈔。　**迷你句** Bills, please.

完整句 I don't want to have too many coins. Can I chang it into bills?

換成100塊的紙鈔可以嗎？
Are $100s okay?

我想要兌現這張旅行支票。　**迷你句** I want to cash this traveler's check.

完整句 Would you cash this traveler's check?

好的，您想要怎麼換？
Ok, how would you like it?

我想要換一些零錢。　**迷你句** I want some small change.

完整句 May I have some change?

您想要換多少？
How much do you want?

請問要在哪裡換錢？　**迷你句** Where can I exchange money?

完整句 Where is the money exchange counter?

您可以到『貨幣兌換處』換錢。
You can go to the "Currency Exchange" to exchange money.

[Things to Know] 一定要知道的**旅行常識**

　　若需要攜帶大筆錢財，不想帶現金，當地提款又不方便，可以考慮購買旅行支票。旅行支票以美金計價，用簽名方式驗證身分，不必擔心被偷，因為竊賊無法使用該旅行支票，而且購買人也可以 24HR 申請補發。旅行支票的匯率，通常會比在當地換錢來得好，可說是到未知國家最方便的取錢法。

[Must be...] 這個時候最需要的一句話！

👄 為什麼我沒看到我的行李？
迷你句 I can't find my luggage.
完整句 Why can't I find my luggage?

🔊 很抱歉，行李卸載有點延遲。
I am sorry, there is a delay for unloading the baggage.

👄 我有一件行李遺失了。
迷你句 One bag was missing.
完整句 One piece of my luggage is missing.

🔊 請給我您的行李托運條。
Can I have your baggage check-in slip?

👄 我找不到我的行李箱。
迷你句 Where is my suitcase?
完整句 I can't find my suitcase everywhere.

🔊 抱歉，您的行李箱在下一班飛機上。
Sorry, it will arrive on the next flight.

👄 請幫我檢查一下我的行李有沒有上飛機。
迷你句 What is the status of my suitcase?
完整句 Can you check if my luggage made it to the flight?

🔊 很抱歉，您的行李並沒有上飛機。
Sorry, but your luggage didn't make it on the flight.

👄 我現在應該要怎麼辦呢？
迷你句 What should I do?
完整句 What can I do now?

🔊 我們可以將行李寄到您的飯店。
We can have it delivered to your hotel.

😊 我的行李箱上面有我的名條。

迷你句 My luggage is tagged.

完整句 There is my name tag on my luggage.

👂 好的,我們的人正在尋找您的行李。
Ok, we are looking for it.

😊 我的行李箱裡有很重要的東西。

迷你句 My suitcase is important.

完整句 There is something very expensive in my suitcase.

👂 請填寫這張表格我馬上為您查詢。
Please fill out this form; I will go check for you right away.

😊 你們會將找到的行李送到我的住處嗎?

迷你句 Will you deliver it to me?

完整句 Will you deliver my luggage to me if you find it?

👂 是的,我們會直接送到您的飯店。
Yes, we will deliver it to your hotel directly.

😊 我的行李損壞得很嚴重,你們要怎麼賠我?

迷你句 I demand compensation.

完整句 My baggage is seriously damaged, how are you going to deal with it?

👂 別擔心,我們會負起所有責任。
Don't worry; we will take all the responsibility.

[Vocabulary] 生字不用另外查字典!

01 行李 luggage

02 卸載 unload

03 延遲 delay

04 遺失 miss

05 托運條 check-in slip

06 行李箱 suitcase

07 狀態 status

08 寄送 deliver

09 名條 name tag

10 尋找 look for

11 負責任 take responsibility

12 賠償 compensation

：你要會說的一句話　　🔊：你會聽到的問／答　　　MP3 Track ▶ 023

[Must be...] 這個時候最需要的一句話！

😊 請問洗手間在哪裡？

迷你句 Where is the toilet?

完整句 Excuse me, do you know where the restroom is?

🔊 洗手間在走廊最末端。
The restroom is at the end of this corridor.

😊 請問哪裡有餐廳？

迷你句 Where is the restaurant?

完整句 Do you know where the restaurant is?

🔊 餐廳在三樓。
Restaurants are on the third floor.

😊 請問 B 航廈怎麼走？

迷你句 Where is terminal B?

完整句 Could you tell me how can I get to terminal B?

🔊 你可以搭航站巴士去那裡。
You can take the shuttle bus to terminal B.

😊 請問機場咖啡廳要怎麼走？

迷你句 How do I get to the airport café?

完整句 Can you give me direction to the airport café?

🔊 就在候機室後方。
It is right behind the lounge.

😊 我想要找機場保安人員。

迷你句 I need a security guard.

完整句 I need to find the airport security agent.

🔊 您可以使用黃色的電話跟保安人員連絡。
You can use the yellow phone to talk to the security agent.

😎 請問機場有書店嗎？

迷你句 Any bookstores?

完整句 Is there any bookstores in the airport?

👂 書店在 B1。
The bookstores are located on B1.

😎 請問服務台在哪裡？

迷你句 I need the information desk.

完整句 Where is the information desk?

👂 直走到底您就會看到了。
Go straight to the end then you will find it.

😎 請問機場巴士在哪裡？

迷你句 Is there a shuttle?

完整句 Where can I find the airport shuttle bus?

👂 在 1 號出口那裡。
It is at exit No.1.

😎 請問計程車要在哪裡搭？

迷你句 Are there taxis?

完整句 Where is the taxi services?

👂 計程車站在東出口。
The taxi service is at the east exit.

[Things to Know] 一定要知道的**旅行常識**

在一些航空業發達的國家，因為要容納來自世界各國的飛機，機場往往建得很大，也因此航廈分散，不能靠步行到達。若在航空站迷路，可向航警或櫃檯人員詢問，航站間通常會有接駁巴士定時發車，或是以輕軌捷運相互連結。

07 客訴航空公司

👄：你要會說的一句話　🔗：你會聽到的問／答

[Must be...] 這個時候最需要的一句話！

👄 他們的顧客服務很糟。

迷你句 The service is awful.

完整句 Their customer service is really poor.

🔗 發生什麼事了嗎？
Please tell us what happened so we can do our best to help.

👄 空服員的態度非常惡劣。

迷你句 They have an attitude problem.

完整句 The flight attendants have really bad attitude.

🔗 您可以詳細告訴我事情的經過嗎？
Can you tell me more about that? We need to know more to help.

👄 地勤人員沒將我的行李全程托運。

迷你句 They made a mistake with my luggage.

完整句 The ground crew didn't check my luggage all the way.

🔗 很抱歉您的行李遺失了。
We are very sorry that your luggage is missing.

👄 這真是非常不愉快的飛行經驗。

迷你句 That was an unpleasant journey.

完整句 That was a very unpleasant flight experience.

🔗 我們感到很抱歉。
We are sorry to hear that.

👄 登機櫃台的地勤人員什麼都不會。

迷你句 The ground crew needs more training.

完整句 The ground staff at the check-in counter were not helpful at all.

🔗 我會將資訊傳達給管理團隊。
I will pass this message to the management team.

你們的空服員種族歧視。

（迷你句）Your cabin crew is racist.

（完整句）What your cabin crew said was racist.

很抱歉,您可以告訴我們是哪位空服員嗎?
We're very sorry. Do you mind telling us which one of the crew said such a thing to you?

他們沒先通知我,就把我的座位換掉。

（迷你句）They made a mistake with my seat.

（完整句）They changed my seat without telling me first.

可以再告訴我們一些細節嗎?
Could you tell us more details about this?

空服員沒有說這個飛機餐不是素食的。

（迷你句）This is not vegetarian.

（完整句）The cabin crew didn't tell me that it wasn't for vegetarians.

很抱歉。我們會賠償。
We're sorry and we'll compensate you.

你們要怎麼賠償我?

（迷你句）How will you make it up to me?

（完整句）What would you do to make it up to me?

我們的主管會與您說明。
The official will let you know more details about the compensation.

[Things to Know] 一定要知道的**旅行常識**

若航空公司把行李運丟了、搞錯機位或是態度不佳,可以向櫃檯人員或是撥電話客訴。航空業與旅客交易的金額較大,因此在服務方面不會馬虎,而且一般信用卡買機票都會附送保險,也多會負責旅客的損失。雖然如此,旅客還是要把旅遊流程弄清楚,把出錯的風險降到最低,才是最保險的作法。

旅遊常用句型 + 超多替換字，套入馬上用！

入境過海關 (1)

● 我是來這兒 _____ 的。

I'm here _____.

01 觀光 **for sightseeing**
02 度假 **on vacation**
03 出差 **on business**
04 念書 **to study**
05 找朋友 **to visit a friend**
06 參加研討會 **to attend a seminar**

入境過海關 (2)

● 拜訪期間我會住在 _____。

I will be staying _____ during my visit.

01 朋友家 **at my friend's place**
02 我姑姑家 **at my aunt's place**
03 圓山飯店 **in the Grand Hotel**
04 一間青年旅館 **in a youth hostel**
05 學校宿舍 **in the school dormitory**
06 員工宿舍 **in the staff dormitory**

轉機

● 我總是在轉機中停時去 _____。

I always go to the _____ during the layover.

01 美髮廳 **salon**
02 免稅商店 **duty free shop**
03 水療 **spa**
04 按摩中心 **massage area**
05 書店 **bookstore**
06 美食區 **food court**

行李不見了

● 我的 _____ 沒有出現在行李輸送帶上。

My _____ didn't show up on the luggage carousel.

01 行李 luggage
02 袋子 bag
03 行李箱 suitcase
04 旅行袋 travel bag
05 託運行李 checked luggage
06 背包 backpack

在航空站迷路

● 可以請你告訴我怎麼去 _____ 嗎？

Can you tell me how to get to _____?

01 第一航廈 Terminal 1
02 三十二號登機門 Gate 32
03 國際航廈 International Terminal
04 入境大廳 the arrivals hall
05 出境大廳 the departure lounge
06 國內航廈 Domestic Terminal

客訴航空公司

● 我要對 _____ 提出申訴。

I want to file a complaint on _____.

01 我受損的行李 my damaged luggage
02 機位超賣 the overbooking
03 我遺失的行李 my lost luggage
04 航班延遲 the flight delay
05 機上服務 the in-flight service
06 機上餐點 the in-flight meals

機場到市區、飯店的交通

到了當地機場，旅行真正開始了！但是機場往往在離市中心很遠的地方，所以要事先知道從機場到市中心、飯店的交通，才不至於帶著一大堆行李，卻又不知道怎麼離開機場。通常，機場到市區的交通工具有以下幾種：

01【巴士】

通常巴士會經過市區許多交通樞紐，如有需要可以考慮。機場巴士會有放置大型行李的地方，工作人員通常會幫你把行李貼上識別證，以防別人或自己拿錯行李。

02【地鐵】

搭地鐵是最便宜、也很快就能到達市區的方式，只是有些國家的地鐵站沒有手扶梯和電梯，而攜帶大型行李的人較不適合搭地鐵，因為扛行李會很累，也怕地鐵站的人潮會增加行李遺失的風險。

03【火車】

火車也是到市區的交通方式之

一。要注意的是，有時候在市區的火車站，會離真正的市中心很遠，所以要注意在市區內部的交通問題。

04【接駁車】

如果你已經預約了國外的學校或是營隊，可以請對方出車接你，雖然費用會比其他交通方式貴上很多，但是比較方便。如果有預約高級飯店，也可以與飯店詢問有無免費或付費的機場巴士。

05【計程車】

計程車絕對是最從機場到市區最便利的方式，但是收費較高。要注意有些國家的計程車，對旅客的收費會比對當地人高。與計程車司機語言上的溝通，也是個要克服的問題。

PART 04
住飯店

[Must be...] 這個時候最需要的一句話！

👄 請問你們有哪幾種套房？
　迷你句 Are there different rooms?
　完整句 What type of suits do you have?

👂 您可以參考我們的目錄。
You can check our catalogue.

👄 請問雙人房多少錢？
　迷你句 How much is a double room?
　完整句 How much does a double room cost?

👂 雙人房一個晚上200美元。
It is $200 per night for a double room.

👄 請問現在有優惠活動嗎？
　迷你句 What is the special?
　完整句 What is the special offer now?

👂 抱歉，我們現在沒有任何優惠活動。
Sorry, we don't offer any special price now.

👄 請問可以打折嗎？
　迷你句 Any discount?
　完整句 Can I have a discount?

👂 抱歉，旺季沒有折扣。
Sorry, there is no discount in the peak season.

👄 請問哪一種房間的價位較高？
　迷你句 What is the expensive one?
　完整句 Which room is the most expensive one?

👂 湖景套房收費較高。
We charge more for a lake view suite.

請問雙人房和家庭套房哪個比較好？
迷你句 Which one is better?
完整句 Which room is better, double room or family suite?

家庭套房比較適合您的需求。
The family suite is ideal for your needs.

請問平日有折扣嗎？
迷你句 Any discount during weekdays?
完整句 Is there any discount during weekdays?

有，平日有打八折。
Yes, you will have 20% off during weekdays.

你能報一下貴飯店的房價嗎？
迷你句 What are the prices of your hotel?
完整句 Could you tell me the prices of your hotel?

我們的房價從200美元到500美元不等。
Our room rates range from $200 to $500.

請問住一個星期要多少錢？
迷你句 How much for a week?
完整句 How much will it cost for a week?

請問您要住哪一種套房呢？
What type of suite do you like?

[Vocabulary] 生字**不用另外查字典**！

01 套房 **suite**
02 目錄 **catalogue**
03 雙人房 **double room**
04 優惠活動 **special offer**
05 打折 **discount**
06 旺季 **peak season**
07 湖景套房 **lake view suite**
08 家庭套房 **family suite**
09 八折 **20% off**
10 平日 **during weekdays**
11 從......到...... **range from**
12 種類 **type**

[Must be...] 這個時候最需要的一句話！

👄 請問健身房的營業時間是什麼時候？

迷你句 When can I use the gym?

完整句 What are the opening hours for the gym?

👂 營業時間從早上八點到晚上十點。
It is open from 8 a.m. to 10 p.m.

👄 請問飯店裡有游泳池嗎？

迷你句 Do you have a pool?

完整句 Is there a swimming pool in your hotel?

👂 游泳池在 B1。
The swimming pool is on B1.

👄 請問我可以使用傳真機嗎？

迷你句 Is there a fax?

完整句 Can I use the fax machine?

👂 沒問題，傳真機就在會議室旁邊。
Sure, the fax machine is right beside the meeting room.

👄 請問有網路可以使用嗎？

迷你句 Is Internet available?

完整句 Can I use the Internet in your hotel?

👂 是的，我們有提供免費的網路服務。
Yes, we provide complimentary Internet access.

👄 請問電梯在哪裡？

迷你句 Where is the elevator?

完整句 Can you show me where the elevator is?

👂 電梯就在服務台右手邊。
The elevator is at the right hand side of the front desk.

😮 請問我可以在哪裡獲得更多的資訊？

迷你句 How can I know more from you?

完整句 Where can I get more information?

👂 您可以到服務台諮詢。
You can go to the front desk.

😮 請問飯店裡有幾個逃生門？

迷你句 How many emergency exits do you have?

完整句 How many emergency exits do you have in this hotel?

👂 每個樓層各有四個逃生門。
There are four exits on each floor.

😮 請問酒吧營業到幾點？

迷你句 When does the bar close?

完整句 Can you tell me how late does the bar open?

👂 營業到凌晨一點鐘。
The bar closes at 1a.m.

😮 請問哪裡可以唱卡拉OK？

迷你句 Where can I sing karaoke?

完整句 Is there a place where I can sing karaoke?

👂 抱歉，飯店裡沒有卡拉OK設備。
Sorry, there is no karaoke in this hotel.

[Vocabulary] 生字不用另外查字典！

01 健身房 **gym**

02 營業時間 **opening hours**

03 游泳池 **swimming pool**

04 傳真機 **fax machine**

05 網路 **Internet**

06 附加的 **complimentary**

07 電梯 **elevator**

08 資訊 **information**

09 服務台 **front desk**

10 逃生門 **emergency exit**

11 酒吧 **bar**

12 卡拉OK **karaoke**

[Must be...] 這個時候最需要的一句話！

我想要入房。　　(迷你句) Check-in, please.
　　　　　　　　(完整句) I need to check-in.

請問您有在網路上先預訂嗎？
Did you register online?

我們有五個人。　(迷你句) Party of five.
　　　　　　　　(完整句) There will be five of us.

請問要住在一起嗎？
Would you like to share one room?

這是我的訂房號　(迷你句) Here is my reservation.
碼。　　　　　　(完整句) I have my reservation number.

好的，請給我您的護照。
Ok, please give me your passport.

我已經在網路上預　(迷你句) I booked a room.
訂房間了。　　　　(完整句) I reserved a room online.

太好了！請問先生貴姓？
Great! What is your name, Sir?

請給我房間鑰匙。　(迷你句) My room key, please.
　　　　　　　　　(完整句) Would you please give me my room
　　　　　　　　　　　　　key?

在這裡，您的房間在 18 樓。
Here, your room is on the 18th floor.

👄 我已經在你們的線上訂房系統完成付款。

迷你句 I have already paid.

完整句 I have already paid for the rate through your online booking system.

👂 好的，請問您的預定編號是？
Ok, please tell me your registration number.

👄 請問今天晚上有空房嗎？

迷你句 Can I get a room for tonight?

完整句 Do you have a room for tonight?

👂 請問是要單人房嗎？
Do you want a single room?

👄 請給我一間面海的房間。

迷你句 A room with a sea view.

完整句 I would like to have a room with an ocean view.

👂 這樣收費會高一點，請問這樣可以嗎？
That will cost more; will that be ok with you?

👄 我想要延長幾天的住宿。

迷你句 I want to extend.

完整句 I would like to extend my stay.

👂 請問要延長幾天呢？
How many days would you like to extend?

[Things to Know] 一定要知道的**旅行常識**

　　飯店報到的時間通常在下午三點左右，如果有需要提早入住，也可以在訂房時詢問，若不是太熱門的日子，飯店多半會給予通融。到飯店辦理入住時，櫃檯人員通常會要您出示護照並提供信用卡，讓他們做一個過卡的動作，先向你的信用卡發卡銀行預取一個額度，作為保證金，預收房客在飯店房間內打電話或是使用房間內付費飲料或點心等的費用。但是別擔心，若是入住期間都沒有產生房費之外的費用，這筆錢當然就不會出現在信用卡帳單上。

飯店設備介紹

許多飯店都備有娛樂設備,如健身房和游泳池。由於歐美的健身風氣盛,因此使用健身房的人會相當多,如要使用,記得先預約。在市中心的飯店,游泳池多位於頂樓,且為了住宿的家庭,通常附有兒童池。

【常見生字】

飯店大廳	lobby	服務台	reception desk
客房	room	樓梯	stair
酒吧	bar	廚房	kitchen
健身房	gym	游泳池	swimming pool

【最常用的旅行句】

01 我會在大廳等你。

I'll be waiting for you at the lobby.

02 健身房開到幾點?

When does the gym close?

03 使用廚房需要付費嗎?

Is it free to use the kitchen?

04 我們有宵禁,所以前台會在晚上11點關閉。

We had a curfew, so the reception desk will be closed at 11 p.m.

逛地球旅遊專欄 飯店房間設備介紹

到了房間，最好先檢查所有電器用品是否都可以用，再確認床單、毛巾等用品是否備齊了。現在有許多小旅館為了環保，已經不再提供牙刷、毛巾等一次性清潔用品，預訂旅館時最好先詢問。

【常見生字】

電燈	light	電視	television
洗手間	rest room	冰箱	refrigerator
冷氣	air-conditioner	暖氣	heat
地毯	carpet	床單	sheet
網路	Internet	無線網路	wi-fi

【最常用的旅行句】

01 房間裡的電視壞掉了。

The television is not working.

02 我想要換一組新的床單。

I would like to have a new set of sheet.

03 無線網路的帳號密碼是什麼？

What's the wi-fi username and password?

● : 你要會說的一句話　　🔊 : 你會聽到的問／答　　**MP3** Track ▶ 028

[Must be...] 這個時候最需要的一句話！

😊 這個房間夠大嗎？　　迷你句 Is it big enough?

完整句 Is the room spacious enough?

🔊 我相信這房間足夠您使用。
I am sure this room will be perfect for you.

😊 我找不到電燈開關。　　迷你句 Where is the light?

完整句 I can't find the light switch.

🔊 電燈開關就在牆壁上。
The light switch is on the wall.

😊 請問房間裡有微波爐嗎？　　迷你句 Is there a microwave?

完整句 Is there a microwave in the room?

🔊 微波爐在冰箱上方。
The microwave is above the refrigerator.

😊 請問房間裡的酒吧可以使用嗎？　　迷你句 Can I use the mini bar?

完整句 May I use the mini bar in my room?

🔊 您可以免費使用酒吧，但吧台上的酒若要開瓶，就要收費。
You can use the mini bar for free. But we charge for the alcohol on the table.

😊 請問有提供按摩服務嗎？　　迷你句 Do you have massage?

完整句 Do you provide massage service?

🔊 按摩服務每次要收費20美元。
Massage service costs $20 each time.

💬 請問打網球一個小時要多少錢？

迷你句 How much per hour?

完整句 How much is it per hour to play tennis?

👂 打網球不用錢。
It is all free to use.

💬 請問健身房裡的跑步機要如何使用？

迷你句 How do I use the treadmills?

完整句 Can you tell us how to use the treadmills in the gym?

👂 健身房裡有專業指導員可以教您。
There is a professional gym instructor who can teach you.

💬 請問使用房間內的電視需要收費嗎？

迷你句 Is it free to watch TV?

完整句 Is it free to watch the TV in my room?

👂 我們有六個免付費頻道供您選擇。
We have six free channels to choose from.

💬 我想要用飲水機。

迷你句 How do I use the drinking fountain?

完整句 Can you show me how to use the drinking fountain?

👂 按熱水鍵前，請先按紅色按鈕。
Press the red button before you press "hot water".

[Vocabulary] 生字不用另外查字典！

01 房間 room

02 電燈 light

03 開關 switch

04 微波爐 microwave

05 冰箱 refrigerator

06 按摩服務 massage service

07 打網球 play tennis

08 跑步機 treadmills

09 健身教練 gym instructor

10 免付費頻道 free channels

11 飲水機 drinking fountain

12 紅色按鈕 red button

[Must be...] 這個時候最需要的一句話！

👄 請問你們的客房服務是 24 小時的嗎？

迷你句 Is it 24 hours?

完整句 Do you offer room service for 24 hrs a day?

👂 是的，有需要請隨時通知我們。
Yes, just give us a call whenever you need to.

👄 請問你們現在還有客房服務嗎？

迷你句 Is it too late for service?

完整句 Do you still offer room service now?

👂 是的，我們還有在服務。
No, room service is still available.

👄 我想要叫晚餐的客房服務。

迷你句 Can I order dinner?

完整句 I would like to have room service for dinner.

👂 您的餐點將在三十分鐘內送到。
Your order will be ready in 30 minutes.

👄 可以請你們現在過來整理房間嗎？

迷你句 I need my room to be cleaned.

完整句 Will it be ok to clean the room now?

👂 請問您的房間號碼是？
What is your room number?

👄 可以再給我一個枕頭嗎？

迷你句 I want one more pillow.

完整句 Could you give me one more pillow?

👂 請問是 6814 號房嗎？
Is it room No.6814?

😮 請在明天早上八點叫我起床。

(迷你句) Wake me up at 8 o'clock in the morning.

(完整句) Would you please give me a wakeup call at 8 o'clock tomorrow morning?

👂 沒問題。
That won't be a problem.

😮 我想洗這些衣服。

(迷你句) I need laundry service.

(完整句) I would like to have this laundry done.

👂 請您填寫一下這張洗衣單。
Would you please fill out this laundry list?

😮 請問我什麼時候可以取回洗的衣服呢？

(迷你句) When will it be done?

(完整句) When can I get my laundry back?

👂 我們明天早上就會送過來。
We will send it back tomorrow morning.

😮 請問有提供行李搬運服務嗎？

(迷你句) Are there porters?

(完整句) Is there a porter service available?

👂 有的，請問有需要嗎？
Yes, do you need one?

[Words to Use] 替換字放空格，一句多用!!

- 你們現在有提供_____嗎？
  Do you provide _____ now?

01 客房服務 room service   **02** 接駁服務 shuttle service

03 洗衣服務 laundry service   **04** 行李搬運服務 a porter service

05 晨喚服務 wakeup call service   **06** 按摩服務 massage service

06 飯店餐廳／酒吧

👄：你要會說的一句話　🔊：你會聽到的問／答　　**MP3** Track ▶ 030

[Must be...] 這個時候最需要的一句話！

👄 請問今日特餐是什麼？
迷你句 What's the special?
完整句 What is today's special?

🔊 今日特餐是牛排。
Steak is today's special.

👄 我可以點 B 餐嗎？
迷你句 I will have set meal B.
完整句 Can I have the set meal B?

🔊 好的，還需要什麼嗎？
Ok, anything else?

👄 我有晚餐券。
迷你句 Here is the voucher.
完整句 I have a dinner voucher.

🔊 好的，請自行取用自助餐。
Please help yourself to the buffet.

👄 請將帳記在5385號房。
迷你句 Bill it to 5385.
完整句 Please put the bill in room 5385.

🔊 當然，您還需要其他服務嗎？
Sure, do you need any other service?

👄 請給我一杯咖啡。
迷你句 Coffee, please.
完整句 I would like to have a cup of coffee.

🔊 您要冰的還是熱的？
Would you like iced or hot coffee?

😊 請幫我續杯。　**迷你句** Refill it, please.
　　　　　　　　完整句 Can I get a refill?

👂 好的，我馬上來。
Ok, I will be right back.

😊 請問這張兌換券要如何使用？　**迷你句** How do I use this?
　　　　　　　　完整句 How should I use this voucher?

👂 您可以兌換一杯無酒精飲料。
You can get a free soft drink with it.

😊 請問今天晚上有什麼表演嗎？　**迷你句** Any dinner show?
　　　　　　　　完整句 Will there be any dinner show tonight?

👂 今天晚上有個知名樂團的表演。
There is a live show by a famous band tonight.

😊 請問有酒單嗎？　**迷你句** Can I see the wine list?
　　　　　　　　完整句 Do you have a wine list? I may want to have some.

👂 給您。您喜歡喝哪一種口感的酒呢？
Here you are. What type of wine do you prefer?

[Vocabulary] 生字不用另外查字典！

01 今日特餐 today's special
02 牛排 steak
03 B餐 meal B
04 晚餐券 dinner voucher
05 自助餐 buffet
06 一杯咖啡 a cup of coffee
07 續杯 get a refill
08 馬上回來 right back
09 無酒精飲料 soft drink
10 表演 show
11 知名樂團 famous band
12 酒單 wine list

[Must be...] 這個時候最需要的一句話！

😮 請幫我們退房。　**迷你句** Check out, please.

　　　　　　　完整句 Can you help us check out?

👂 您的房間號碼是幾號？
What is your room number?

😮 8769房要退房。　**迷你句** Checking out of 8769.

　　　　　　　完整句 We are going to check out from 8769.

👂 請問您想要怎麼付費呢？
How would you like to pay?

😮 可以讓我看一下我的費用總額嗎？　**迷你句** Can I check the bill?

　　　　　　　完整句 Can I check the total charge of my stay?

👂 好的，請幫我們核對一下資料。
Sure, please check to see whether your information is correct.

😮 請刷我的卡付費。　**迷你句** Leave it on the card.

　　　　　　　完整句 Please charge it to my credit card.

👂 請給我您的信用卡。
Please give me your credit card.

😮 請問您還有我的信用卡資料嗎？　**迷你句** You should have my details.

　　　　　　　完整句 Do you still have my credit card information?

👂 有的，請稍候。
Yes, please wait a moment.

請問這筆費用是什麼？
迷你句 What is this for?
完整句 What is this charging for?

那是您的長途電話費用。
It is a long distance phone call charge.

這是我的房間鑰匙。
迷你句 Here is my room key.
完整句 Here is the key of my room.

請核對一下您的帳單並在這裡簽名。
Please check your receipt and sign your name here.

我喝了冰箱裡的礦泉水和啤酒。
迷你句 I drank a bottle of water and a beer.
完整句 I had a bottle of water and a beer from refrigerator.

這樣總共 5 塊錢美金。
The charge will be $5.

帳單金額有錯誤。
迷你句 This bill is wrong.
完整句 The amount is wrong.

很抱歉，請讓我再算一次。
Sorry, let me check it again.

[Vocabulary] 生字**不用另外查字典**！

01 退房 check out
02 房間號碼 room number
03 付費 pay
04 費用總額 total charge
05 資料 information
06 信用卡 credit card
07 長途電話 long distance phone call
08 鑰匙 key
09 帳單 receipt
10 簽名 sign
11 礦泉水 a bottle of water
12 冰箱 refrigerator

：你要會說的一句話　　：你會聽到的問/答　　**MP3** Track ▶ 032

[Must be...] 這個時候最需要的一句話！

空調壞掉了。　　**迷你句** The air-con is broken.

完整句 The air conditioner is not working.

請問是哪間房？
May I have your room number?

房間裡沒有熱水。　　**迷你句** No hot water here.

完整句 There is no hat water in the room.

您可以使用在走廊盡頭的飲水機。
You can use the drinking fountain at the end of the hallway.

咖啡機無法使用。　　**迷你句** The coffee maker is not working.

完整句 The coffee maker is broken down.

我們會派人去修理。
We will send someone up to get it repaired.

麻煩請派人到我房間來一下好嗎？　　**迷你句** Could you send someone up?

完整句 Please send someone up to my room.

請問有什麼問題嗎？
What is the problem?

廁所故障了。　　**迷你句** I can't use the toilet.

完整句 The toilet is out of order.

我們馬上過去檢查。
We will check on it right away.

我的門打不開。　　　　迷你句 I can't open the door.

完整句 I can't get my door unlocked.

讓我示範給您看。
Let me show you.

請問你們可以現在　　　迷你句 Could you fix it now?
過來修嗎？
完整句 Please fix it immediately.

好的，我馬上到。
Sure, I will be right there.

馬桶不能沖水。　　　　迷你句 The toilet is stuck.

完整句 The toilet won't flash.

好的，請填寫這張維修單。
Ok, please fill out this repair form.

空調不夠冷。　　　　　迷你句 The air-con is not cold.

完整句 The air conditioner is not cold
enough.

我馬上請維修人員過去看。
I will report it to the maintenance right away.

[Things to Know] 一定要知道的**旅行常識**

進到飯店房間後，最好把全部電器包含電燈都打開，檢查是否故障，其次就是檢查衛浴設備。最後再看看寢具是否有短少，毛巾是否乾淨。若遇到房間內的任何設備出狀況，無論是電視沒影像、空調壞掉、洗臉臺堵塞還是馬桶不能沖水，都要記得盡快打電話通知櫃檯，請他們派人過來處理。一般如果問題沒辦法即時解決，飯店都會幫房客換一間房間。若是沒有同等房型的空房，這時候免費升等恐怕是必要的。

109

😖：你要會說的一句話　👂：你會聽到的問／答　　**MP3** Track ▶ 033

[Must be...] 這個時候最需要的一句話！

👄 這間房間有菸味。　**迷你句** It smells smoky.
　完整句 This room smells smoky.

👂 您想要換一間房嗎？
Would you like to move to another room?

👄 這間房間對我們來說太小了。　**迷你句** It is too small.
　完整句 This room is too small to use.

👂 我們還剩下一間家庭房。
We still have one family room.

👄 可以幫我們換其它的房間嗎？　**迷你句** Can we change rooms?
　完整句 Can you find another room for us?

👂 抱歉，今晚的住房率已滿。
Sorry, we are fully booked today.

👄 我不喜歡這間房間。　**迷你句** I don't like this room.
　完整句 This room is not my idea.

👂 很抱歉，但是我們目前沒有其它的單人房。
I am sorry, but we don't have any single rooms available at the moment.

👄 這間房間的景色很差。　**迷你句** The view is really bad.
　完整句 The view in my room is really bad.

👂 您介意我幫您換到另一個樓層的房間嗎？
Would you mind if I put you in another room on an other floor?

隔壁房的旅客很吵。

迷你句 My neighbor is noisy.

完整句 The people next door is too noisy.

我們會另外幫您找一間房間。
We will find another room for you.

請問加一張床要多少錢？

迷你句 How much for an extra bed?

完整句 How much do you charge for an extra bed?

加一張床要40塊美金。
It costs $40 for an extra bed.

請問可以加一張床嗎？

迷你句 I need one more bed.

完整句 Can I have an extra bed?

好的，我們會派人過去幫您。
Ok, we will send someone to help you.

我的房間太靠近電梯了。

迷你句 My room is next to the elevator.

完整句 My room is too close to the elevator.

我們馬上幫您換房。
We will switch rooms for you right away.

[Things to Know] 一定要知道的**旅行常識**

在許多歐美的旅館裡，常常會在床頭櫃的抽屜裡發現聖經。或許有人會覺得毛骨悚然，但其實是因為歐美有許多基督、天主教徒，習慣在睡前禱告，旅館因此放了聖經。如果是這個原因覺得房間不吉利，倒是可以安心，因為並不代表該房間發生過什麼壞事。

[Must be...] 這個時候最需要的一句話！

👄 我忘記帶我的鑰匙了。
迷你句 I forgot my key.
完整句 I forgot to bring my key.

🔊 我可以給您另一支鑰匙。
I can give you another key.

👄 我的鑰匙不見了。
迷你句 My key is missing.
完整句 I lost my room key.

🔊 請問您住幾號房。
Which room are you staying in?

👄 我把自己反鎖在門外了。
迷你句 I am locked out.
完整句 I locked myself out.

🔊 我們會重啟您的房門。
We will have to reactivate your room.

👄 我房間的鑰匙壞掉了。
迷你句 It is broken.
完整句 My room key is not working.

🔊 請讓我看一下您的鑰匙。
May I have your room key?

👄 請問有人撿到我的手錶嗎？
迷你句 Did anyone find my watch?
完整句 I am wondering if someone found my watch.

🔊 您的手錶在這裡。
We do have your watch.

我的錢包掉了。　**迷你句** I lost my purse.

完整句 I can't find my purse.

您可以到服務台詢問。
You can go to the front desk.

請問我可以看一下　**迷你句** Can I check the lost and found box?
失物招領盒嗎？
完整句 May I take a look at the lost and found box?

請問您掉了什麼嗎？
Did you lose something?

如果有人撿到我的　**迷你句** Contact me if someone finds it.
筆記型電腦，請通
知我。　**完整句** Please let me know if someone found my laptop.

請留下您的手機號碼。
Please leave your cell phone number.

我掉了大約 300 塊　**迷你句** I lost $300.
美金。
完整句 I lost money. It is about $300.

請填寫這份財務遺失單。
Please fill out this Lost Property Form, please.

[Words to Use] 替換字放空格，一句多用!!

- 如果有人撿到我的_____請通知我。
  Please contact me if someone found my _____.

01 筆記型電腦 **laptop**　　　　**02** 護照 **passport**

03 錢包 **wallet**　　　　**04** 手錶 **watch**

05 房間鑰匙 **room key**　　　**06** 手機 **cell phone**

113

[Must be...] 這個時候最需要的一句話！

我想要客訴。
迷你句 I want to make a complaint.
完整句 I have some advice for your hotel.

請問是關於什麼呢？
What is it about?

我可以找經理談嗎？
迷你句 I need to see your manager.
完整句 May I speak to your manager?

請問發生什麼事了嗎？
What happened?

我對我的房間不滿意。
迷你句 I don't like my room.
完整句 This room is not what I expected.

可以詳細地告訴我嗎？
Can you tell me more about it?

服務生的態度很差。
迷你句 The waiter has a bad attitude.
完整句 I am not satisfied with your service.

我們會反應您的意見。
We will report your comment.

我要填寫顧客意見表。
迷你句 I need the Customer Satisfaction List.
完整句 I want to fill out the Customer Satisfaction List.

意見表可以在服務台領取。
You can find the list at the front desk.

😐 我要退款。　　　迷你句 I want to have a refund.
　　　　　　　　　完整句 Can I have total refund?

👂 抱歉，我們只能賠償部分損失。
Sorry, we can only pay for a part.

😐 我需要降價。　　迷你句 Please give me discount.
　　　　　　　　　完整句 I want to have discount.

👂 我們能夠給您打 5 折。
We can offer you 50% off.

😐 我需要獲得賠償。　迷你句 Please give me indemnification.
　　　　　　　　　　完整句 I want to have indemnification.

👂 請先讓我跟經理談談。
Please let me speak to the manager first.

😐 你們能給我什麼賠償？　迷你句 What is the compensation?
　　　　　　　　　　　完整句 What kinds of compensation can I
　　　　　　　　　　　　　　get from this?

👂 我們可以給您飯店的折價券。
We can offer you a coupon for our hotel.

[Things to Know] 一定要知道的**旅行常識**

　　如果飯店、旅館房內設備損壞、與當初下訂時的優惠不符，請直接與飯店櫃檯或行政人員反應。通常會得到住宿費的折扣、餐券或者是下次住宿的優惠。但若是在背包客居多的青年旅館，許多東西則是堪用即可，畢竟住宿費比較便宜，住宿的訴求不同。

旅遊常用句型＋超多替換字，套入馬上用！

詢問房價

● _____ 一晚費用多少？

What is the price of a _____ for one night?

01 單人房 single room

02 三人房 triple room

03 雙床房 twin room

04 家庭套房 family suite

05 雙人房 double room

06 豪華客房 deluxe room

詢問房間設備

● 我想知道房間內有沒有 _____。

I'm wondering if there's a/an _____ in the room.

01 暖氣 heater

02 冰箱 fridge

03 保險箱 safe deposit box

04 浴缸 bathtub

05 熨斗 iron

06 熱水瓶 water boiler

我想要……的房間

● 我們比較想要有 _____ 的房間。

We prefer a room with a/an _____.

01 海景 ocean view

02 山景 mountain view

03 湖景 lake view

04 市景 city view

05 港景 harbor view

06 陽台 balcony

如何使用房內設備

● 我不知道怎麼 _____。你可以派一個人過來嗎？
I have problems _____. Could you send someone over?

01 打開電視 **turning on the TV**　　**02** 將空調溫度調高 **turning up the air con**
03 使用保險箱 **using the safe deposit box**　**04** 將暖氣溫度調低 **turning down the heat**
05 設定鬧鐘 **setting the alarm clock**　**06** 使用咖啡機 **using the coffee maker**

房內設備有問題

● 我房內的 _____ 不能用。
The _____ in my room is not working.

01 空調 **air conditioning**　　　**02** 電話 **telephone**
03 電視遙控器 **TV remote control**　**04** 傳真機 **fax machine**
05 咖啡機 **coffee maker**　　　　**06** 免治馬桶 **bidet toilet**

換房間／加床位

● 我想知道我們可不可以 _____。
I'd like to know if we could _____.

01 多加一張床 **have an extra bed**
02 有一個嬰兒澡盆 **have a baby bathtub**
03 有一張嬰兒床 **have a baby cot**
04 換房間 **change our room**
05 再加一個枕頭 **have one more pillow**
06 多加一條被子 **have one more blanket**

旅館種類介紹

旅途當中最重要的就是住宿了，好的旅館能讓你好好休息，消除一天的疲勞。但相對地，各式旅館價錢差異也大，該如何挑個符合期待的旅館就相當重要了。看看下面哪種旅館適合你吧！

01【一般旅館】

即使是歸類於旅館（Hotel），住宿品質也是差異很大。簡單地說，旅館的優劣與價錢高低，是由汽車旅遊指南星等服務評等（Mobile Travel Guide Rating Service Stars）所列出的星級來評價旅館。五星級為頂級旅館，價格也最貴。一星級則屬於還算可以提供舒適的住宿環境，價格較經濟實惠。

02【汽車旅館】

在美國地廣人稀，郊區就很容易看到汽車旅館（Motel）。沒有豪華氣派的門面或裝飾，提供給旅人一個簡單的住宿環境。通常汽車旅館就是簡單一、兩層樓，可以把汽車停在最靠近房間的位子，方便進出。

03【民宿】

就如同台灣一樣，歐美許多的民宿 B&B（Bed & Breakfast）也富有各式各樣變化，充分表達出在地風情與主人的生活哲學。通常這類民宿房間數較少，訂位不易，價格也不見得便宜，但卻是可以體驗當地生活的最佳選擇。

04【青年旅館】

大部分的青年旅館（Hostel）除了有房間住宿外，還會提供「床位」住宿。所以若是一個人旅行，就可以用相當便宜的價格住宿，與各地來的旅人同住一間房間。喜歡以有限經費四處旅遊，並結交各國各地朋友的人來說，青年旅館最適合。

PART 05
吃四方

[Must be...] 這個時候最需要的一句話！

👄 我正在找一間好吃的日式餐廳。
- **迷你句** Any good Japanese restaurants?
- **完整句** I am looking for a decent Japanese restaurant.

👂 你可以試試山崎，他們有好吃的日本菜。
You should try Yamasaki; they have got decent Japanese food.

👄 你知道任何當地好吃的餐廳嗎？
- **迷你句** Any good local restaurants?
- **完整句** Do you know any local restaurants with good food?

👂 有一家好吃的印度餐廳叫蓮花。
There is a good Indian restaurant called Lotus.

👄 有外帶中國菜的好地方嗎？
- **迷你句** Any good Chinese takeout?
- **完整句** Is there any good Chinese takeout place?

👂 轉角有一家不錯的中國菜館。
There is a good Chinese restaurant around the corner.

👄 請問這家熟食店的東西好吃嗎？
- **迷你句** Is this deli good?
- **完整句** Is the food in this deli good?

👂 這家熟食店的東西都很好吃。
The food in this deli is generally delicious.

👄 請問這個鎮上最有名的餐館是哪間？
- **迷你句** Which restaurant is the best?
- **完整句** Can you tell me the best restaurant in this town?

👂 莉莉的餐館是個個鎮上最棒的。
Lily's restaurant is the best one in this town.

😮 我不知道哪裡有餐廳。

迷你句 Where is the restaurant?

完整句 Can you show me where the restaurant is?

🗨 直走左轉你就會看到了。
Go straight and turn to the left then you will find it.

😮 你能推薦我一個好餐館嗎？

迷你句 Can you recommend one to me?

完整句 Can you recommend me a good restaurant?

🗨 你可以參考旅遊指南。
You can check the tour guide.

😮 哪家餐廳有提供美味的本地料裡？

迷你句 Which restaurant serves good local food?

完整句 Do you know a restaurant serving good local food?

🗨 飯店裡那一家的料理很棒。
The one in the hotel is good.

😮 請問有吃到飽的餐廳嗎？

迷你句 Is there an all-you-can-eat restaurant?

完整句 Do you know an all-you-can-eat restaurant?

🗨 這附近有幾家。
There are several around here.

[Words to Use] 替換字放空格，一句多用!!

- 這間餐廳的＿＿＿＿很好吃。
  This restaurant makes delicious ＿＿＿＿.

01 龍蝦 **lobsters**

02 炸雞 **fried chicken**

03 燉飯 **risotto**

04 千層麵 **lasagna**

05 牛排 **steak**

06 古巴三明治 **Cuba sandwiches**

各種用餐地點介紹

旅途中的異國美食是最讓人難忘的，但若有經濟預算的情況下，如何同時兼顧荷包及胃呢？想要吃得道地，不一定餐餐都要上館子。選擇不同類型的飲食，反而更能體會當地風情。

01【餐廳】

花費指數：★★★★★

餐廳價格都從台幣600多元起，而許多國外餐廳習慣結帳後再加上小費，因此若餐餐都在餐廳吃，很容易超出預算；但餐廳往往衛生條件較佳，也可以一次性地品嘗到當地的美食。

02【吃到飽】

花費指數: ★★★

吃到飽接受度廣，付一定的金額可以享受各式各樣的食物，不限食量，是給不想要花大錢，但卻要想要吃很飽的人的好選擇。

03【速食店】

花費指數: ★★

速食店接受度也較廣，但因為每個國家的速食店仍有些許在地化，會有與其它國家不一樣的餐點，也不至於吃不到當地的口味，因此到當地旅遊時，不妨也去試試。

04【咖啡廳】

花費指數: ★★

旅遊途中累了，尋找一間有氣氛的咖啡廳，享受輕食、放鬆自己，是旅遊中小小的幸福之一。咖啡廳的價位較一般餐廳便宜，也有簡單的三明治、或蛋糕餐點可供選擇，適合不想吃正餐的時候。

05【路邊攤販】

花費指數: ★

想要了解當地美食，最快的方法就是前往市集；市集裡有最道地的料理、價格也很平易近人，透過與小販們的交流，更可以了解當地人民的飲食習慣，但要注意衛生。

逛地球旅遊專欄 各國超有名美食

在上一篇提及了許多不同種類餐廳的介紹，現在來介紹各國平價、容易尋找、當地人也喜歡的美食。到了當地旅遊時，一定要試試！

01【美國超有名】

在美國街頭常見推車攤販，或是一應俱全的餐車。通常餐車販賣的食物，是美國人常吃的熱狗、漢堡；有時花不到一元美金，就可享有披薩加小杯可樂，划算至極。

02【紐、澳超有名】

紐、澳的路邊攤常見 Sea Food BBQ（烤海鮮），多賣炸魚、海鮮這類的食物。有時候花不到台幣 100 元，就可以買到很多炸魚、炸薯條，吃得開心，又可以餵飽五臟廟。而海鮮類的食物因為食材新鮮，價格會稍貴。

03【加拿大超有名】

加拿大有兩間有名連鎖咖啡店：一間是 Tim Hortons，價位較星巴克咖啡便宜，另有多樣的甜甜圈以及提供午餐和湯類。另外一間是 Second Cup，目前為止加拿大有三百多家的分店，是第一間提供行動上網的咖啡店，咖啡口味選擇多！

04【英國超有名】

英國人習慣吃三明治，因為快速且方便帶著走。在英國有間有名的連鎖三明治餐廳Pret a Manger，該餐廳強調食材新鮮、口味多樣。實在可納為省錢旅遊的好選擇。

: 你要會說的一句話　　:你會聽到的問／答

MP3 Track ▶ 037

[**Must be...**] 這個時候最需要的一句話！

👄 我要訂兩個位子。　　**迷你句** Table for two, please.

完整句 I would like to make reservation for two.

👂 請問要訂幾點呢？
What time do you prefer?

👄 我們明天晚上八點　**迷你句** At 8 p.m. tomorrow night.
會到。
完整句 We would like to come at 8p.m. tomorrow night.

👂 請問有幾位？
How many of you will there be?

👄 我們有兩個大人一　**迷你句** Two adults and a child, please.
個小孩。
完整句 There will be two adults and one child.

👂 請問是明天晚上八點的時間嗎？
8 p.m. tomorrow?

👄 請問我們的訂位可　**迷你句** Will you hold it if we are late?
保留多久呢？
完整句 How long will you hold the reservation for us?

👂 我們會保留訂位 10 分鐘。
We will hold the reservation for 10 minutes.

👄 我們想要靠窗的桌　**迷你句** A table by window is the best.
子。
完整句 We prefer the seat by window.

👂 沒問題，我們已經幫您留了位子。
Sure, we saved a table for you.

我們需要 8 個人的位子。 （迷你句）Table for 8, please.

（完整句）We need a table for 8.

好的。我們會幫你們併桌。
Okay. We will mov two tables together for you.

我們想要包廂。 （迷你句）Can we have a booth?

（完整句）A booth table will be great.

好，我去安排。
Ok, I will manage it.

我們已經預約了。 （迷你句）I made a reservation.

（完整句）We've already made a reservation.

很好，請問貴姓？
Great, may I have your name?

我們有五位。 （迷你句）Five, please.

（完整句）We have five people.

您對座位有任何偏好嗎？
Do you have any preference for the seat?

[Vocabulary] 生字不用另外查字典！

01 訂位子 make reservation　02 人人 adult
03 保留訂位 hold the reservation　04 靠窗 by window
05 要求併桌 have a table tighter　06 包廂 booth
07 預約 reservation　08 偏好 preference
09 準時 on time　10 遲到 delay
11 留位子 save a table　12 安排 manage

:你要會說的一句話　　:你會聽到的問／答　　**MP3** Track ▶ 038

[**Must be...**] 這個時候最需要的一句話！

😋 我要外帶。

迷你句 Takeout, please.

完整句 I want to take out.

👂 外帶可以在此點餐。
You can order your food here for takeout.

😋 請問你們有外送嗎？

迷你句 Do you deliver?

完整句 Do you have delivery?

👂 有的，請問要點什麼？
Yes, what do you need?

😋 請問外帶要收取服務費嗎？

迷你句 Do you charge for takeout?

完整句 How much money do you charge for takeout?

👂 外帶不需要收取服務費。
There is no service charge for takeout orders.

😋 我們要內用。

迷你句 For here.

完整句 We want to eat here.

👂 如果要內用請等候帶位。
Please wait to be seated if you are dining in.

😋 我們要點外帶的東西。

迷你句 We want takeout.

完整句 We want to order some for takeout.

👂 好的，這是我們的外帶表格。
Ok, here is our takeout form.

😙 請問外送要多少錢？

(迷你句) How much for delivery?

(完整句) How much do you charge for delivery?

👂 我們外送是免費的。
There is also a free delivery option.

😙 請問你們有餃子外帶嗎？

(迷你句) Can I order dumplings for takeout?

(完整句) Do you have dumplings to take away?

👂 有的，您需要多少？
Yes, how many do you want?

😙 請給我外帶一份中薯和一杯大可樂。

(迷你句) A medium fries and a large coke to go.

(完整句) I would like a medium fries and a large Coke to go.

👂 好的，請稍等一下。
Ok, please wait a moment.

😙 請問今天有什麼可以外帶？

(迷你句) What can I take out?

(完整句) What is the takeout menu you have today?

👂 我們今天的外帶食物只有春捲。
We only have spring rolls today for takeout.

[Vocabulary] 生字不用另外查字典！

01 外帶 **take out**

02 外送 **delivery**

03 點餐 **order food**

04 服務費 **service charge**

05 內用 **eat here**

06 等候 **wait**

07 就餐 **dine in**

08 外帶表格 **takeout form**

09 餃子 **dumpling**

10 一份中薯 **a medium fries**

11 一杯大可樂 **a large coke**

12 春捲 **spring roll**

常見烹調法／食材

01【烹調法】

煎	fry	炒	stir fry
炸	deep fry	燉	stew
烤（用烤架）	grill	烤（用烤箱）	bake
煮（液體）	boil	蒸	steam

【最常用的旅行句】

我們昨天晚上煮了番茄牛肉湯。

We stewed the tomatoes with beef last night.

02【常見食材】

牛肉	beef	豬肉	pork
雞肉	chicken	魚肉	fish
青菜	vegetable	水果	fruit
海鮮	seafood	雞蛋	egg

【最常用的旅行句】

01 我不吃牛肉。

I don't eat beef.

02 我對海鮮過敏。

I'm allergic to seafood.

常見調味料／味道

01【調味料】

醋	vinegar	醬油	soy sauce
鹽	salt	糖	sugar
醬	sauce	沙拉油	salad
胡椒	pepper	薑	ginger
蒜	garlic	辣椒	hot pepper
蠔油	oyster sauce	奶油	butter

【最常用的旅行句】

我們的麵包需要多一點奶油。

We need more butter for the bread.

02【味道】

酸	sour	甜	sweet
苦	bitter	辣	spicy
鹹	salty		

【最常用的旅行句】

01 我想要一道比較不辣的菜。

   I would like to have something less spicy.

02 這道湯本來就酸酸的嗎？

   Is this soup supposed to taste so sour?

04 點餐／看中文菜單

👄：你要會說的一句話　　🎧：你會聽到的問／答　　**MP3** Track ▶ 039

[Must be...] 這個時候最需要的一句話！

👄 請問你們有中文菜單嗎？
　迷你句 I want a Chinese menu.
　完整句 Do you have Chinese menu?

🎧 有的，需要點餐請叫我。
　Here you are. Call me when you are ready.

👄 可以請你幫我介紹一下這道菜嗎？
　迷你句 What is this?
　完整句 Could you explain this dish for us?

🎧 好的，請問您問的是哪一個？
　Ok, which one do you want to know about?

👄 請問有兒童菜單嗎？
　迷你句 Do you have a kid's menu?
　完整句 Do you have a menu for children?

🎧 有的，請問需要幾份？
　Yes, how many do you need?

👄 請問無酒精飲料在哪裡點？
　迷你句 Where are the soft drinks?
　完整句 Where can I find soft drinks?

🎧 無酒精飲料在菜單的後面。
　Soft drinks are on the back of the menu.

👄 我找不到這道菜。
　迷你句 I can't find this.
　完整句 Where is this dish? I didn't see it on the menu.

🎧 很抱歉，這道菜已經停止供應了。
　Sorry, this one is not available anymore.

130

😮 請給我酒單。　　**迷你句** Wine list, please.

　　　　　　　　完整句 Please give me the wine list.

👂 好的，酒單在這裡。
Sure, here is the wine list.

😮 我的開胃菜是馬鈴薯泥。　**迷你句** I will start with mashed potatoes.

　　　　　　　　完整句 I will have mashed potato as a starter.

👂 請問需要哪一種醬汁呢？
Which sauce would you like?

😮 我想要加點沙拉。　**迷你句** Japanese Salad as an extra.

　　　　　　　　完整句 Can we have some extra Japanese Salad?

👂 好的，我幫您拿一些過來。
Ok, I will get you some.

😮 我們要兩個。　　**迷你句** Make it two.

　　　　　　　　完整句 Can we have two of those?

👂 好的，要點一些飲料嗎？
Sure, can I get you anything to drink?

[Vocabulary] 生字**不用另外查字典**！

01 中文菜單 **Chinese menu**
02 介紹 **explain**
03 主餐 **entrée**
04 兒童菜單 **kid's menu**
05 無酒精飲料 **soft drink**
06 菜 **dish**
07 供應 **available**
08 酒單 **wine list**
09 馬鈴薯 **mashed potato**
10 醬汁 **sauce**
11 沙拉 **salad**
12 飲料 **something to drink**

05 點餐需求

👄：你要會說的一句話　💬：你會聽到的問/答

 **MP3** Track ▶ 040

[Must be...] 這個時候最需要的一句話！

👄 請問你們的雞翅有什麼口味？
迷你句 What are your chicken wing flavors?
完整句 What are the flavors of your chicken wings?

💬 我們有烤肉以及蜂蜜大蒜口味的雞翅。
We have BBQ and honey garlic chicken wings.

👄 我喜歡辣的食物。
迷你句 Any spicy foods?
完整句 I like spicy foods.

💬 或許您可以試試宮保雞丁。
Maybe you can try The Palace Chicken.

👄 我的餐不要太辣。
迷你句 I would like it mild.
完整句 Can you make the dish not too spicy for me?

💬 我會請廚房留心。
I will tell the kitchen.

👄 請問這個奶油蛋糕會很甜嗎？
迷你句 Is that very sweet?
完整句 Would the cream cake be very sweet?

💬 不會，我相信您會喜歡的。
No, I am sure you will like it.

👄 你們有什麼口味的冰淇淋？
迷你句 What flavors do you have?
完整句 What flavors of ice cream do you have?

💬 我們有草莓和鳳梨口味。
We have strawberry and pineapple.

132

請問你們的三明治是哪種起司？
迷你句 What kind of cheese?
完整句 What kind of cheese do you use for sandwich?

我們使用切達起司。
We use cheddar cheese for our sandwich.

請問大蒜麵包的味道會很濃嗎？
迷你句 Is it strong?
完整句 Is the smell of garlic bread very strong?

是的，它的蒜味很濃。
Yes, the garlic bread is very garlicky.

我的牛排要半熟的。
迷你句 Medium, please.
完整句 I would like medium, please.

請問您要多大的呢？
How about the size?

我吃素。
迷你句 I am a vegetarian.
完整句 I only eat vegetables.

請您參考這份菜單。
You can check this menu.

[Words to Use] 替換字放空格，一句多用!!

- 我對＿＿過敏。
  I am allergic to＿＿＿.

01 蝦子 **shrimps**

02 海鮮 **seafood**

03 雞蛋 **egg**

04 花生 **peanuts**

05 巧克力 **chocolate**

06 乳製品 **dairy products**

飲料／酒類介紹

01【基本酒類】

紅酒	red wine	白酒	white wine
威士忌	whisky	雪利酒	sherry
伏特加	vodka	白蘭地	brandy

02【基礎調酒】

螺絲起子	Screwdriver	萊姆伏特加	Vodka Lime
龍舌蘭日出	Tequila Sunrise	柯夢波丹	Cosmopolitan
新加坡司令	Singapore Sling	邁泰	Mai Tai
杏仁酸酒	Amaretto Sour	性慾海灘	Sex on the Beach
曼哈頓	Manhattan	鹹狗	Salty Dog
獵豔	Hunter	長島冰茶	Long Island Ice Tea
血腥瑪莉	Bloody Mary	深水炸彈	Deep Bomb

03【常見飲料】

汽水	soda	果汁	juice
啤酒	beer	紅茶	black tea
綠茶	green tea	無酒精飲料	soft drink
可口可樂	coke	咖啡	coffee
豆漿	soymilk	奶精	coffee mate

逛地球旅遊專欄 **點心／水果介紹**

01【常見點心】

餅乾	cracker	蛋糕	cake
冰淇淋	ice cream	巧克力	chocolate
提拉米蘇	Tiramisu	布丁	pudding
起司	cheese	瑪芬蛋糕	muffin
堅果	nut	甜餅乾	cookies
貝果	bagel	椒鹽脆餅乾	pretzel
圓鬆餅	pancake	格子鬆餅	waffle

【最常用的旅行句】

我要一份雙份起司貝果。

I would like a bagel with double cheese.

02【常見水果】

蘋果	apple	梨	pear
鳳梨	pineapple	西瓜	watermelon
櫻桃	cherry	葡萄	grape

【最常用的旅行句】

你們有賣黃肉的西瓜嗎？

Do you have yellow watermelon?

06 點飲料／餐前酒

👄：你要會説的一句話　🔊：你會聽到的問／答

[Must be...] 這個時候最需要的一句話！

👄 請問你們有什麼飲料？
迷你句 What soft drinks are there?
完整句 What kind of soft drinks do you have?

🔊 請參考菜單後面的飲料項目。
The soft drinks list is on the back of the menu.

👄 請問你們有奶昔嗎？
迷你句 Do you have shakes?
完整句 Do you have any milk shake?

🔊 您想要哪一種口味？
What flavor do you like?

👄 我要柳橙汁。
迷你句 Orange juice, please.
完整句 Can I have some orange juice?

🔊 抱歉，柳橙汁賣完了。
Sorry, orange juice is sold out.

👄 請問你們有薑汁汽水或柳橙汽水嗎？
迷你句 Ginger ale or orange pop?
完整句 Do you have ginger ale or orange soda?

🔊 沒有，但是我們有蔓越莓汁。
No, but we have cranberry juice.

👄 我想要一杯拿鐵。
迷你句 Latte, please.
完整句 I want a latte.

🔊 請問要冰的還是熱的？
Do you want it iced or hot?

請換一杯給我。　**迷你句** I want another one.
　　　　　　　　完整句 Please change another one for me.

請問您的飲料怎麼了嗎？
What is wrong with your drinks?

可以推薦我一杯雞　**迷你句** What is your recommendation?
尾酒嗎？　　　　　**完整句** Can you recommend me a cocktail?

請參考我們的酒單。
Here is our wine list.

請給我一杯威士忌　**迷你句** A whisky on the rocks, please.
加冰塊。　　　　　**完整句** Please give me whisky on rocks.

這是您要的酒。
Here is your drink.

我想要一瓶紅酒。　**迷你句** A bottle of red wine.
　　　　　　　　完整句 I would like to order a bottle of red
　　　　　　　　　　　　 wine.

請問您要哪個年分的呢？
What year would you like?

[Words to Use] 替換字放空格，一句多用!!

- 我想要一杯_____。謝謝。
  I would like a/an _____. Thanks.

01 (一瓶)紅酒 **a bottle of red wine**　　02 奶昔 **milk shake**

03 雞尾酒 **cocktail**　　　　　　　　04 薑汁汽水 **ginger ale**

05 蔓越莓汁 **cranberry juice**　　　　06 柳橙汁 **orange juice**

07 點甜點

:你要會說的一句話 🔈 :你會聽到的問/答

MP3 Track ▶ 042

[Must be...] 這個時候最需要的一句話!

👄 請問你們有什麼甜點?

迷你句 What desserts are there?

完整句 What do you have for desserts?

🔈 您可以試試我們的蘋果派。
You should try our apple pie.

👄 我可以看一下你們的甜點菜單嗎?

迷你句 I want to see the dessert menu.

完整句 Can I take a look at your dessert menu?

🔈 甜點菜單就在飲料項目的旁邊。
The dessert menu is beside the drinks list.

👄 請問你們的蘋果派有多大?

迷你句 Is it big?

完整句 How big is your apple pie?

🔈 普通大小,您想要試試看嗎?
The size is normal. Would you like to try some?

👄 請問你們有哪幾種水果?

迷你句 What kinds of fruit do you have?

完整句 I would like to know the types of fruit you serve.

🔈 我們的菜單上有樣本可以參考。
There are samples in our menu.

👄 請問你們有低卡路里的甜點嗎?

迷你句 Any low-cal desserts?

完整句 Do you have any low-calorie desserts?

🔈 冰沙是個不錯的選擇。
Sherbet would be good.

我要一個提拉米蘇蛋糕。　**(迷你句)** A tiramisu.

(完整句) I would like a tiramisu.

需要搭配任何飲料嗎？
Do you need any drinks?

請問有沒有熱的甜點？　**(迷你句)** Any hot desserts?

(完整句) Do you have any hot desserts?

來一杯熱奶茶怎麼樣呢？
How about a cup of hot milk tea?

我的咖啡不要加糖。　**(迷你句)** I don't like sugar.

(完整句) Please give me black coffee.

請問需要奶精嗎？
Do you need coffee mate?

我不需要甜點。　**(迷你句)** I don't need it.

(完整句) I will skip the desserts.

來點新鮮水果怎麼樣呢？
How about some fresh fruit?

[Words to Use] 替換字放空格，一句多用!!

- 我甜點要來一份＿＿＿＿。
  I'll have a/an ＿＿＿＿ for dessert.

01 英式麵包布丁 **bread & butter pudding**

02 提拉米蘇 **tiramisu**

03 巧克力布朗尼 **chocolate brownie**

04 紅絲絨杯子蛋糕 **red velvet cupcake**

05 蘋果派 **apple pie**

06 草莓乳脂鬆糕 **strawberry trifle**

08 請服務生幫忙

:你要會說的一句話　：你會聽到的問／答

[Must be...] 這個時候最需要的一句話！

這道菜的最佳吃法是？
迷你句 What is the right way to eat it?
完整句 What is the best way to have this dish?

讓我教您怎麼吃。
Let me show you how to eat it.

請問這道菜有特定的吃法嗎？
迷你句 Is there a correct way?
完整句 Is there a certain way to eat this dish?

沒有，您可以找您喜歡的方式來吃。
No, you can eat it freely.

請問這個口袋餅要怎麼吃？
迷你句 How do you eat this?
完整句 How do you eat this pita sandwiches?

您可以直接用手吃。
You can just eat it with your hands.

請問這道菜需要沾醬嗎？
迷你句 Do I need the sauce?
完整句 Do I have to eat it with the sauce?

醬料和蔬菜一起吃會更好吃。
It tastes better if you mix the sauce and the vegetables together.

請問可以幫我們拍張照嗎？
迷你句 Can you take a photo for us?
完整句 Would you please take a picture for us?

當然沒有問題。
That won't be a problem.

服務生！

迷你句 Excuse me!

完整句 Excuse me, waiter!

請問有什麼可以效勞的嗎？
How can I help you?

我把我的叉子弄掉了。

迷你句 I dropped my fork.

完整句 My fork fell to the ground.

我幫您拿過新的。
I will get you a new one.

請幫我們拿一些小盤子來。

迷你句 I need some small plates.

完整句 Could you bring us some small plates?

我馬上拿過來。
Coming right up.

我們吃完了。

迷你句 We are done with this.

完整句 We are finished with this.

請讓我幫您收拾桌面。
Let me clean the table for you.

[Things to Know] 一定要知道的**旅行常識**

在歐美文化中，許多餐廳服務生對食物的常識，是非常廣博的，因此不覺得自己只是在服務別人的「服務生」，也是對該餐廳料理的專家。因此我們在問服務生問題、請他們幫忙時，也務必要當個有禮貌的遊客。

[Must be...] 這個時候最需要的一句話！

請幫我打包這些食
物。
迷你句 Doggy bag, please.
完整句 Could you wrap this up to go?

好的，我去拿食物袋。
Yes, I will get you a doggie bag.

請給我一些食物
袋。
迷你句 I need some doggie bags.
完整句 Would you please give me some doggie bags?

在這裡，我可以幫您打包。
Here, I can help you pack this up.

這是你的小費。
迷你句 Here you go.
完整句 Here is your tip.

非常感謝您，祝您有個愉快的一天。
Thank you. Have a nice day.

小費要給多少？
迷你句 How much is the tip?
完整句 How much would the tip usually be?

小費通常是您帳單的一成半。
The tip is usually 15% of your bill.

請將它們分開包。
迷你句 Separate them, please.
完整句 Please pack them in different boxes.

這醬料也要包嗎？
Do you want the dressing packed as well?

😮 不要打包薯條。 **（迷你句）** Leave this fries.

（完整句） Don't pack the fries.

👂 好的，還需要什麼嗎？
Ok, need anything else?

😮 我要買單。 **（迷你句）** Check, please.

（完整句） Just the bill, please.

👂 請問要怎麼付款？
How would you like to pay?

😮 我們要各付各的。 **（迷你句）** Go Dutch, please.

（完整句） We would like to pay separately.

👂 沒問題，先生。
Certainly, Sir.

😮 請問我要付多少？ **（迷你句）** How much is it?

（完整句） How much is my share?

👂 包含小費總共30塊美金。
It is $30 including the tip.

[Things to Know] 一定要知道的**旅行常識**

　　歐美的美食文化中，很少把吃不完的東西打包回家。他們會打包走的食物，多半是要「給家中狗狗吃的食物」。但是現在許多人也覺得，東西不吃完也不帶走很浪費，所以若是你想要將吃不下的美食打包帶走，也不用覺得難為情了。

10 這道菜不OK

👄：你要會說的一句話　👂：你會聽到的問／答

[Must be...] 這個時候最需要的一句話！

👄 你們的食物沒有熟。

迷你句 Your dish is quite raw.

完整句 Your dish is not cooked enough.

👂 請問是哪一道菜？
Which dish do you mean?

👄 這三明治吃起來真糟。

迷你句 That is really bad.

完整句 This sandwich taste really awful.

👂 我們會告知廚房的。
We will report it to the kitchen.

👄 我覺得這道菜有點鹹。

迷你句 This is too salty.

完整句 I think this dish is too salty.

👂 我們馬上為您換菜。
We will change it for you right away.

👄 這盤菜裡有頭髮。

迷你句 There is hair in it.

完整句 We found some hair in this dish.

👂 很抱歉，這盤菜不收費。
Sorry to hear that. There will be no charge for this dish.

👄 我點的是可樂不是汽水。

迷你句 I did not order soda, it was a cola.

完整句 I thought I ordered a cola not a soda.

👂 很抱歉，我去拿可樂過來。
I am sorry; I will go get a cola for you.

這麵煮過頭了。 (迷你句) The noodles are overdone.

(完整句) The noodles are over cooked.

我們幫您換一盤新的。
We will bring you another dish.

請幫我催一下廚房。 (迷你句) Please check on my order.

(完整句) Would you check on my order, please.

是的，馬上來。
Yes, right away.

這杯茶不夠熱。 (迷你句) It is cold.

(完整句) This tea is not hot enough.

我們會換一杯給您。
We will get you another one.

我沒有要求放辣椒。 (迷你句) I didn't order the spicy one.

(完整句) I don't think I've ordered a spicy one.

抱歉，立刻幫您換一盤。
Sorry, let me get a new one for you.

[Words to Use] 替換字放空格，一句多用!!

- 我們沒有點_____。
  We didn't order the _____.

  01 烤雞 roasted chicken
  02 糖醋排骨 sweet & sour pork
  03 炸魚薯條 fish & fries
  04 口袋餅 pita sandwiches
  05 菲力牛排 filet mignon
  06 義大利麵 spaghetti

11 抱怨服務差勁

👄：你要會說的一句話　🔊：你會聽到的問/答

[Must be...] 這個時候最需要的一句話！

👄 這不是我們點的。　**迷你句** We did not order this.

完整句 This is not what we ordered.

🔊 抱歉，我們端錯菜了。
Sorry, we brought you the wrong dish.

👄 請問我的餐何時會好？　**迷你句** How long for our food?

完整句 When will our food be ready?

🔊 您的餐點就快好了。
Your food will be ready in a minute.

👄 我們沒有點烤雞。　**迷你句** We did not order roasted chicken.

完整句 I don't think we have ordered the roast chicken.

🔊 很抱歉，我點錯了。
I am sorry that I took the wrong order.

👄 我們已經等超過一個小時了。　**迷你句** It has been over an hour.

完整句 We have been waiting for over an one hour.

🔊 我去廚房看一下。
I will check with the kitchen.

👄 我的菜還沒來。　**迷你句** My order hasn't come yet.

完整句 I am still waiting for my meal.

🔊 您什麼時候點的餐？
When did you order?

我們花太久的時間在等待。
迷你句 We've spent too much time waiting.
完整句 We have been wasting so much time on waiting.

抱歉讓您久等了。
Sorry to keep you waiting.

為什麼讓我們等這麼久？
迷你句 Why does it take so long?
完整句 Why do you keep us waiting so long?

抱歉，今晚太多客人了。
Sorry, we have too many customers tonight.

你應該要給我點優惠。
迷你句 I want a discount.
完整句 You should offer some discount for me.

我們一定會在帳單上扣掉這道菜的費用。
We will be sure to cross out the dish from the bill.

你們的服務態度太惡劣了。
迷你句 Your service was really bad.
完整句 You had a really bad attitude.

我們保證這樣的事不會再發生了。
We promise such a thing will never happen again.

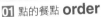

[Vocabulary] 生字不用另外查字典！

01 點的餐點 **order**
02 等待 **waiting**
03 上錯菜 **wrong dish**
04 準備好了 **ready**
05 很多時間 **too much time**
06 客人 **customer**
07 扣除 **cross out**
08 帳單 **bill**
09 服務 **service**
10 態度 **attitude**
11 糟糕 **bad**
12 優惠 **discount**

旅遊常用句型 + 超多替換字，套入馬上用！

尋找餐廳

● 我今天想吃 _____ 料理。

I am in the mood for _____ food today.

01 中式 **Chinese**	02 韓式 **Korean**
03 義大利 **Italian**	04 西班牙 **Spanish**
05 日式 **Japanese**	06 泰式 **Thai**

要求推薦餐點

● 你會建議哪一道做為 _____ ？

What would you suggest for the _____?

01 開胃菜 **appetizer/starter**	02 附餐 **side dish**
03 主餐（肉類）**entrée**	04 甜點 **dessert**
05 主菜 **main course**	06 餐前酒 **aperitif**

待餐 / 候位時間

● _____ 要等多久 ？

How long do we have to wait for _____?

01 一張四個人的餐桌 **a table for four**	02 一張露天餐桌 **an outdoor table**
03 一張靠窗的餐桌 **a table by the window**	04 一間私人包廂 **a private booth**
05 我們外帶的餐點 **our takeout**	06 我們點的餐 **our order**

點餐

● 我今天要試試你們的 ＿＿＿＿＿。

I am going to try your ＿＿＿＿ today.

01 主廚推薦 chef's recommendation

02 特餐 special

03 最受歡迎的餐點 most popular dish

04 招牌菜 signature dish

05 無菜單料理 chef's tasting menu

06 商業套餐 business set

要求服務生協助

● 不好意思，可以請你給我 ＿＿＿＿＿ 嗎？

Excuse me, may I have ＿＿＿＿, please?

01 一支叉子 a fork

02 一雙筷子 a pair of chopsticks

03 菜單 the menu

04 一些餐巾紙 some napkins

05 帳單 the bill

06 一個乾淨的盤子 a clean plate

這道菜不 OK

● 這道菜對我來說 ＿＿＿＿。

I'm afraid this dish is ＿＿＿＿ for me.

01 煮過頭了 overcooked

02 太乾了 too dry

03 沒煮熟 undercooked

04 太油膩了 too greasy

05 調味不足 under-seasoned

06 太鹹了 too salty

各國必吃特色美食

各國氣候、地形不同,自然會有不同的食材,孕育各自精彩的美食文化。快來看看有什麼是在當地不可錯過的超級美食!

01【在美國必吃】

美式食物多是我們熟悉的三明治、漢堡、生菜沙拉。以高熱量、大分量、氣氛熱絡聞名。雖然美式食物對健康會造成負擔,但是的確是十分美味。美國也很流行早餐加午餐一起吃,稱為 brunch,尤其是在週末及假日時,許多 brunch 店更是一位難求。

02【在加拿大必吃】

加拿大與美國雖然飲食文化差異不大,但有兩樣東西卻是不可不知:楓糖與冰酒。每年 3、4 月春天來臨時,加拿大的楓糖農場就會開放給觀光客,可以觀看他們採集楓汁、品嘗新鮮的楓糖;而冰酒則是使用成熟且結霜的葡萄來製酒,糖分極高。

03【在英國必吃】

英國的大街小巷,都可看到炸魚 & 炸薯條(fish & chips),魚多為鱈魚。傳統的英式下午茶也不可錯過 —— 經典的三層甜點盤和英國茶。下午茶是以前英國貴族的消遣,所以分量少、價格較高。

04【在紐、澳必吃】

由於畜牧業發達,牛奶、起司製品種類多、牛、羊肉的菜餚比例也高,小羊排是不可錯過的紐澳美食。紐西蘭的鹹派相當有名,內餡包雞肉、牛肉、蛋及培根等,在許多小店都可買到。還有一種特別的甜點叫 pavlova,是用蛋清打成泡去做甜點,口味極甜。

PART 06
交通工具

：你要會說的一句話　🗣：你會聽到的問／答　**MP3** Track ▶ 047

[Must be...] 這個時候最需要的一句話！

請問到中央公園最好的方法是？
- 迷你句 How to get to Central Park?
- 完整句 What is the best way to get to Central Park?

🗣 您可以騎腳踏車過去。
You can get there by bike.

請問我要怎麼到三河醫院？
- 迷你句 Where is Three Rivers Hospital?
- 完整句 How can I get to Three Rivers Hospital?

🗣 恐怕您得搭火車才行。
I am afraid you have to take the train.

請問這個地址要怎麼走？
- 迷你句 How can I get to here?
- 完整句 How can I get to this address?

🗣 您用走的就可以了。
You can go there on foot.

請問這家超市離這裡很遠嗎？
- 迷你句 Is this supermarket very far?
- 完整句 Is this supermarket far from here?

🗣 搭公車只要十分鐘。
It takes ten minutes to the supetmarket by bus.

請問您可以載我到巴士站嗎？
- 迷你句 I need a lift.
- 完整句 Can you give me a ride to there?

🗣 我可以載你到巴士站。
I can drop you off at the bus stop.

請問巴士站在哪裡？

迷你句 Where is the bus stop?

完整句 Can you tell me where the bus stop is?

巴士站就在前方轉角處。
The bus stop is right around the corner.

請問市政廳在這附近嗎？

迷你句 Is city hall nearby?

完整句 Is the city hall anywhere around here?

那邊那棟白色的大樓就是市政廳了。
The white building over there is the city hall.

您可以告訴我，我現在在哪裡嗎？

迷你句 Where am I?

完整句 Can you tell me where I am now?

您在金斯頓大道和華爾街的交叉口。
You are at the intersection of Kensington Avenue and Wall Street.

你知道要怎麼去郵局嗎？

迷你句 Where is the post office?

完整句 Can you show me how to get to the post office?

直走右轉你就會看到了。
Go straight and turn to the right then you will find it.

[Words to Use] 替換字放空格，一句多用!!

- 請問我要怎麼到_____？
  How do I get to _____?

01 中央公園 the Central Park

02 三河醫院 Three Rivers Hospital

03 超市 the supermarket

04 購物中心 the mall

05 市政廳 the city hall

06 郵局 the post office

[Must be...] 這個時候最需要的一句話！

👄 請問巴士營運到幾點？

迷你句 When is the last bus?

完整句 I would like to know the operating hour of the bus.

🗣 它只營運到半夜。
It only operates until midnight.

👄 請問火車幾點開？

迷你句 What time does it leave?

完整句 When will the train depart?

🗣 請問您搭的是哪一班火車？
Which train will you take?

👄 請問下一班巴士幾點？

迷你句 When is the next bus?

完整句 What time is the next bus?

🗣 下一班巴士 5 分鐘內就會到。
The next bus will be here in 5 minutes.

👄 請問這班火車會準時到嗎？

迷你句 Is it on time?

完整句 Will the train be on time?

🗣 恐怕會晚 10 分鐘。
I am afraid it will be 10 minutes late.

👄 請問有下午 5 點往馬德里的火車嗎？

迷你句 How about the train to Madrid around 5 p.m.?

完整句 Is there any train leaving for Madrid around 5 p.m.?

🗣 有一班下午 5 點 30 分往馬德里的火車。
There is 5:30 p.m. train leaving for Madrid.

請問有時刻表嗎？ **迷你句** I need a timetable.

完整句 I would like to know where to get a timetable.

請問您是要哪一種類型的？
What kind of timetable do you need?

我看不懂時刻表。 **迷你句** I don't understand it.

完整句 I don't quite understand the timetable.

我來幫您解釋。
Let me explain it to you.

請問這巴士多久來一班？ **迷你句** How often does it come?

完整句 How often does the bus come?

每十分鐘來一班。
The bus comes every 10 minutes.

請問這班火車是直達車嗎？ **迷你句** Is it an express?

完整句 Is this train an express?

不是，這是普通列車。
No, it is a local train.

[Words to Use] 替換字放空格，一句多用!!

- 這班＿＿＿＿幾點開往芝加哥？
  What time does the ＿＿＿＿leave for Chicago?

01 巴士 **bus**

02 火車 **train**

03 觀光遊覽車 **tourist coach**

04 渡船 **ferry**

05 飛機 **flight**

06 船 **boat**

[Must be...] 這個時候最需要的一句話！

請問我可以用走的到那裡嗎？
迷你句 Can I walk there?
完整句 Can I get there on foot?

可以，用走的不會太遠。
Yes, it is not far.

請問走路過去要幾分鐘？
迷你句 How long will it take?
完整句 How many minutes on foot?

走過去要花 15 分鐘。
It takes 15 minutes on foot.

我得找租自行車的店。
迷你句 Is there a bike rental shop?
完整句 I need to find a bike rental shop.

公園附近有很多租自行車的店。
There are a lot of bike rental shops around the park.

請問我的自行車可以停哪裡？
迷你句 Is there bike parking?
完整句 Where can I park my bike?

那裡是自行車專用的停車區。
There are dedicated areas for bike parking.

請問我可以將自行車帶上火車嗎？
迷你句 Do trains take bikes?
完整句 Is it ok to take my bike on the train?

當然，您可以帶上火車。
Sure, you can bring it on the train.

請問這附近有自行車道嗎？

迷你句 Where is the bike path?

完整句 Is there a bike path nearby?

自行車道就在人行道旁邊。
The path beside the pavement is the bike path.

請問騎自行車過去大概要多久？

迷你句 How long will it take?

完整句 How long does it take by bike?

只要 5 分鐘就到了。
It only takes 5 minutes.

請問騎自行車過去可以嗎？

迷你句 Can I ride the bike?

完整句 Is it possible to get there by bike?

騎自行車去，恐怕得花很長的時間。
I am afraid it will take too much time by bike.

我不知道該如何走過去？

迷你句 How can I walk there?

完整句 I don't know how to walk to there.

我用地圖跟你說。
I can show you on the map.

[Things to Know] 一定要知道的**旅行常識**

自行車在許多歐洲國家就像臺灣的機車一樣，是大部分居民的主要交通工具。許多國家都有非常完善的自行車道，而且他們的火車或地鐵是可以帶自行車上去的。如果想去歐洲國家短途旅行，騎自行車真的很不錯，不僅比徒步輕鬆，還可以慢慢地欣賞沿路風景；若要拜訪另一個城市，把自行車帶上火車就行了。是不是很吸引人呢？趕快和當地一些專門協辦腳踏車旅行或是提供腳踏車租賃的旅行社聯繫吧！

[Must be...] 這個時候最需要的一句話！

😊 請問你們有旅行車嗎？
> **迷你句** Do you have any wagons?
>
> **完整句** Do you have any wagons available?

👂 抱歉，我們目前只有小型車。
Sorry, we only have compact cars available right now.

😊 我想要跑車。
> **迷你句** A sports car.
>
> **完整句** I would like some sports cars.

👂 跑車的價錢比較高。
There will be a higher charge for a sports car.

😊 我在找休旅車。
> **迷你句** I need an SUV.
>
> **完整句** I am looking for an SUV.

👂 我想這台車會符合您的需求。
I think this one will suit your needs.

😊 請問有什麼樣的車呢？
> **迷你句** What do you have?
>
> **完整句** What kinds of cars do you have?

👂 這裡有很多種車子可以供您挑選。
There are many cars that you can choose from.

😊 請問最經濟的選項是？
> **迷你句** What is the cheapest?
>
> **完整句** What is the most economic option?

👂 請問您的預算是多少呢？
What is your rough budget?

請問租一天要多少錢？
(迷你句) What is the daily rate?
(完整句) What is the rate for one-day car rental?

單日基本費 150 美元。
The daily basic rate is $150.

請問有加收保險費嗎？
(迷你句) Is insurance extra?
(完整句) Do you charge extra for insurance?

是的，您需要付保險費。
Yes, you will have to pay for the insurance.

請問休旅車比小轎車貴多少？
(迷你句) How much extra is an SUV over a compact?
(完整句) What is the price difference between an SUV and a compact?

休旅車要多 30 美金。
It is $30 more if you need an SUV instead.

怎麼樣可以比較便宜呢？
(迷你句) Can the price be cheaper?
(完整句) How can I get a cheaper price?

如果租長期的話可以便宜一點。
You can get a cheaper rate if you make a long-term rental.

[Vocabulary] 生字不用另外查字典！

01 旅行車 **wagon**
02 小型車 **compact car**
03 跑車 **sports car**
04 休旅車 **SUV**
05 符合 **suit**
06 挑選 **choose**
07 經濟的 **economic**
08 選項 **option**
09 預算 **budget**
10 基本費 **basic rate**
11 保險費 **insurance**
12 租期 **rental**

05 購買車票

👄：你要會說的一句話　　👂：你會聽到的問／答　　**MP3** Track ▶ 051

[Must be...] 這個時候最需要的一句話！

👄 我們要搭下午 5 點半的接駁車。
迷你句 We need to take the 5:30 p.m. bus.
完整句 We have to take the 5:30 p.m. shuttle.

👂 很抱歉，那班車已經額滿了。
Sorry, the shuttle bus is fully booked.

👄 請問地鐵票要去哪裡買？
迷你句 I need a subway ticket.
完整句 Where can we get the subway ticket?

👂 您可以在自動售票機買票。
You can get a ticket at the ticket vending machine.

👄 請問這個代幣是要做什麼用的？
迷你句 What is this for?
完整句 How can I use these tokens?

👂 地鐵出口會用到。
The token lets you out at your stop.

👄 請問等候區有售票機嗎？
迷你句 Is there a ticket machine?
完整句 Is there a vending machine in the waiting area?

👂 每個等候區都有一個售票機。
There is a ticket vending machine at each waiting area.

👄 我要一張到墨西哥市的車票。
迷你句 To Mexico City, please.
完整句 Can I have a ticket to Mexico City?

👂 請問您要單程還是來回票？
Do you need a one way or round trip ticket?

😊 我需要來回車票。 (迷你句) Return ticket, please.
(完整句) I need a round trip ticket.

👂 請問您哪一天要回來？
Which day do you want to come back?

😊 回程票先不要劃位。 (迷你句) Can I have an open return?
(完整句) Can you make the return ticket open?

👂 好的，兩張都不要劃嗎？
Ok, both tickets?

😊 我要買兩張車票。 (迷你句) Two tickets, please.
(完整句) I need two tickets.

👂 請問您要到哪裡？
What is your destination?

😊 請問我可以在哪邊買票？ (迷你句) Where can I get a ticket?
(完整句) Where should I purchase a ticket?

👂 您可以在任何一個車站買票。
You can buy one at any station.

[Words to Use] 替換字放空格，一句多用!!

- 可以請你教我如何_____？
  Could you show me how to _____?

01 使用自動購票機 use the ticket vending machine

02 使用代幣 use the tokens

03 使用加值機 use the add value machine

04 購買地鐵票 buy the subway tickets

05 購買捷運卡 buy the metro card

06 幫我的捷運卡加值 add value to my metro card

😊：你要會說的一句話　🔔：你會聽到的問／答　🎵 **MP3** Track ▶ 052

[Must be...] 這個時候最需要的一句話！

😊 我可以拿一份地鐵
地圖嗎？

(迷你句) Can I have a map?

(完整句) May I have a subway map?

👂 當然，請自行取用。
Sure, please help yourself.

😊 請問這些地鐵地圖
是免費的嗎？

(迷你句) Are these all free?

(完整句) Are those subway maps free?

👂 是的，請問有什麼需要嗎？
Yes, do you need anything?

😊 請問我應該搭哪一
條線到 42 號街？

(迷你句) Which one should I take?

(完整句) Which line should I take to go to
42nd Street?

👂 請搭一號線。
Take line no.1, please.

😊 請問我應該在哪裡
轉車到華爾街？

(迷你句) Where should I transfer?

(完整句) Where should I transfer trains for
Wall Street?

👂 您可以在 42 號街轉車。
You can transfer at 42nd Street.

😊 請問這條線的終點
站是哪裡？

(迷你句) Where is the end?

(完整句) Where is the end of this line?

👂 您可以參考地鐵的地圖。
You can check the subway map.

請問有到那裡的直達車嗎？

迷你句 Is there a direct bus?

完整句 Is there any bus that goes there directly?

抱歉，您必須要轉車。
Sorry, you will have to transfer.

請問我需要轉車嗎？

迷你句 Do I need to transfer?

完整句 Do I have to transfer the train?

請問您的目的地是？
What is your destination?

請問哪裡可以搭直達車？

迷你句 Where is the direct train?

完整句 Where can I get the directly train?

您必須要到另一個月台。
You have to go to another platform.

請問你會看這個地鐵圖嗎？

迷你句 Can you read it?

完整句 Can you read the subway map?

當然，需要我幫忙嗎？
Of course, do you need any help?

[Vocabulary] 生字**不用另外查字典**！

01 地鐵 **subway**

02 地圖 **map**

03 華爾街 **Wall Street**

04 終點站 **end**

05 直達車 **direct bus**

06 轉車 **transfer**

07 月臺 **platform**

08 看 **read**

09 幫忙 **help**

10 參考 **check**

11 一號線 **line no.1**

12 請行取用 **help yourself**

07 車費要多少錢

😊：你要會說的一句話　🔈：你會聽到的問／答

[Must be...] 這個時候最需要的一句話！

😊 請問計程車費多少錢？

迷你句 How much is it?

完整句 How much is the taxi fare?

🔈 300美金。
It is $300

😊 請問計程車費怎麼算？

迷你句 How do you charge?

完整句 How do you charge if I want to take taxi?

🔈 我們每五百公尺收費 2 美元。
We charge $2 for every 500 meters.

😊 請問有夜間計費嗎？

迷你句 Are there other rates?

完整句 Is there a nighttime rate?

🔈 有的，夜間收費較便宜。
Yes, the nighttime rate is cheaper.

😊 我可以使用後車廂嗎？

迷你句 Can I use the trunk?

完整句 Is your trunk available to use?

🔈 使用後車廂要加收 5 美元。
We charge an extra $5 if you need to use the trunk.

😊 請問有任何優惠嗎？

迷你句 Can I have a discount?

完整句 Can I get any discount?

🔈 如果您從旅館叫車可以打 95 折。
You can get a 5% discount if you reserve the taxi from the hotel.

😒 我覺得你多收我錢。

迷你句 That price seems high.

完整句 I think you over-charged me.

👂 因為您必須要付高速公路通行費。
It is high because you have to pay for the highway toll.

😒 請問學生票多少錢？

迷你句 How much is the student ticket?

完整句 How much does a student ticket cost?

👂 學生票只要 2 塊錢美金。
The student ticket costs only $2.

😒 請問到市區的公車要多少錢？

迷你句 How much is it to downtown?

完整句 How much is the bus to downtown?

👂 我不太確定，大約 30 塊美金。
I am not sure, maybe $30.

😒 請問回數票跟優待票的差別在哪裡？

迷你句 Are these two different?

完整句 What is the difference between transfer ticket and coupon ticket?

👂 或許您可以去問問服務台。
Maybe you can ask at the information desk.

[Words to Use] 替換字放空格，一句多用!!

● 從飯店到機場的_____大概要多少？
What's the approximate _____ from the hotel to the airport?

01 計程車資 **taxi fare**

02 公車費 **bus fare**

03 火車車費 **train fare**

04 豪華巴士費用 **limousine fare**

05 接駁車費 **shuttle bus fare**

06 車資 **fare for a vehicle ride**

08 開車廂放行李

[Must be...] 這個時候最需要的一句話！

👄 我的行李太多了。　**迷你句** I have too much luggage.
　　　　　　　　　　完整句 I have got a lot of luggage with me.

👂 請問您需要用後車廂嗎？
Do you need to use the trunk?

👄 我需要用後車廂。　**迷你句** It will go in the back.
　　　　　　　　　　完整句 I will need to use the trunk.

👂 我來幫您放行李。
I'll help you to load the luggage.

👄 請問後車廂的空間　**迷你句** Is it big enough?
夠嗎？　　　　　　**完整句** Do you have enough space in the trunk?

👂 後車廂應該能放得下您所有的行李。
The trunk should be big enough for all your luggage.

👄 這袋子放不進後　**迷你句** It is too big.
座。　　　　　　**完整句** This bag won't fit in the back seat.

👂 您得把袋子放進後車廂裡。
You need to put this bag in the trunk.

👄 可以幫我打開後車　**迷你句** Please open it.
廂嗎？　　　　　**完整句** Can you open the trunk for me?

👂 當然，請讓我來幫您。
Sure, let me help you with this.

請幫我放這個袋子。

迷你句 Can you help me?

完整句 Please help me put this bag.

好的，讓我先把後車廂打開。
Ok, let me open the trunk first.

零錢不用找了。

迷你句 Keep the change.

完整句 You can keep the change.

謝謝您的小費。
Thanks for your tip.

可以請你幫我把行李搬到後車廂嗎？

迷你句 Can you help me?

完整句 Can you help me put my luggage in the trunk?

可以，但是我要 5 塊錢美金的小費。
Yes. A $5 tip would be prefered.

這是你的小費。

迷你句 Your tip.

完整句 Here is your tip.

謝謝，您真大方。
Thanks, you are so generous.

[Vocabulary] 生字不用另外查字典！

01 行李 luggage

02 後車箱 trunk

03 空間 space

04 袋子 bag

05 後座 back seat

06 放 load

07 打開 open

08 零錢 change

09 小費 tip

10 足夠 enough

11 需要 need

12 大方 generous

09 司機，我要下車！

：你要會說的一句話　　：你會聽到的問／答　　**MP3** Track ▶ 055

[Must be...] 這個時候最需要的一句話！

😊 我要去綜合醫院。
迷你句 General Hospital, please.
完整句 I need to go to the General Hospital.

👂 請問您有地址嗎？
Do you have the address?

😊 我要去這裡。
迷你句 Please take me here.
完整句 This is where I want to go.

👂 沒問題，我可以載您到那裡。
No problem, I can take you there.

😊 這是我要去的地址。
迷你句 I am going here.
完整句 Here is the address that I need to be at.

👂 好的，這個地方不會太遠。
This place is not too far away.

😊 請問你可以載我到這個地方嗎？
迷你句 Please take me there.
完整句 Can you take me to this place?

👂 我得看一下地圖才行。
I have to look at the map.

😊 請問你知道這裡是什麼地方嗎？
迷你句 Do you know where it is?
完整句 Do you have any idea where this place is?

👂 抱歉我不清楚那裡是哪裡。
Sorry, I don't know where this place is.

請在這裡停車。　　**迷你句** This is it.

　　　　　　　　完整句 Stop here, please.

停在這個旅館嗎？
At this hotel?

可以請你在前面一　**迷你句** Please pull up a little closer.
點的地方停車嗎？　**完整句** Could you pull up a little further?

好的，請問這裡可以嗎？
Ok, here?

請問我要怎麼下　**迷你句** How can I get off?
車？　　　　　　**完整句** How can I get off the bus at the stop
　　　　　　　　　　　　I want?

只要拉下車鈴就可以了。
Just ring the bell.

不好意思，我要在　**迷你句** Excuse me, this is my stop.
這裡下車。　　　　**完整句** Excuse me, I want to get off here.

好的，別忘記您的行李。
Ok, don't forget your luggage.

[Vocabulary] 生字不用另外查字典！

01 綜合醫院 General Hospital 　 02 地址 address

03 沒問題 no problem 　 04 停下 stop

05 旅館 hotel 　 06 停車 pull up

07 下車鈴 bell 　 08 行李 luggage

09 忘記 forget 　 10 地圖 map

11 拉下車鈴 ring the bell 　 12 遙遠 far away

[Must be...] 這個時候最需要的一句話！

😮 請問我應該在哪裡轉車到華爾街？

迷你句 Where should I transfer?

完整句 Where should I transfer trains for Wall Street?

👂 您可以在 42 號街轉車。
You can tranfser at 42nd Street.

😮 請問有到那裡的直達車嗎？

迷你句 Is there a direct bus?

完整句 Is there any bus that goes there directly?

👂 抱歉，您必須要轉車。
Sorry, you have to transfer.

😮 請問我需要轉車嗎？

迷你句 Do I need to transfer?

完整句 Do I have to transfer the train?

👂 請問您的目的地是？
Where are you going?

😮 請問我要怎麼到這裡？

迷你句 How can I get to here?

完整句 Can you tell me how can I get to here?

👂 您必須要搭電車然後再轉火車。
You should take the subway first, then take a train.

😮 不好意思，我找不到出口。

迷你句 Excuse me, where is the exit?

完整句 Excuse me, I can't find the exit.

👂 請問您在找哪一個出口呢？
Which exit are you looking for?

請告訴我最近的出口在哪。

迷你句 Where is the nearest exit?

完整句 Can you tell me where is the nearest exit?

一直往前走您就會看到了。
Go straight and you will find it.

請問我要轉幾次車？

迷你句 I need to transfer how many times?

完整句 How many times do I need to transfer?

您需要轉3次車。
You have to transfer three times.

請問到洛杉磯要轉機嗎？

迷你句 Do I need to transfer?

完整句 Should I need to transfer to LA?

是的，您必須要在西雅圖轉機。
Yes, you have to transfer planes in Seattle.

請問東出口在哪裡？

迷你句 Where is the Eastern exit?

完整句 I can't find the Eastern exit.

東出口是在大廳的右手邊。
The exit is on the right hand side of the lobby.

[Words to Use] 替換字放空格，一句多用!!

- 我要到_____應該在哪一站換車？
  Which stop should I change trains if I want to go to the _____?

01 馬偕醫院 **Mackay Hospital**　　**02** 希爾頓飯店 **Hilton Hotel**

03 星光大道 **Avenue of Stars**　　**04** 艾菲爾鐵塔 **Eifel Tower**

05 西敏寺 **Westminster Abbey**　　**06** 希思羅機場 **Heathrow Airport**

[Must be...] 這個時候最需要的一句話！

👄 請問坐一趟輪船要多少錢？

迷你句 How much is it?

完整句 How much does it cost for a ferry tour?

🔊 一趟要 50 塊美金。
It cost $50 for one trip.

👄 請問一趟航程要多久？

迷你句 For how long?

完整句 How long is the tour?

🔊 大約兩個小時。
About two hours for one tour.

👄 請問輪船一天有幾班航次？

迷你句 How many voyages a day?

完整句 How many voyages are there in a day?

🔊 一天有 6 個航班。
There are 6 voyages in a day.

👄 請問坐飛機去倫敦要多久？

迷你句 How long is it?

完整句 How long does it take to fly to London?

🔊 大概需要 13 個小時。
It will take about 13 hours.

👄 我應該搭飛機還是火車呢？

迷你句 Which one should I take?

完整句 Should I take airplane or train?

🔊 坐飛機會比火車來的快。
Going by plane is faster than by train.

😕 坐飛機回家太貴了。
迷你句 It is expensive.
完整句 It is expensive to go home by plane.

👂 或許你可以考慮搭船。
Maybe you can take a ship.

😕 請問今天纜車會開放嗎？
迷你句 Is it open today?
完整句 Does the cable cars run today?

👂 很抱歉，今天風太大了。
Sorry, it is too windy today.

😕 請問我要怎麼上山？
迷你句 How can I get to the top?
完整句 Can you tell me how to get to the top?

👂 您可以搭乘纜車上山。
The cable cars will get you up to the top.

😕 我想要搭纜車。
迷你句 I want to take the cable car.
完整句 I would like to ride up in the cable car.

👂 您可以到售票機買票。
You can get the ticket from the vending machine.

[Vocabulary] 生字不用另外查字典！

01 加油 refuel the car
02 加油站 gas station
03 超市 convenient store
04 汽油 gas
05 汽油（英）petrol
06 半自助加油站 self serve station
07 加侖 gallon
08 現金 cash
09 洗窗服務 window cleaning
10 確定 sure
11 信用卡 credit card
12 付費 pay

12 加油站

：你要會說的一句話　：你會聽到的問／答

[Must be...] 這個時候最需要的一句話！

我需要加油。　　**迷你句** I need some gas.
　　　　　　　　完整句 We need to refuel the car.

請問您要加多少？
How much gas do you need?

請問哪裡有加油
站？
　　　　　　　　迷你句 Where is the gas station?
　　　　　　　　完整句 Can you show me where the gas
　　　　　　　　station is?

超商附近就有一間加油站。
There is one near the convenience store.

請問最近的加油站
在哪裡？
　　　　　　　　迷你句 Which way to the gas station?
　　　　　　　　完整句 Where is the closest gas station?

我不清楚這附近有沒有。
I am not sure if there is one around here.

請幫我加滿。　　**迷你句** Fill it up, please.
　　　　　　　　完整句 Fill up the tank, please.

請問您需要哪種汽油？
What type of gas do you need?

我要加 30 塊美金
的汽油。
　　　　　　　　迷你句 $30, please.
　　　　　　　　完整句 I need $30 of petrol.

好的，請問要用信用卡付費嗎？
Ok, pay by credit card?

請問這是半自助加油站嗎？

迷你句 Self serve?

完整句 Is this a self serve station?

是的，請自己加油。
Yes, please fill it by yourself.

請問目前的油價是多少？

迷你句 How much is it?

完整句 How much is the gas now?

今天的油價是 1 加侖 1 塊半。
It is $1.50 per gallon today.

我要付現金。

迷你句 Cash, please.

完整句 I would like to pay by cash.

好的，請問有需要洗窗服務嗎？
Ok, do you need our window cleaning service?

我不確定有沒有加滿。

迷你句 Is it full?

完整句 I am not sure if it's filled.

我可以幫您看一下。
I can check on it.

[Things to Know] 一定要知道的**旅行常識**

在歐洲，加油站幾乎都是沒有加油員的，也就是說，所有的加油站都是要自己動手加油。在加油機旁邊有個拋棄式手套的抽取盒，車主戴上後自己去拿油槍加油，然後自己再去收銀台付錢，或是直接刷卡付款。旁邊還有紙巾盒，方便車主們加油後擦手。要注意不可以因為沒有店員，就逕自加油後離開，因為每個加油站都有監視器，如果逃跑的話，警察會循車牌找到你。

常見交通號誌

若遇見警察要你停車，務必以最快速度停下來配合檢查，因為國外警察的權力大，不配合的可能會惹禍上身。

【常見生字】

停	STOP	禁止鳴笛	No Honking
禁止通行	No Passing	交叉路口	Diverted Traffic
高速入口	Entry to Motorway	不准停車	No Parking
慢車道	Slow Lane	快車道	Fast Lane
限速	Speed Limit	此路封閉	Road Closed
前方橋低	Low Bridge Ahead	彎道危險	Dangerous Bend
人行橫道	Pedestrian Crossing	小心袋鼠	Be Careful of Kangaroo
不准左轉	Keep Right	不准右轉	Keep Left
左轉	Turn Left	右轉	Turn Right
不准超車	No Overtaking	不准掉頭	No Turns
入口	Entrance		

【最常用的旅行句】

01 不要在這裡停車。有個不准停車的標誌。

Don't pull over. It says No Parking over there.

02 我沒看到停車場的入口。

I didn't see the entrance of the parking lot.

在美國租車

要在美國旅遊,除非都待在大城市,否則沒有開車,就等於無法自由移動。在美國,有許多景點都不在城市裡,也有許多名勝是沒有大眾交通工具可以到達的。美國公路發達,到了美國,你會發現租車是遊歷美國最好的方式。

【租車介紹】

在地廣人稀的美國,除了在幾個如紐約、舊金山、芝加哥等大城有較方便的大眾交通工具,一般普羅大眾還是開車代步。所以在美國旅遊,租車是少不了的。不管是商務出差或外出旅遊,租車絕對是在各地旅遊交通工具的第一首選。租車在美國是個相當大的產業,百家爭鳴,也因此租車公司選擇多也容易搶到便宜。

【租車車款】

各家租車公司都有不同車款可選擇,一般從小到大可分為經濟型(Economy),小型車(Compact),中型車(Mid-Size),大型車(Full-Size),休旅車(SUV),豪華車(Premium),七或九人坐車

(Mini-Van)。經濟型、小型車車款就如同一般小型轎車,可乘坐五人與體積不大的行李。若行李較多且大件,可視情況選擇較大車款。

【租車價格】

由於在美國一般租車公司較大的客群是來自商務客,平常工作日的租車價格就略高,從 $50-$150 不等。因此多數租車公司在週末都會有很低的費率,有時低價一天 $10 就可以租到車。而若是租超過五天,租車公司則會適用另一價格稱 Weekly rate。

[Must be...] 這個時候最需要的一句話！

👄 可以告訴我第二月台在哪裡嗎？
迷你句 Where is the platform 2?
完整句 Can you show me where the platform 2 is?

📄 第二月台在第一月台對面。
It's over there, in front of platform 1.

👄 請問這是往台北的火車月台嗎？
迷你句 Can I catch the Taipei train here?
完整句 Is this the platform for train to Taipei?

📄 不，這是往高雄的火車月台。
No, this is the platform for the train to Kaohsiung.

👄 請問我要怎麼到第二月台？
迷你句 How can I get there?
完整句 How can I get to the platform 2?

📄 您可以搭電梯。
You can take the elevator.

👄 我迷路了。
迷你句 I am lost.
完整句 I don't know where I am.

📄 您可以參考樓層圖。
You can check the floor map.

👄 請問售票處在哪裡？
迷你句 Where is the ticket office?
完整句 I would like to know where the ticket office is.

📄 售票處就在服務台的旁邊。
It is just next to the information desk.

我過站了。　　　**迷你句** I missed my stop.

完整句 I missed my stop which I'm supposed to get off.

您本來要在哪一站下車？
What was your stop?

我該怎麼辦？　　**迷你句** What should I do?

完整句 What can I do now?

恐怕您得搭另一台車回去了。
I am afraid you have to go back by another train.

我沒搭上車。　　**迷你句** I missed my train.

完整句 I failed to catch the train I was about to take.

別擔心，請讓我看看您的車票。
Don't worry; let me see your ticket.

我得在下一站下車。　**迷你句** I have to get off.

完整句 I have to get off at next stop.

好的，下車請小心。
Ok, be careful when you get off the bus.

[Words to Use] 替換字放空格，一句多用!!

- 這輛車加的是_____。
  This car takes _____.

01 一般汽油 **Regular 87**　　　02 特級汽油 **Plus 89**

03 高級汽油 **Premium 91**　　　04 超高級汽油 **Ultra 93**

05 無鉛汽油 **unleaded 95/98**　　06 柴油 **diesel**

👄：你要會說的一句話　👂：你會聽到的問／答　**MP3** Track ▶ 060

[Must be...] 這個時候最需要的一句話！

👄 請問我搭錯車了嗎？
迷你句 Is it wrong?
完整句 Am I on the correct train?

👂 是的，您搭錯車了。
Yes, this is not your train.

👄 請問這是藍線嗎？
迷你句 Is it the blue line?
完整句 Is this the blue line?

👂 不，您恐怕搭錯線了。
No, I am afraid you took the wrong bus.

👄 我搭錯車了。
迷你句 I took the wrong train.
完整句 This is not the train I should take.

👂 您得馬上在下一站下車。
You have to take off the train at the next stop.

👄 這不是往動物園的車，對嗎？
迷你句 Am I on the wrong bus?
完整句 This is the bus to the zoo, isn't it?

👂 不，這不是往動物園的車。
No, it's not the bus to the zoo.

👄 請問下一班公車得等多久？
迷你句 When is the next bus?
完整句 How long do I have to wait for the next bus?

👂 您得等上一個小時。
You have to wait for an hour.

請問往雪梨的火車開走了嗎？

迷你句 Did the train to Sydeny leave?

完整句 Did the train bound for Sydney just leave?

是的，您的火車剛開走。
Yes, your train just left.

請問往動物園的公車在哪裡？

迷你句 Where is the bus to the zoo?

完整句 Can you tell me where the bus to the zoo is?

對不起，往動物園的最後一班車剛開走。
I am sorry, the last bus to the zoo just left.

請問退票有什麼規定嗎？

迷你句 Any refund rules?

完整句 Are there any regulations for refunding the ticket?

退票要收取服務費。
There will be a service charge if you need to refund the ticket.

我買錯票了，請問我可以退票嗎？

迷你句 Can I have a refund?

完整句 I bought the wrong ticket, can I have a refund?

很抱歉，這張票無法退錢。
Sorry, this ticket is non-refundable.

[Words to Use] 替換字放空格，一句多用!!

- 糟糕，我搭錯＿＿＿了。
  Oops, I took the wrong ＿＿＿＿.

  01 公車 bus

  02 火車 train

  03 電車 tram

  04 路線 line

  05 渡船 ferry

  06 船 boat

15 發生車禍

：你要會說的一句話　：你會聽到的問／答　**MP3** Track ▶ 061

[**Must be...**] 這個時候最需要的一句話！

我出車禍了。
迷你句 I had an accident.
完整句 I had a car accident.

我可以幫您報警。
I can help you to call the police.

我被一輛車撞到。
迷你句 A car hit me.
完整句 I was hit by a car.

您有受傷嗎？
Did you get hurt?

我撞毀了我的車子。
迷你句 I wrote it off.
完整句 I totaled my car.

您得跟您的保險公司連絡。
You have to contact your insurance company.

這是肇事逃逸。
迷你句 It was a hit-and-run.
完整句 He did not stop after he bumped the person.

請問您記得他的車牌號碼嗎？
Do you remember the license plate number?

我在 1 號公路上，請盡快過來處理。
迷你句 Please send someone to the no.1 highway.
完整句 I am on no.1 highway, please send someone to help me.

請問需要救護車嗎？
Do you need an ambulance?

他酒後駕車。　　　（迷你句）He was drunk-driving.

（完整句）He drove after drinking.

我會幫他做酒測。
I will give him a breathalyzer test.

他因為要超車所以　（迷你句）He was trying to overtake me when
撞到我。　　　　　　he hit me.

（完整句）He hit me because he was trying to overtake me.

請問您有任何證人嗎？
Are there any witness?

有人闖紅燈。　　　（迷你句）A man ran the traffic light.

（完整句）Someone ran through the traffic light.

我可以幫您作證。
I can be your witness.

請打這個電話給我　（迷你句）Please call my parents at this number.
的爸媽。

（完整句）Please call this number and contact my parents.

還有什麼我可以幫忙的嗎？
Anything I can help you with?

[Vocabulary] 生字不用另外查字典！

01 車禍 car accident

02 肇事逃逸 hit-and-run

03 受傷 hurt

04 保險公司 insurance company

05 連絡 contact

06 逃逸 run

07 車牌號碼 license plate number

08 闖紅燈 run the traffic light

09 證人 witness

10 駕駛 drive

11 酒測 breath test

12 公路 highway

16 汽車抛錨／爆胎／沒油

：你要會說的一句話　：你會聽到的問／答

[Must be...] 這個時候最需要的一句話！

我的車子抛錨了。
迷你句 It just stopped.
完整句 My car just broke down and didn't go anymore.

我可以載您一程。
I can give you a ride.

請問你可以幫我換輪胎嗎？
迷你句 I need help with a flat.
完整句 Can you help me changing the wheel?

沒問題，請問是要換哪一個？
Of course. Which one do you need to change?

我需要道路救援。
迷你句 Can you send help?
完整句 I need roadside assistance.

我可幫您打電話。
I can help you to make the call.

我的車子發不動。
迷你句 It won't start.
完整句 My car won't start.

您的引擎壞掉了。
Your engine is dead.

請問最近的修理廠在哪裡？
迷你句 How far to the garage?
完整句 Where is the closest garage?

在華盛頓大道上有一間。
There is one on Washington Avenue.

請問我的車子怎麼了？
迷你句 What is wrong?
完整句 What is wrong with my car?

您的車子過熱了。
Your car is overheating.

請問拖吊到修理廠要錢嗎？
迷你句 Do I have to pay the towing fee?
完整句 Is there a charge for towing it back to garage?

是的，這是必須的。
Yes, it is necessary.

我需要把車送到修車廠。
迷你句 I need to get my car repaired.
完整句 I am going to have it repaired in a garage.

我們來拖吊您的車子。
We will tow your car.

我忘記給車子加油了。
迷你句 I forgot to refuel the car.
完整句 My car is running out of the gas.

我可以載你一程到加油站。
I can give you a lift to the gas station.

[Words to Use] 替換字放空格，一句多用!!

● 我們的車_____了。我現在該怎麼做？
Our car had a/an _____. Now what should I do?

01 爆胎 flat tire
02 電瓶沒電 flat battery
03 漏油 fluid leak
04 引擎故障 engine failure
05 拋錨 breakdown
06 閃警示紅燈 red flashing light that blinks

旅遊常用句型＋超多替換字，套入馬上用！

問路

● 可以告訴我最近的 ＿＿＿ 在哪裡嗎？
Can you tell me where the nearest ＿＿＿ is?

01 火車站 train station
02 計程車站 taxi stand
03 捷運站 MRT station
04 地鐵站 subway station
05 公車站 bus stop
06 遊客中心 tourist center

自己租車

● 我週末需要租一台 ＿＿＿。
I need to rent a ＿＿＿ for the weekend.

01 休旅車 SUV
02 跑車 sports car
03 小型車 compact
04 敞篷車 convertible
05 中型車 intermediate
06 廂型車 mini-van

詢問票價

● 一張 ＿＿＿ 多少錢？
How much do you charge for a/an ＿＿＿?

01 成人票 adult ticket
02 老人票 senior ticket
03 兒童票 child's ticket
04 一日通行票 Day Pass
05 優惠票 concession ticket
06 月票 Monthly Pass

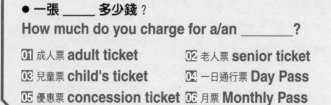

各種交通工具

● 在這城市遊走的最佳方式就是搭 _____。

The best way to get around the city is by _____.

01 公車 **bus**　　　　**02** 汽車 **car**

03 捷運 **MRT**　　　　**04** 輕軌電車 **light rail**

05 地鐵 **subway**　　　**06** 腳踏車 **bike**

要求下車

● 可以請你讓我在 _____ 下車嗎？

Would you please drop me off at _____?

01 餐廳門口 **the restaurant**　　**02** 車站 **the station**

03 飯店門口 **the hotel**　　　　**04** 轉角 **the corner**

05 機場 **the airport**　　　　**06** 下個路口 **the next junction**

詢問如何搭車

● 如果我想去 _____ 應該搭哪一線？

Which line should I take if I want to go to _____?

01 大都會藝術博物館 **Metropolitan Museum of Art**

02 東京鐵塔 **Tokyo Tower**

03 白金漢宮 **Buckingham Palace**

04 比佛利山莊 **Beverly Hills**

05 羅浮宮 **the Louvre Museum**

06 香榭大道 **the Champs Elysees**

租車注意事項

歐美的大眾交通工具多只在大城市中，若要離開市中心去市郊旅遊，則一定需要開車。以下是租車（在美國租車叫 car rental，在英國叫 car hire）的注意事項。

01【租車地點】

在機場都有各大租車公司駐點，也因此價格都較便宜。機場租車通常都是24HR營業，較具彈性。但要注意有時在機場租車有機場稅的徵收，所以可先多加比價。而在市區租車，通常價格略高，容易發生沒車可租的情況。且營業時間較短，甚至週末不營業，容易造成行程安排的不便。

02【租車保險】

在美國若不幸發生事故，後續處理常常是精神與時間的大損失。而租車公司的保險也琳琅滿目，建議事前先研究購買所需要的保險。

03【租車油資】

租車公司在把車交給你前，通常車子裡的油箱都是加滿的。租車公司要求租方在車子歸還時，油箱都必須是滿的。你可以事前加購一桶汽油，通常此時油價會與市面上加油相似，或是回程時再把油加滿還車。若要方便，當然就是選擇前者。但是需考量即使你沒有把那桶汽油用完，租車公司是不會退款的。但若你未事前購買一桶汽油，也未加滿還車，此時租車公司將會以汽油市價兩至三倍收費。

PART 07
到處玩

01 找到遊客中心

：你要會說的一句話 ⏵：你會聽到的問／答　**MP3** Track ▶ 063

[Must be...] 這個時候最需要的一句話！

請問你知道什麼地方的風景不錯嗎？
迷你句 Is there a place with a nice view?
完整句 Do you know any place with a nice view?

塔上的風景不錯。
There is a great view from the tower.

請問附近有什麼地方適合年輕人遊玩嗎？
迷你句 Any good place for young people around here?
完整句 Do you know any good place for young people to have fun around here?

這附近有幾間夜店。
We have a few night clubs nearby.

我想要見識一下紐約的風光。
迷你句 I want to see the sights of New York.
完整句 I would like to see the New York sights.

您對觀光團有興趣嗎？
Are you interested in a tour?

請問你推薦哪個觀光行程？
迷你句 Do you have any suggestions?
完整句 What do you recommend for sightseeing?

您可以試試 B 行程。
You can try tour B.

請問我可以到哪裡一日遊呢？
迷你句 Where can I go for a one-day trip?
完整句 Do you know any nice one-day tour?

您可以參考我們的旅遊導覽。
You can check our tour guide.

請問我必須要跟團才可以去這裡嗎？

迷你句 Do I have to join a tour?

完整句 Do I have to join a tour to go there?

當然不用，您可以自行前往。
Of course not, you can go there on your own.

請問我們可以拿一份導覽手冊嗎？

迷你句 Can we get one?

完整句 Can we have one of a guidebook?

當然。你也可以考慮參加旅行團。
Sure. You can also think about joining a tour.

請給我們一份中文語音導覽。

迷你句 We need a Chinese-speaking guide.

完整句 Please give us a Chinese-speaking guide.

抱歉，我們只有英文版的語音導覽。
Sorry, we only have English-speaking guides.

請問我要去哪裡拿活動一覽表？

迷你句 Where can I get the show guide?

完整句 Can you tell me where can I have a show guide?

您可以到旅客服務中心拿。
You can get one at the passenger service center.

[Things to Know] 一定要知道的**旅行常識**

到了目的地後，若不知道要怎麼開始玩，可以找到旅客服務中心，好好運用裡頭提供的資源。以下列出大型旅客服務中心會提供的服務：旅遊資訊諮詢服務、旅遊景區景點宣傳品索取、推薦旅遊路線、代售景區（點）門票、旅遊紀念商品展示、接待旅遊投訴、救援救助服務。

02 請人幫忙拍照

：你要會說的一句話　：你會聽到的問／答

[Must be...] 這個時候最需要的一句話！

請幫我們拍照。
迷你句 Can you take a picture for us?
完整句 Can you help us take a picture?

當然，你們想要在哪拍？
Sure, where would you like to take it?

請幫我跟米奇拍照。
迷你句 I want to have a picture with Mickey.
完整句 Could you take a picture for Mickey and me?

當然沒有問題。
That won't be a problem.

請跟我合照好嗎？
迷你句 Can we take a picture together?
完整句 Would you like to take a picture with me?

好啊，我的朋友可以幫我們拍。
Ok, my friend can take the picture for us.

我想要以這棟建築物為背景。
迷你句 I want this building in the background.
完整句 I want to have this building in the background.

您想要拍直的還是橫的？
Do you want the picture to be portrait or landscape?

請問這裡可以拍照嗎？
迷你句 Can I take a picture here?
完整句 Is it okay to take pictures here?

抱歉，這裡禁止拍照。
Sorry, it is prohibited to take pictures here.

👄 我想要買一捲底片。
迷你句 I need a roll of film.
完整句 I want to buy a roll of film.

👂 這樣 10 塊錢美金。
It is $10.

👄 請問洗一捲底片要多少錢呢？
迷你句 How much is it?
完整句 How much is it to develop a roll of film?

👂 洗一捲要 20 塊美金。
It costs $20 for a roll of film.

👄 請問要多久才會好呢？
迷你句 How long will it take?
完整句 How long will it take for the film to be developed?

👂 您必須要等 30 分鐘。
You have to wait for 30 minutes.

👄 請問有 36 張、400 度的底片嗎？
迷你句 Do you have this kind of film?
完整句 Do you have a roll of 36 pictures, ISO 400 films?

👂 有的，請問要幾捲？
Yes, how many do you want?

[Vocabulary] 生字不用另外查字典！

01 拍照 take a picture
02 沒有問題 no problcm
03 建築物 building
04 背景 background
05 肖像 portrait
06 風景 landscape
07 禁止 prohibit
08 一捲底片 a roll of film
09 等待 wait for
10 美金 dollar
11 買 buy
12 花費 cost

03 來買門票

：你要會說的一句話　　：你會聽到的問／答

 **MP3** Track ▶ 065

[Must be...] 這個時候最需要的一句話！

👄 我要兩張成人票。　**迷你句** Two adults, please.
　　　　　　　　　完整句 Can we have two adults ticket?

👂 請問要買幾點的？
What time do you want?

👄 請問入場費要多少錢？　**迷你句** How much is it?
　　　　　　　　　　　完整句 How much is the admission fee?

👂 成人一張10塊美金。
It is $10 for adults.

👄 請問您們有賣季票嗎？　**迷你句** Are there season passes?
　　　　　　　　　　　完整句 Do you have seasonal passes?

👂 有的，請問您需要幾張？
Yes, how many do you need?

👄 我要買家庭票？　**迷你句** One family pass, please.
　　　　　　　　完整句 We would like to purchase a family pass.

👂 請出示會員卡。
Please show me your membership card.

👄 請問三歲以下的兒童可以免費入場嗎？　**迷你句** Are kids free?
　　　　　　　　　　　　　　　　　完整句 Are children under three free for entrance?

👂 是的，三歲以下的兒童不需收費。
Yes, there is no charge for children under three.

三個大人兩個小孩。

迷你句 We have three adults and two children.

完整句 I want three adult tickets and two children tickets.

買家庭票會比較便宜。
It will be cheaper if you buy a family pass.

請問有任何折扣嗎？

迷你句 Any discount?

完整句 Is there any discount?

請問您是我們公司的會員嗎？
Are you a member of our company?

請問入場時間是什麼時候？

迷你句 What time can we enter?

完整句 What is the open time for this park?

從早上9點開到晚上8點。
It's open from 9 a.m. to 8 p.m.

我要兩張星光票。

迷你句 Two night passes, please.

完整句 I need two night passes, please.

這是您的票，下午6點可以進場。
Here are your tickets; you can get in at 6 p.m.

[Vocabulary] 生字不用另外查字典！

01 成人票 adults ticket

02 入場費 admission fee

03 季票 seasonal pass

04 家庭票 family pass

05 入口 entrance

06 兒童 kid

07 折扣 discount

08 會員 member

09 公司 company

10 入場 enter

11 星光票 night pass

12 進場 get in

👄：你要會説的一句話　　🗣：你會聽到的問/答　　🎧 **MP3** Track ▶ 066

[Must be...] 這個時候最需要的一句話！

👄 請問現在哪齣音樂劇最熱門？
- **迷你句** What is the hit musical right now?
- **完整句** What musical is popular right now?

🎧 「貓」劇現在仍在上映中。
"Cats" is still playing.

👄 請問我要到哪裡看「貓」劇呢？
- **迷你句** Where can I see it?
- **完整句** Where is "Cats" playing?

🎧 就在市區的劇院。
At the theater downtown.

👄 我想參觀比佛利山莊。
- **迷你句** I want to visit Beverly Hills.
- **完整句** I would like to see Beverly Hills.

🎧 我們可以為您安排。
We can arrange that for you.

👄 我可以參觀 NBC 電台嗎？
- **迷你句** Can I visit NBC?
- **完整句** Can I see the NBC Studios?

🎧 您得參加觀光團。
You have to join the tour.

👄 請問我可以在這裡預約嗎？
- **迷你句** Can I register here?
- **完整句** Can I make a reservation here?

🎧 可以，請留下您的個人資料。
Yes, please write down your personal information.

我想要選晚餐航遊行程。

迷你句 I want this dinner tour.

完整句 I want to take the dinner cruise.

好的，請讓我先幫您訂位。
Ok, let me book a reservation for you.

請問可以幫我弄一張票嗎？

迷你句 Can you get me a ticket?

完整句 Could you get a ticket for me?

當然，您想參加哪個觀光團？
Sure, which tour do you want to join?

我想在迪士尼樂園待上幾天。

迷你句 I want to be in Disneyland for a few days.

完整句 I would like to spend a few days at Disneyland.

您想要住在哪間飯店呢？
Which hotel would you like to stay at?

我想去當地的跳蚤市場。

迷你句 I want to go to the flea market.

完整句 I would like to go to the local flea market.

您想要看什麼呢？
What would you like to see?

[Words to Use] 替換字放空格，一句多用!!

● 我等不及要參觀_____了。
I can't wait to visit the _____.

01 NBC電台 **NBC Studios**　　**02** 比佛利山莊 **Beverly Hills**

03 迪士尼樂園 **Disneyland**　　**04** 紫禁城 **Forbidden City**

05 牛津大學 **Oxford University**　　**06** 羅浮宮 **Le Louvre**

[Must be...] 這個時候最需要的一句話！

請問這個行程要多少人才成行？

迷你句 How many at least?

完整句 What is the minimum number of person for this tour?

🎧 至少要 10 個人才可以。
It will be 10 at least.

請問我們會住哪一間飯店？

迷你句 Which hotel?

完整句 Which hotel are we going to stay at?

🎧 我們現在還不確定。
We are not sure right now.

請問這趟旅程的行程表呢？

迷你句 Is there an itinerary?

完整句 What is the itinerary for this tour?

🎧 所有的行程都在這小冊子上。
The itinerary is listed on this brochure.

請問有包含餐點嗎？

迷你句 Are meals included?

完整句 Does it include all the meals?

🎧 是的，房價包含了所有餐點。
Yes, all the meals are included in the price.

請問市區觀光團有名額限制嗎？

迷你句 Are there any limits?

完整句 Does this city tour group has any limited amount?

🎧 我們一團只收十個人。
We only take 10 members.

可以告訴我行程計畫嗎？

迷你句 I want to know about the tour.

完整句 Please tell me about the tour.

您想知道什麼？
What do you want to know?

我們可以得知更進一步的資訊嗎？

迷你句 Can we know more about it?

完整句 May we have some further information?

您可以上我們的網站查詢。
You can check on our website.

請問這些旅遊行程有什麼差別？

迷你句 What is the difference?

完整句 What is the difference between these tours?

這個行程有包含晚餐。
This one includes dinner.

我可以只參加這個旅遊的一部分嗎？

迷你句 Can I join only a part of it?

完整句 Can I take only a part of the tour?

很抱歉，這是個全天的行程。
Sorry, it is a whole-day tour.

[Vocabulary] 生字不用另外查字典！

01 行程 **tour**

02 至少 **at least**

03 最少的人數 **minimum number**

04 飯店 **hotel**

05 停留 **stay**

06 行程表 **itinerary**

07 小冊子 **brochure**

08 包含 **include**

09 餐點 **meal**

10 進一步資訊 **further information**

11 網站 **website**

12 晚餐 **dinner**

●：你要會說的一句話　　🗨：你會聽到的問／答　　**MP3** Track ▶ 068

[Must be...] 這個時候最需要的一句話！

👄 請問遠洋客輪之旅的日期是？

迷你句 What are the dates of the cruise?

完整句 What are the dates for the ocean liner tour?

🗨 遠洋客輪之旅從 9 月 14 日開始，為期一星期。
It starts on 14th September and lasts a week.

👄 請問這個旅遊的時間多長？

迷你句 How long is it?

完整句 How long will the tour take?

🗨 大概要兩個小時的時間。
It lasts for two hours.

👄 請問幾點出發？

迷你句 When does it start?

完整句 What time do you leave?

🗨 我們早上九點出發。
We leave at 9 a.m.

👄 請問從哪裡出發？

迷你句 Where does it start?

完整句 Where does it leave from?

🗨 從飯店出發。
It starts at the hotel.

👄 請問我們幾點會回來？

迷你句 When will we be back here?

完整句 What time will we come back?

🗨 我們晚上六點會回來這裡。
We will be back here by 6p.m.

這個行程要花上幾天？

迷你句 How many days?

完整句 How many days will this tour take?

大概要花上3天的時間。
It takes about 3 days.

請問會去華爾街嗎？

迷你句 Does it go to Wall Street?

完整句 Is Wall Street included in the tour?

是的，這也包含在行程裡。
Yes, it is included in this tour.

請問這是半天的旅程嗎？

迷你句 Half-day tour?

完整句 Is it a half-day tour?

不是，這是全天的旅程。
No, it is a full-day tour.

請問我們會有自由時間嗎？

迷你句 Any free time?

完整句 Do we have free time?

是的，你們有兩個小時的自由時間。
Yes, you have 2 hours of free time.

[Things to Know] 一定要知道的**旅行常識**

有別於團體旅遊，吃的玩的逛的可能都會受到限制，想要依照自己的行程、計劃以及品味來旅行的人，不妨為自己好好規劃一次自助旅行。初次拜訪一個城市，又不想為了怎麼搭地鐵、看地圖找景點而傷腦筋的話，不妨考慮參加當地的巴士旅遊。可以輕鬆地在最短時間內，將城市裡的重要景點一次看個夠！你可以選擇要不要有導遊沿路導覽，也可以選擇自由觀光旅遊，可以讓你在限定時間內自由在各景點上下車，隨興安排自己的行程。這種旅遊方式對觀光客來說，也是一大福音！

：你要會說的一句話　：你會聽到的問／答　**MP3** Track ▶ 069

[**Must be...**] 這個**時候**最需要的一句話！

請問到西班牙的行程要多少錢？

迷你句 How much for the Spain trip?

完整句 How much will the tour to Spain cost?

一個人1500塊美元。
It will be $1500 per person.

請問這個行程多少錢？

迷你句 How much is it?

完整句 How much does this tour cost?

50塊美金，並且不可以退費。
It is $50, and non-refundable.

請問這筆費用是什麼？

迷你句 What is this?

完整句 What is this charge for?

這筆費用是保險費。
It is the insurance.

請問這個價錢包含什麼？

迷你句 What does the price include?

完整句 What is included in the price?

包含了門票和午餐。
It includes the admission and lunch.

請問這個價錢有包含餐費嗎？

迷你句 Including meals?

完整句 Does the price include meals?

沒有，餐費要額外計算。
No, that would be extra.

請問我們會在飯店留宿嗎？

迷你句 Will we stay in the hotel?

完整句 Are we going to stay in hotel?

是的，會住在一間五星級飯店。
Yes, at a five-star hotel.

請問我們會搭乘哪種交通工具？

迷你句 How will we get there?

完整句 What kind of transportation will we take?

您可以從清單裡挑選。
You can pick from the list.

請問我們需要保險嗎？

迷你句 Any insurance?

完整句 Do we have to buy the insurance?

是的，這是不可避免的。
Yes, it is unavoidable.

請問有團體優惠嗎？

迷你句 Is there a group discount?

完整句 Are there a group discount?

有的，十個人或十人以上有優惠。
Yes, for a group of 10 or more.

[Vocabulary] 生字不用另外查字典！

01 行程 trip
02 一個人 per person
03 退費 non-refundable
04 保險費 insurance
05 價錢 price
06 門票 admission
07 午餐 lunch
08 額外 extra
09 一餐 meal
10 五星級飯店 five-star hotel
11 交通工具 transportation
12 清單 list

[Must be...] 這個時候最需要的一句話！

😮 請問你們有圖畫明信片嗎？

迷你句 Do you have any postcards?

完整句 Are there any picture postcards available?

👂 您可以到紀念品商店看看。
You can go to the souvenir store.

😮 請問遊行幾點開始？

迷你句 When does it start?

完整句 What time does the parade start?

👂 晚上 6 點開始遊行。
The parade starts at 6 p.m.

😮 請問下一次導覽的時間是什麼時候？

迷你句 When is the next guided tour?

完整句 When does the next guide tour begin?

👂 下一次導覽 10 分鐘內就要開始了。
The next guided tour starts in 10 minutes.

😮 請問我們會在這裡待多久？

迷你句 How long will we stay?

完整句 How long will we be here?

👂 我們會在這裡待上一個小時。
We will be here for an hour.

😮 請問我們有多久的時間？

迷你句 For how long?

完整句 How much tine do we have?

👂 我不太確定，好像是一個半小時。
I am not sure, maybe a half hour.

請問我們有時間可以購物嗎？
迷你句 Any time for shopping?
完整句 Do we have time to buy things?

你們有兩個小時可以購物和吃午餐。
You have 2 hours for shopping and lunch.

我們應該幾點回來？
迷你句 When should we return?
完整句 What time should we be back?

4 點在這裡集合。
Please be here at 4 p.m.

請問我們幾點會結束？
迷你句 When will we be back?
完整句 What time will we finish the tour?

下午 5 點會結束行程。
It will end at 5p.m.

請問我們現在要往哪裡走？
迷你句 Where are we going?
完整句 Where are we headed to?

我們要去參觀好萊塢劇場。
We are going to visit the Hollywood Bowl.

[Vocabulary] 生字不用另外查字典！

01 日期 **date**
02 遠洋客輪 **ocean lincr**
03 旅行 **tour**
04 出發 **start**
05 華爾街 **Wall Street**
06 自由時間 **free time**
07 巡遊 **cruise**
08 持續 **last**
09 離開 **leave**
10 包含 **include**
11 半天 **half-day**
12 全天 **full-day**

觀光行程常見標語

還在找想要參加的行程嗎？收集了一堆傳單，到處晃了晃，先認識以下
詞彙，才能選到最適合自己的行程唷！

01【描述行程花費】

· 不收門票 admission is free
· 向所有人開放 free entry for all.
· 持本廣告 85 折優惠 15% off with this flyer
· 票價包括所有費用 all-inclusive ticket
· （票價）優惠 concessions
· 全季12歲以下的兒童半價

　children under 12 half price throughout season
· 欲知詳情請來電

　for more detailed information please call
· 買成人票，兒童免費

　free children admission with full paying adult
· 兒童優惠 child reductions
· 24小時內收半價

　under 24 hours a 50% charge may be levied

02【描述行程時間】

· 旅遊活動全天進行 tours are held throughout the day
· 遊程兩個小時 tours take up to two hours
· 全天開放 access all day

03【描述行程內容】

- 觀光遊覽最佳季節 Sightseeing at its best!
- 提供購物機會 shopping offers
- 安全可靠 safe and reliable
- 旅遊配有現場英語解說 tours have live english commentary

04【描述注意事項】

- 預訂 reservations
- 預訂座位 reserved seating
- 建議所有乘客購買旅遊保險

  all passengers are strongly advised to obtain travel insurance.
- 旅遊需要提前定票 all tours require advance booking.
- 接站地點和接站時間 pick up points and times
- 提前預定，避免錯過

  advanced booking is essential to avoid disappointment

05【描述行程伙食】

- 提供自助餐 cafeteria available
- 提供素食餐 vegetarian meals available
- 包含餐費 meals included
- 不包含餐費 meals excluded
- 可自己做飯 self-catering

[Must be...] 這個時候最需要的一句話！

我以為入場費只要 10 塊錢美金。
迷你句 I thought it was $10.
完整句 I thought the admission fee was only $10.

抱歉，我們最近調漲了。
Sorry, we raised the fee recently.

我沒帶到會員卡。
迷你句 I forgot my card.
完整句 I didn't bring my membership card.

那您就必須付全額。
Then you have to pay full price.

可以給我們特價嗎？
迷你句 Give us a discount, please.
完整句 Can you just give us discount price?

很抱歉，只有老人有優惠。
Sorry, the special price is only for seniors.

為什麼我們必須付全額？
迷你句 Why do you charge us full price?
完整句 Why do we have to pay the full price?

旺季只有一種價格。
There is only one price in peak season.

我可以跟你們的經理談談嗎？
迷你句 Is your supervisor here?
完整句 Can I talk to your manager?

好的，請等一下。
Ok, please wait a minute.

你拿錯票給我了。　**迷你句** This ticket is wrong.

完整句 You gave me the wrong ticket.

抱歉，我馬上給您另一張。
Sorry, I will give another one right away.

我要使用折價卷？　**迷你句** Here is the coupon.

完整句 Can I use this coupon?

抱歉，折價券無法在假日使用。
Sorry, this coupon is not valid on weekends.

你少找給我 1 塊錢　**迷你句** You short changed me.
美金。　**完整句** It is still short with $1.

抱歉，這是您的 1 塊錢。
Sorry, here is your $1.

我買錯票了。　**迷你句** It is the wrong ticket.

完整句 I bought the wrong ticket.

請讓我看一下您的收據。
May I have your receipt, please.

[Vocabulary] 生字不用另外查字典！

01 入場費 admission

02 調漲 raise

03 費用 fee

04 會員卡 membership card

05 付全額 pay full price

06 特價 discount price

07 老人 senior

08 優惠 special price

09 旺季 peak season

10 經理 manager

11 無效的 not valid

12 折價卷 coupon

旅遊常用句型 + 超多替換字，套入馬上用！

遊客中心

● 我需要這城市的 _____。

I need a/an _____ of the city.

01 地圖 map
02 捷運路線圖 MRT route map
03 旅遊手冊 travel brochure
04 遊客通行證 tourist pass
05 旅遊指南 sightseeing guide
06 美食指南 gourmet guide

請人幫忙拍照

●你可以幫我們在 _____ 前照一張相嗎？

Will you take a picture of us in front of the _____?

01 噴泉 fountain
02 建築物 building
03 雕像 statue
04 寺廟 temple
05 瀑布 waterfall
06 美術館 gallery

購買門票

● 我們得排很長的隊伍買 _____ 門票。

We have to wait in a long line to buy the _____ tickets.

01 音樂會 concert
02 博物館 museum
03 音樂劇 opera
04 展覽 exhibition
05 美術館 art gallery
06 入場 admission

詢問行程內容

● 我需要更多有關你們 ＿＿＿ 行程的細節。
I need more details about your ＿＿＿＿ package.

01 城市一日遊 city day tour　02 機加酒 flight & accommodation

03 遊輪 cruise　04 賞櫻 cherry blossom

05 團體旅遊 group tour　06 滑雪假期 ski vacation

詢問行程費用

● 旅遊行程費用有包含 ＿＿＿ 嗎？
Is ＿＿＿ included in the tour package?

01 午餐 lunch　02 機票 flight ticket

03 旅遊保險 travel insurance　04 住宿 accommodation

05 入場門票 admission ticket　06 交通費 transportation

最著名的娛樂

● 這城市以其 ＿＿＿ 聞名。
The city is famous for its ＿＿＿＿.

01 美食 cuisine　02 手工藝品 handicrafts

03 小吃 snacks　04 歷史遺產 historical legacy

05 高端時尚 high fashion　06 （陸上）景色 landscapes

戶外活動介紹

除了逛街血拼、大啖美食外，還有什麼有趣好玩的活動，讓你能有個難忘回憶的旅程呢？

01【滑雪】

位於亞熱帶的台灣，看到雪的機會不多，更別說是滑雪了，所以趁這個機會來體驗這刺激又好玩的活動。滑雪有分兩種：單板（Snowboard） 與雙板（Ski），端看個人喜好選擇，有人說 ski 滑起來優雅且入門容易，喜歡追求速度又熱愛酷炫東西的人就會愛上 snowboard。雖然滑雪是個刺激又容易上癮的活動，但危險性較高，上場前別忘了戴好安全帽與護具。最好能再找個教練帶入門，就能好好享受滑雪樂趣。

02【高空跳傘】

天氣好的話，又想追求極限，不妨來試試看高空跳傘（Skydiving）。跳傘目前在台灣僅有軍方特種部隊才能體驗的活動，而在歐美早已不稀奇。高空跳傘事前會要求簽署切結書，再由專業教練講解注意事項與穿戴套帶。最後就搭乘小型飛機至 4,500 公尺高空，由教練帶你縱身往下跳，挑戰自我的極限。高空跳傘約一次 USD$200-250 不等，若想要再錄影留念，再加約 $100 會有另位教練貼身記錄從搭機，跳機一直到落地過程。這絕對會是你難忘的回憶，與體驗人生的一大挑戰。

03【熱氣球】

如果跳傘太過激烈，那麼來試試看乘坐熱氣球（Hot Air Balloon）吧。搭熱氣球可以讓你慢慢的享受周邊風景，通常熱氣球都會挑在風景優美的郊區。若時間能搭配得好，在日出或日落時更是浪漫滿分的體驗。乘坐一次熱氣球的價位與高空跳傘差不多，約 $200-250，乘坐時間約一小時。

PART 08
到處買

：你要會說的一句話　🗨：你會聽到的問／答　**MP3** Track ▶ 072

[**Must be...**] 這個時候最需要的一句話！

請問你們的店在哪裡？
迷你句 Where is your store?
完整句 Where is your store located?

🗨 就在紀念大樓的旁邊。
Just right besides the Memorial building.

請問你們店的地址在哪裡？
迷你句 The address?
完整句 What is your store's address?

🗨 我們的地址是華爾街 222 號。
Our address is 222 Wall Street.

請問你們的營業時間為何？
迷你句 When do you open?
完整句 What are your store's opening hours?

🗨 我們從早上11點營業到晚上10點。
We are open from 11a.m. to 10p.m.

請問你們的店營業到幾點？
迷你句 How late are you open?
完整句 What time do you close?

🗨 我們開到午夜。
We are open till midnight.

請問你們週末有營業嗎？
迷你句 Weekends as well?
完整句 Do you open on the weekends?

🗨 不，我們週末和假日沒有營業。
No, we aren't open on the weekends or holidays.

請問你們有分店嗎？
迷你句 Any branches?
完整句 Do you have any branches?

沒有，我們只有一間店。
No, we only have one store.

請問你們有幾間分店？
迷你句 How many branches?
完整句 How many branches do you have?

我們在美國擁有超過50間分店。
We have over 50 branches in US.

請問你們和分店有什麼不同嗎？
迷你句 What is the difference?
完整句 What is the difference between your store and other branches?

其他分店有具有當地特色的商品。
There are some different local items in other branches.

請問你們在台灣有設分店嗎？
迷你句 Any branch in Taiwan?
完整句 Do you have a branch in Taiwan?

不，我想沒有。
No, I don't think so.

[Vocabulary] 生字不用另外查字典！

01 商店 **store**
02 紀念大樓 **Memorial building**
03 店址 **address**
04 華爾街 **Wall Street**
05 營業時間 **store hours**
06 午夜 **midnight**
07 週末 **weekend**
08 假日 **holiday**
09 分店 **branches**
10 不同 **difference**
11 當地特色商品 **local item**
12 旁邊 **beside**

：你要會說的一句話　🗨：你會聽到的問／答　**MP3** Track ▶ 073

[Must be...] 這個時候最需要的一句話！

我可以看一下那個手提袋嗎？
迷你句 I would like to see that handbag.
完整句 Can I have a look at that handbag?

您想要看哪一個？
Which one do you want to see?

我正在找一條西裝褲。
迷你句 I want dress pants.
完整句 I am looking for a pair of dressing pants.

您在找哪一種款式呢？
What type are you looking for?

請問這是誰設計的？
迷你句 Who is the designer?
完整句 What is the name of the designer?

這是蒂娜傑克森設計的。
It was designed by Tina Jackson.

我在找能禦寒的背心。
迷你句 A vest for cold weather.
完整句 I am looking for a vest which designed for cold weather.

或許您可以試試這件。
Maybe you can try this one.

請問這個靴子還有其他顏色嗎？
迷你句 Any other colors?
完整句 What color options do I have for this boots?

有5種顏色供您選擇。
We have 5 colors for you to choose from.

請問這件襯衫有黑色的嗎？

迷你句 A black one?

完整句 Do you have this shirt in black?

這件襯衫有黑色和紅色兩種。
This shirt comes in red and black.

請問這是什麼材質？

迷你句 What is it made of?

完整句 What kind of material is this made of?

我們使用的材質為羊毛。
The material we used is fleece.

請問這些襯衫是棉的嗎？

迷你句 Are they cotton?

完整句 Are these shirt made of cotton?

是的，這是百分之百棉花。
Yes, they are made of 100% cotton.

我正在找一雙羊毛手套。

迷你句 I want wool gloves.

完整句 I am looking for a pair of wool gloves.

您想要什麼顏色的？
What color do you like?

[Words to Use] 替換字放空格，一句多用!!

● 我想找_____。
I am looking for a/an _____.

01 （一雙）羊毛手套 **pair of wool gloves**

02 （一條）西裝褲 **pair of dressing pants**

03 （一件）套頭毛衣 **pullover sweater**

04 條紋襯衫 **stripe shirt**

05 百褶裙 **pleated skirt**

06 黑色蕾絲洋裝 **black lace dress**

😊：你要會説的一句話　🗨：你會聽到的問／答　**MP3** Track ▶ 074

[Must be...] 這個時候最需要的一句話！

😊 請問這粉底有防曬嗎？

迷你句 Is this also sun block?

完整句 Does this foundation have sun protection?

🗨 沒有，您可以試試旁邊那一種。
No, you can try the one next to that one.

😊 我需要洗面乳。

迷你句 I need a cleanser.

完整句 I need a facial cleanser.

🗨 請問您是哪一種肌膚？
What type of skin do you have?

😊 這個眼影的顏色對我來説太亮了。

迷你句 It is too bright for me.

完整句 The color of this eye shadow is too bright to me.

🗨 我換個給您。
I will give you a different one.

😊 可以給我一些眼霜的樣品嗎？

迷你句 Do you have eye cream samples?

完整句 Can I have some samples of this eye cream?

🗨 如果您消費超過50美元，就能免費獲得一個樣品。
You can get a free sample if you spend over $50.

😊 請問這是新推出的產品嗎？

迷你句 Is this new?

完整句 Is this the new item?

🗨 這是我們的每週特別版。
This is our weekly special bundle.

請問這眼線好用嗎？
迷你句 Is this good?
完整句 Is this eyeliner good?

當然，需要我幫妳畫一點嗎？
Of course, do you want me to put on the eyeliner for you?

我想試試這口紅。
迷你句 I want to try this lipstick.
完整句 I would like to try this lipstick.

您喜歡哪種色彩濃度？
What shade would you like?

你可以幫我推薦嗎？
迷你句 Any suggestions?
完整句 Can you recommend one for me?

沒問題，您想要找哪一方面的產品？
Sure, what kind of product are you looking for?

我可以試用這個嗎？
迷你句 Can I try this?
完整句 Can I try some of this?

可以，你可以在手上試一點。
Yes, you can try some on your hand first.

[Vocabulary] 生字不用另外查字典！

01 粉底 foundation
02 防曬 sun block
03 洗面乳 facial cleanser
04 肌膚 skin
05 顏色 color
06 眼霜 eye cream
07 樣品 sample
08 免費 free
09 新推出的產品 new item
10 每週特別版 weekly special bundle
11 眼線筆 eyeliner
12 口紅 lipstick

04 買食物

:你要會說的一句話　　:你會聽到的問／答

[Must be...] 這個時候最需要的一句話！

請問哪裡有起司？　迷你句 Where is the cheese?
完整句 Where can I find cheese?

你可以在麵包店找到。
You can find it in a bakery.

請問這裡有麵包店嗎？　迷你句 Do you have a bakery here?
完整句 Is there a bakery around here?

我想超市旁邊應該有一間。
I think there is one next to the supermarket.

我要買披薩。　迷你句 I want a pizza.
完整句 I would like to buy a pizza.

您想要哪一種口味？
Which flavor do you want?

我可以在哪裡買到熱食？　迷你句 I want to buy some hot food.
完整句 Where can I buy hot food?

您可以在熟食店買熱食。
You can buy some hot food at the deli.

請問蔬果在哪裡？　迷你句 Where are the vegetables?
完整句 Where can I find some vegetables?

蔬菜和水果在農產品區。
Vegetables and fruits are in the produce department.

有什麼產品比較便宜嗎？
迷你句 Any cheaper products?
完整句 Is there any products on sale?

有，自有品牌的洋芋片全部特價。
Yes, the store brand chips are all on sale.

請問有有機產品嗎？
迷你句 Do you have organic products?
完整句 Is there any organic products?

您可以到 3 號走道看看。
You can try to find them in aisle 3.

請問哪裡有賣冰淇淋？
迷你句 Where is the ice cream?
完整句 On which aisle can I find ice cream?

冰淇淋在3號走道。
You can find ice cream in aisle 3.

請問賣東方食品區在哪裡？
迷你句 Any oriental foods?
完整句 Where is the oriental food?

抱歉，我們沒有東方食品區。
Sorry, we don't have an oriental food section.

[Words to Use] 替換字放空格，一句多用!!

● 我可以在哪裡買到＿＿＿？
Where can I get some ＿＿＿?

01 熟食 prepared food

02 蔬果 vegetables

03 水果 fruits

04 有機產品 organic products

05 冷凍食品 frozen food

06 乳製品 dairy products

05 買首飾珠寶

👄：你要會説的一句話　📢：你會聽到的問／答

 **MP3** Track ▶ 076

[Must be...] 這個時候最需要的一句話！

👄 我要買玉項鍊當禮物。

迷你句 A jade necklace.

完整句 I want to buy a jade necklace as a gift.

📢 您可以看看這一區。
You can take a look at this section.

👄 請問這個金鐲子是幾 K 金？

迷你句 What carat gold is this?

完整句 How many carat is this gold bracelet?

📢 那是 20K 金的鐲子。
This bracelet is 20 carat gold.

👄 請問有 20K 金的金飾嗎？

迷你句 Do you have any 20-carat gold items?

完整句 I am looking for a 20-carats gold product.

📢 抱歉，我們只有 14K 金的。
Sorry, we only carry 14-carats gold items.

👄 我想要買戒指。

迷你句 I am looking for a ring.

完整句 I would like to buy a ring.

📢 您在找多大的戒指呢？
What size ring are you looking for?

👄 這個戒指太大了。

迷你句 It is too big.

完整句 The ring is too big for me.

📢 我們可以幫您換尺寸。
We can get you a different size.

222

我要琥珀做的墜子。
(迷你句) I want an amber pendant.
(完整句) I want a pendant made of amber.

這一款賣得很好。
This one sells very well.

請問有翡翠嗎?
(迷你句) Do you have jadeite?
(完整句) Is there any jadeites in your store?

是的,我們有許多翡翠製成的產品。
Yes, we have many items made of jadeite.

請問這是純金的嗎?
(迷你句) Is this pure gold?
(完整句) Is it made of pure gold?

是鍍金的,但是非常精美。
It is gold-plated but quite delicate.

我想要有紅寶石墜子的項鍊。
(迷你句) I want one with a ruby pendant.
(完整句) I would like to have one with ruby pendant.

好的,我要確認有無庫存。
Okay. Let me check if it's in stock.

[Words to Use] 替換字放空格,一句多用!!

● 可以讓我看看你們店裡的_____嗎?
Can you show me the _____ in your store?

01 翡翠 jadeite

02 琥珀墜子 amber pendants

03 戒指 rings

04 金飾 gold products

05 玉項鍊 jade necklaces

06 金鐲子 gold bracelets

06 買電器用品

[Must be...] 這個時候最需要的一句話！

👄 我在找水壺。
迷你句 Do you have kettles?
完整句 I am looking for a kettle.

👂 水壺在11走道。
They're in aisle 11.

👄 請問你們這台吹風機還有貨嗎？
迷你句 I would like this hair dryer.
完整句 Do you have this hair dryer in stock?

👂 不好意思，這台吹風機缺貨。
Sorry, it is out of stock.

👄 我需要空氣清淨機。
迷你句 An air filter.
完整句 I need something to clean the air.

👂 我們這台目前正在特價。
We have this model of air filter on special now.

👄 請問這台電腦多少錢？
迷你句 How much is it?
完整句 How much does this computer cost?

👂 要美金800塊錢。
It costs $800.

👄 請問哪一種商品最熱門？
迷你句 Which is the most popular one?
完整句 What is the most popular product?

👂 這款電視最熱門。
This TV is the most popular one.

請問還有其他的樣式嗎？
迷你句 Other styles?
完整句 Are there any other styles?

它有其他不同的顏色選擇。
We have some different colors from this one.

請問大部分的人都買什麼當禮物呢？
迷你句 The most popular gift?
完整句 What do most people buy as a gift?

這個壓力鍋是個很不錯的禮物選擇。
This pressure cooker is a great option for a gift.

有什麼適合小孩子的商品嗎？
迷你句 Anything for children?
完整句 Do you have any products for children?

這個電動遊戲機怎麼樣呢？
How about this video game?

請問這個插頭的規格跟台灣的一樣嗎？
迷你句 Can I use this in Taiwan?
完整句 Is the specification of plug as same as Taiwan's?

是的，您可以在台灣使用。
Yes, you can use it in Taiwan.

[Words to Use] 替換字放空格，一句多用!!

● 這個_____有特價嗎？
Is this _____ on sale?

01 平板電腦 **tablet computer**　**02** 氣炸鍋 **airfryer**

03 電動攪拌器 **electric mixer**　**04** 電風扇 **fan**

05 吸塵器 **vacuum cleaner**　**06** 印表機 **printer**

[Must be...] 這個時候最需要的一句話！

👄 請問這些襪子是哪裡做的？
迷你句 Where are they made?
完整句 Where are these socks made?

🎧 這些襪子是印度製造。
They are made in India.

👄 請問這些是中國做的嗎？
迷你句 Made in China?
完整句 Are these made in China?

🎧 不是，我們店裡的商品都是日本生產的。
No, everything in our store is made in Japan.

👄 請問這些填充娃娃是從哪裡進口的？
迷你句 Where were they imported from?
完整句 Where are these stuffed animals imported from?

🎧 這些玩具都是從羅馬尼亞來的。
These toys are manufactured in Romania.

👄 請問它們是來自北美洲嗎？
迷你句 From North America?
完整句 Do they come from North America?

🎧 不，它們是從南美洲來的。
No, they are from South America.

👄 請問這是哪個牌子？
迷你句 What brand is this?
完整句 Who is the maker of this?

🎧 您可以看看標籤。
You can see it on the label.

請問這個做得好不好？
迷你句 Is this made well?
完整句 Is the quality okay?

當然，這是美國製造的。
Of course, it is made in the USA.

我要從哪裡看製造國家呢？
迷你句 Where is this from?
完整句 How can I know the place where the product was made from?

每個商品上都有標籤。
There is a label on each product.

這個商品很特別。
迷你句 It is special.
完整句 This product is very unique.

是的，這些是在地製造的產品。
Yes, they are all locally made products.

我正在找日本生產的相機。
迷你句 I want a camera from Japan.
完整句 I am looking for a camera made in Japan.

抱歉，我們只有韓國產的相機。
Sorry, we only have cameras made in Korea.

[Words to Use] 替換字放空格，一句多用!!

● 請問這個_____是哪裡製造的？
Where was this/were these _____ made?

01 電燈 **lamp**　　02 咖啡機 **coffee make**

03 空氣清淨機 **air filter**　　04 除溼機 **dehumidifier**

05 吹風機 **hair dryer**　　06 電鍋 **rice cooker**

[Must be...] 這個時候最需要的一句話！

👄 我可以試穿這雙鞋子嗎？
迷你句 Can I try these on?
完整句 Can I try on these shoes?

🗣 請問您腳的尺寸是多少？
What size shoe do you wear?

👄 請問這件夾克尺寸多少？
迷你句 What size is this?
完整句 What is the size of this jacket?

🗣 這件是 L。
It is large.

👄 請問這適合我的尺寸嗎？
迷你句 Will this fit me?
完整句 I'm not sure if this my size?

🗣 是的，適合您的尺寸。
Yes, it is your size.

👄 請問你們只有這個尺寸嗎？
迷你句 Any other sizes?
完整句 Is this the only size you have?

🗣 不，我們有很多種尺寸可以供您選擇。
No, we have a variety of sizes.

👄 我不知道我的尺寸。
迷你句 I don't know my size.
完整句 I am not sure what my size is.

🗣 我來幫您。
Let me help you.

請問可以幫我量尺寸嗎？
迷你句 Can you help me?
完整句 Could you measure the size for me?

我非常樂意。
I would be more than happy to.

我找不到我的尺寸。
迷你句 I can't find my size.
完整句 I can't find the one that fits me.

您在找哪一個尺寸呢？
What size are you looking for?

請問你有尺寸大一點的嗎？
迷你句 A bigger one?
完整句 Do you have a bigger size?

有的，請問要哪個尺寸？
Yes, which size do you need?

我要再大一號。
迷你句 One size bigger.
完整句 One size bigger will be good for me.

好的，我馬上去拿您的尺寸。
Ok, I will get your size right away.

[Words to Use] 替換字放空格，一句多用!!

- 這件襯衫有出_____尺寸嗎？
  Does this shirt come in a/an _____ size?

01 特小 **extra-small** 02 小 **small**

03 中 **medium** 04 大 **large**

05 特大 **extra-large** 06 雙特大 **double extra large**

229

👄：你要會說的一句話　🔊：你會聽到的問／答　 **MP3** Track ▶ 080

[Must be...] 這個時候最需要的一句話！

👄 我想要試穿這件黑色的襯衫。
> **迷你句** I want try this in black.
>
> **完整句** I want to try on this shirt in black.

🔊 沒問題，試衣間在那邊。
Sure, there is the fitting room.

👄 請問試衣間在哪裡？
> **迷你句** Where is the fitting room?
>
> **完整句** Could you tell me where the dressing room is?

🔊 讓我帶您去。
Let me show you.

👄 我可以照一下鏡子嗎？
> **迷你句** May I see a mirror?
>
> **完整句** Do you have a mirror here?

🔊 試衣間裡有鏡子。
There is one in the fitting room.

👄 這件尺寸有點太大。
> **迷你句** It is big.
>
> **完整句** It is a little big.

🔊 我們也有小一點的尺寸。
We also have a smaller one.

👄 這個部分太緊了。
> **迷你句** It's too tight here.
>
> **完整句** It is a little too tight around here.

🔊 您要試穿大一點的嗎？
Do you want to try a bigger one?

😮 我看起來如何？ **迷你句** How do I look?

完整句 Do I look okay?

👂 很棒，很適合您。
Great! It fits you well.

😮 請問可以幫我修改腰圍嗎？ **迷你句** Can you fix the waist?

完整句 Can you fix the waist size for me?

👂 可以，但是修改需要花一些時間。
Yes, but it will take some time to do the alternations.

😮 請問訂製這件襯衫要花多久時間。 **迷你句** How long does tailoring take?

完整句 How long will it take to have this shirt tailored?

👂 大約要一週的時間。
It will take about a week.

😮 我要訂製這件衣服。 **迷你句** Can I have this tailored?

完整句 I would like to have this dress tailored.

👂 好的，訂製衣服需要收取 20 美金的費用。
Ok, there is a $20 charge for tailor service.

[Vocabulary] 生字不用另外查字典！

01 襯衫 shirt
02 試衣間 filling room
03 鏡子 mirror
04 緊 tight
05 適合 fit
06 修改 fix
07 腰圍 waist size
08 修改 alternation
09 訂製 tailor
10 試穿 try
11 尺寸 size
12 黑色的 black

231

10 多少錢？有折扣嗎？

：你要會說的一句話　　：你會聽到的問／答　　**MP3** Track ▶ 081

[Must be...] 這個時候最需要的一句話！

這多少錢。

迷你句 How much is it?
完整句 How much does it cost?

這要 25 美金。
It costs $25.

總共多少錢？

迷你句 How much is the total?
完整句 How much is it all together?

這樣總共 300 美元。
Your total is $300.

請問有折扣嗎？

迷你句 Is there a discount?
完整句 Can you give me a discount?

現在這個時候沒有特價活動。
There is no discount at this time.

請問今天有什麼特價？

迷你句 What is on sale today?
完整句 What are the sale items today?

這些襯衫今天打 5 折。
These shirts are 50% off today.

這超過我的預算了。

迷你句 That is over my budget.
完整句 That is more than I planned to spend.

您的預算是多少？
What's your budget?

請問這個打折前是多少錢？

(迷你句) What is the regular price?

(完整句) What was the price before the sale.

原價 150 美元。
The regular price is $150.

這太貴了。

(迷你句) It is overpriced.

(完整句) The price is way higher than I expected.

或許您可以看看特價品區？
Maybe you can take a look at the sale items.

請問你們有低於 50 美元的商品嗎？

(迷你句) Do you have one under $50?

(完整句) I am looking for the item under $50.

有的，我們有許多50美元或價格更低的商品。
Yes, we have many items at that price or less.

我是你們的會員。

(迷你句) I am your member.

(完整句) I have the membership card.

那麼您可以享有 8 折優惠。
Then you can have a 20% discount.

[Words to Use] 替換字放空格，一句多用!!

● 如果我買兩個，你可以給我_____嗎？
Can you give me _____ if I buy two of them?

01 折扣 a discount

02 特價 a special price

03 更優惠的價格 a better price

04 折扣 a rebate

05 打九折 10 percent off

06 打八折 20 percent off

[Must be...] 這個時候最需要的一句話！

😄 可以算我便宜一點嗎？
迷你句 Can it be cheaper?
完整句 Can I have lower price?

👂 您願意出多少呢？
What price are you willing to pay?

😄 可以半價賣我嗎？
迷你句 Can I have it for half price?
完整句 Can you lower the price by half?

👂 好吧，如果您可以多買一些的話。
Well, if you could buy more.

😄 這個價格似乎有點高？
迷你句 It is a little expensive.
完整句 This price seems to be a little high.

👂 如果您買兩個我可以給您折扣。
I can give you a discount if you buy two of them.

😄 你能給我特別優惠嗎？
迷你句 Any special offers?
完整句 Can you give me a special offer?

👂 這要看您買多少。
It depends on how many you are going to buy.

😄 我不會給你超過50美元。
迷你句 $50 at most.
完整句 I won't pay you more than $50.

👂 恐怕沒有討價還價的餘地。
I am afraid there is no room to bargain.

👄 可以給我們打折嗎？　**迷你句** A discount?
完整句 Can you give us a discount?

👂 我們可以給您8折優惠。
We can give you a 20% off discount.

👄 我可以享有會員價嗎？　**迷你句** A member price?
完整句 Can I have member price?

👂 如果您加入會員就可以享有會員價。
You get the member price if you become a member.

👄 請問我可以用折價券嗎？　**迷你句** Can I use this?
完整句 Can I use the coupon?

👂 您不需要用折價券就有折扣。
You don't need any coupons for the discount.

👄 請問這些可以算我5美金就好嗎？　**迷你句** $5 for these, ok?
完整句 Can I take $5 for all of these?

👂 這樣的折扣我們沒有利潤了。
We can't make a profit if I offer you that price.

[Vocabulary] 生字**不用另外查字典**！

01 信用卡 **credit card**　**02** 萬事達卡 **Master card**

03 VISA卡 **VISA card**　**04** 美金 **dollar**

05 收據 **receipt**　**06** 現金 **cash**

07 零錢 **change**　**08** 紙鈔 **bill**

09 折扣卡 **discount card**　**10** 簽名 **sign**

11 免費停車代幣 **free parking token**　**12** 分開 **separate**

[**Must be...**] 這個時候最需要的一句話！

👄 請問我可以用信用卡付帳嗎？
- 迷你句 I will pay by card.
- 完整句 Can I pay with my credit card?

👂 抱歉，我們只收現金。
Sorry, we only take cash.

👄 請問可以刷哪種卡？
- 迷你句 Which credit card can I use?
- 完整句 What kind of cards do you take?

👂 我們收萬事達卡和VISA卡。
We take Master card and VISA .

👄 請問你們收美金嗎？
- 迷你句 Are US dollars ok?
- 完整句 Do you accept US dollars?

👂 是的，我們也可以刷卡。
Yes, and also credit cards.

👄 請給我收據。
- 迷你句 Receipt, please.
- 完整句 Can I have my receipt, please.

👂 好的，您的收據在這。
Yes, here you go.

👄 我想要退20現金。
- 迷你句 $20 cash back, please.
- 完整句 I would like to have $20 cash back.

👂 您要零錢還是紙鈔？
Do you want change or bills?

這是我的折扣卡。　　**迷你句** My discount card.

完整句 Here is my discount card.

好的，您想要怎麼付費？
Ok, how would you like to pay for it?

我要刷卡。　　**迷你句** Pay by credit card.

完整句 I would like to pay by credit cards.

好的，請在這裡簽名。
Ok, please sign here.

我要免費停車代
幣。　　**迷你句** I need a free parking token.

完整句 Can I have my free parking token?

是的，它已經印在您的收據上了。
Yes, it is on your receipt.

請幫我們分開結
帳。　　**迷你句** Separate please.

完整句 Will you give us separate bills?

好的，您要用現金還是信用卡結帳？
Yes. Do you want to pay in cash or credit?

[Vocabulary] 生字不用另外查字典！

01 信用卡 credit card

02 美金 US dollar

03 收據 receipt

04 現金 cash

05 紙鈔 bill

06 零錢 change

07 折扣卡 discount card

08 付款 pay

09 簽名 sign

10 停車代幣 parking token

11 分開帳單 separate bills

12 免費停車 free parking

13 可以退稅嗎？

👄：你要會說的一句話　🔊：你會聽到的問／答

 MP3 Track ▶ 084

[Must be...] 這個時候最需要的一句話！

👄 請問我可以退營業稅嗎？

迷你句 Can I get the tax back?

完整句 Do I get sales tax return?

🔊 您可以在機場提出退營業稅申請。
You can apply for a sales tax return at the airport.

👄 請問我要去哪裡退營業稅？

迷你句 Where do I get the tax back?

完整句 Where can I apply for sales tax return?

🔊 在三樓。
It is on the third floor.

👄 請問我要怎麼退營業稅？

迷你句 How can I get the tax back?

完整句 Can you tell me how can I take sales tax return?

🔊 您需要填寫一些表格。
You have to fill out some application forms.

👄 請問你們有退營業稅表格？

迷你句 I am looking for the application form.

完整句 Do you have sales tax return application form?

🔊 有的，請問您需要多少？
Right, how many do you need?

👄 請問申請退營業稅需要什麼文件嗎？

迷你句 What paperwork is needed?

完整句 What document required when applying for sales tax return?

🔊 需要您的護照和有效登機證。
You will need your passport and a valid boarding pass.

😮 我要怎麼獲得更多這方面的資訊呢？

迷你句 I need further information.

完整句 Where can I know more about it?

👂 您可以撥打這支電話。
You can call this number.

😮 可以給我一張退稅表格嗎？

迷你句 May I have an application form?

完整句 Could I please have an application form?

👂 我去幫您拿一張。
I will go get you one.

😮 請問我符合退營業稅的資格嗎？

迷你句 Can I get it?

完整句 Am I eligible for sale tax return?

👂 是的，有需要申請表格嗎？
Yes, do you need the application form?

😮 我不清楚我能不能夠退稅。

迷你句 I am not sure about it.

完整句 I don't know if I could take sales tax return.

👂 請讓我看看您的收據。
Let me check your receipt.

[Things to Know] 一定要知道的**旅行常識**

　　在免稅店買的東西，因為已經免稅，無法再退稅了；在非免稅店購買物品時，需要填寫退稅單，然後憑退稅單在機場辦理退稅。不過在歐洲也有直接在商場辦理退稅的制度，可先詢問購物中心服務人員。機場退稅都是在行李托運之前辦理，而且承辦人員需要看購買的東西的實品，因此可以在辦理退稅之後，再辦理行李托運。

14 保固維修

[Must be...] 這個時候最需要的一句話！

👄 我需要延長保固。　　**迷你句** Extended warranty, please.
　　　　　　　　　　　完整句 I need the extended warranty.

👂 您可以付費來延長保固。
You can pay for the extended warranty.

👄 請問保固期有多長？　　**迷你句** What is the warranty?
　　　　　　　　　　　　完整句 How long is the warranty good for?

👂 它有一年的保固。
It is a one-year warranty.

👄 請問這個咖啡機還在保固期裡嗎？　**迷你句** Still valid?
　　　　　　　　　　　　　　　　完整句 Is this coffee machine still in valid?

👂 是的，它還在保固期內。
Yes, it is still under warranty.

👄 這台DVD機壞掉了。　　**迷你句** It is broken.
　　　　　　　　　　　完整句 This DVD player is broken.

👂 我們會送回原廠維修。
We will send this to the manufacturer for repairs.

👄 請問這有保固嗎？　　**迷你句** Any warranties?
　　　　　　　　　　　完整句 Does it has any warranties?

👂 是的，所有的廚房用品都有一年的保固。
Yes, there is a one-year warranty on all kitchen appliances.

😕 請問有附合格證書嗎？

迷你句 Does it come with certification?

完整句 Does this come with a certificate of appraisal?

👂 有的，合格證書就在盒子裡面。
Yes the certification is in the box.

😕 請問有送修服務嗎？

迷你句 Any repair service?

完整句 Do you have the auto repair service?

👂 有，但是您必須要負擔一部分的手續費。
Yes, but you will have to pay part of the service fee.

😕 請問可以幫我修理這個嗎？

迷你句 I need it repaired.

完整句 Can I have this repaired?

👂 好的，請讓我看一下您的保證書。
Ok, may I see the warranty?

😕 這個在台灣可以維修嗎？

迷你句 Can I get it repaired in Taiwan?

完整句 What am I supposed to do if it's broken in Taiwan?

👂 我們在台灣的分店會幫您處理。
Out branches in Taiwan will take care of it.

[Vocabulary] 生字不用另外查字典！

01 延長 extend
02 保固 warranty
03 付費 pay for
04 咖啡機 coffee machine
05 在保固期 in valid
06 DVD機 DVD player
07 原廠 manufacture
08 廚房用品 kitchen appliance
09 證書 certificate
10 送修服務 repair service
11 手續費 service fee
12 修理 repair

[Must be...] 這個時候最需要的一句話！

我想要紙袋。
迷你句 Paper bag, please.
完整句 I prefer paper bag.

我們現在購物袋要付費。
We now charge for shopping bags.

請問購物袋要多少錢？
迷你句 How much it is?
完整句 How much does the shopping bag cost?

購物袋要 1 美金。
The shopping bag costs $1.

我自己帶了購物袋來。
迷你句 I have my own.
完整句 I brought my own shopping bags.

很好，需要我幫忙您包裝嗎？
Great, do you need me to help you pack it?

請問可用快遞寄嗎？
迷你句 FedEx it.
完整句 Can you send it by FedEx?

好的，請填寫這張表格。
Ok, please fill out this form.

這個東西有貨的時候請寄給我們。
迷你句 Slip when you receive it.
完整句 Please slip this item to us as soon as it becomes available.

好的，我們會盡快給您。
Yes, we will do it as soon as we can.

請問運費多少錢？

迷你句 What is the shipping cost?

完整句 How much does the shipping cost?

運費要 20 美元。
It costs $20.

可以幫我包裝起來嗎？

迷你句 Pack it, please.

完整句 Can you help me to wrap up as a gift it?

當然，您想要怎麼包？
Sure, how do you want us to pack it?

請幫我把冷凍食品放在一個袋子裡。

迷你句 One bag for frozen foods.

完整句 Can you put all the frozen items in one bag?

好的，這樣可以嗎？
Yes, is this ok?

包裝前請先拿掉標籤。

迷你句 Remove the price first, please.

完整句 Please take the price tag off before packing it.

所有的商品都要拿掉嗎？
For all the items?

[Vocabulary] 生字**不用另外查字典**！

01 紙袋 paper bag

02 付費 charge

03 購物袋 shopping bag

04 帶 bring

05 包裝 pack

06 快遞 FedEx

07 表格 form

08 有貨 available

09 盡快 as soon as possible

10 運費 shipping cost

11 冷凍食品 frozen item

12 標籤 price tag

16 店員太熱情了

：你要會說的一句話　　：你會聽到的問／答　　MP3 Track ▶ 087

[Must be...] 這個時候最需要的一句話！

我只需要一件。
迷你句 I need one.
完整句 I only need one item.

如果您買兩件我們就給您折扣。
We can give you a discount if you buy two.

我現在不想要註冊這個程式。
迷你句 Not today.
完整句 I don't think I will sign up for this program now.

如果您現在註冊就可以享有優惠。
You can get a discount if you sign up for this now.

我不想要辦你們的會員卡。
迷你句 I don't want to be your member.
完整句 I don't think I'll need your membership cards.

如果加入會員，就可以得到特別的禮物。
You will get a special present if you become our member.

我得考慮一下。
迷你句 Let me sleep on it.
完整句 I have to think about it.

這只有今天才有哦。
It is only for today.

我不需要樣品。
迷你句 I don't need it.
完整句 I don't need the free sample, thank you.

這賣得很好哦。
This sells very well.

我不想要試用。 **迷你句** I don't need it.
完整句 I don't want to try the sample.

這真的很不錯哦。
It is really nice.

我這次不想買。 **迷你句** Another time.
完整句 I don't think I will buy it this time.

您可以好好考慮。
You can consider that.

我只是隨便看看而已。 **迷你句** I am just taking a look.
完整句 I am just looking around.

您可以看看我們的新產品。
You can take a look at our new item.

我不確定需不需要。 **迷你句** I am not sure.
完整句 I am still considering.

這是剛推出的產品哦。
It is our new release.

[Words to Use] 替換字放空格，一句多用!!

● 如果加入會員可以得到_____。
You will get _____ if you become our member.

01 特別的禮物 a special present **02** 免費的樣品 a free sample

03 優惠 a discount **04** 美食優惠券 a food coupon

05 免費電影票 a free movie ticket **06** 免費購物袋 a free shopping bag

17 退換貨須知

👄：你要會說的一句話　🗣：你會聽到的問/答

[Must be...] 這個時候最需要的一句話！

👄 這些餅乾要退錢。　　（迷你句）I want a refund for these.
　　　　　　　　　　　（完整句）I need a refund of these crackers.

🗣 這些餅乾怎麼了嗎？
What is wrong with these crackers?

👄 我可以換錢嗎？　　　（迷你句）Can I exchange this money?
　　　　　　　　　　　（完整句）Can I have an exchange?

🗣 當然可以，您想要怎麼換？
Of course, how would you like to change it?

👄 我要退現金。　　　　（迷你句）I will take the money.
　　　　　　　　　　　（完整句）I think I prefer a refund.

🗣 退款需要購買收據。
I need the purchase receipt for a refund.

👄 這個電腦壞掉了。　　（迷你句）It is broken.
　　　　　　　　　　　（完整句）This computer is not working.

🗣 我去找人來修裡。
I will get someone to repair it.

👄 這是我購買的收據。　（迷你句）Here is the receipt.
　　　　　　　　　　　（完整句）I have the purchase receipt.

🗣 好的，請問退款的原因是什麼？
Ok, what is the reason for the refund?

😮 請問可以退款嗎？ 迷你句 Can I have a refund?

完整句 Can I have my money back?

👂 好的，我們可以給您商店退款。
Ok, we can give you a refund.

😮 這個品質不太好。 迷你句 It is not good enough.

完整句 The quality of this is not good.

👂 您要換其它牌子試試看嗎？
Would you like to try a different brand?

😮 請問退貨的規定是 迷你句 What are the rules?
什麼？

完整句 What is your return policy?

👂 大部分的商品都可以在購買後30天內退費。
You can return most of the items within 30 days.

😮 吊牌不見了還可以 迷你句 Can I return it without the tag?
退貨嗎？

完整句 Could I return the good if the tag of it is missing?

👂 我們需要完整吊牌才能退貨。
We only take back the goods with tags with on them.

[Vocabulary] 生字不用另外查字典！

01 餅乾 cracker

02 退錢 refund

03 換零錢 exchange

04 購買 purchase

05 收據 receipt

06 修理 repair

07 原因 reason

08 商店 store

09 品質 quality

10 牌子 brand

11 規定 rule

12 30天內 within 30 days

18 抱怨店家

:你要會說的一句話　:你會聽到的問/答

MP3 Track ▶ 089

[Must be...] 這個時候最需要的一句話！

店員幫不上忙。
迷你句 They were not helpful.
完整句 The store clerk is not very helpful.

他們完全沒有幫助您嗎？
Didn't they give you any help?

服務員的態度不佳。
迷你句 The service is awful.
完整句 The staff got attitude problem.

服務方面呢？
How was the service?

收銀員很粗魯。
迷你句 She was rude.
完整句 The cashier was very reckless.

您需要找客服人員談談嗎？
Do you want to talk to customer service?

他們的服務技巧有待改善。
迷你句 Their service skills need to be improved.
完整句 They should improve their customer service skill.

我會向他們的經理報告。
I will report it to their manager.

那間店的員工都不太友善。
迷你句 They are unfriendly.
完整句 People working in that store are not very friendly.

發生什麼事了嗎？
What was wrong?

😮 我要抱怨一下。　**迷你句** I want to say something.
　　　　　　　　　完整句 I have some complaints.

👂 請說。
I am listening.

😮 他們浪費了我很多　**迷你句** They kept me waiting.
時間。　　　　　　**完整句** They wasted my time.

👂 沒有人幫助您嗎？
Didn't anyone help you?

😮 我發現這邊有個大　**迷你句** I found a big stain on it.
污點。　　　　　　**完整句** There is a huge stain on it.

👂 我馬上去拿另一個給您。
I will get you another one now.

😮 我的心情都變差　**迷你句** I am not happy at all.
了。　　　　　　　**完整句** I am in a bad mood.

👂 抱歉，我們會修正態度。
Sorry, we will correct our attitude.

[Words to Use] 替換字放空格，一句多用!!

● 你們的_____真的需要改進。
You really need to improve your _____.

01 顧客服務 customer service　02 服務態度 service attitude

03 售後服務 after-sales service　04 維修服務 maintenance service

05 退貨政策 return policy　　　06 宅配服務 delivery service

19 找錯錢

😊：你要會說的一句話　　🎧：你會聽到的問／答

[Must be...] 這個時候最需要的一句話！

😊 我覺得你多收我錢。

迷你句 This seems too much.

完整句 I think you over charged me.

🎧 抱歉，我找錯錢了。
Sorry, I made a mistake on your bill.

😊 我覺得你錢算錯了。

迷你句 I think you miscalculated.

完整句 I don't think the number is right.

🎧 真的嗎？請讓我再確認一次。
Really? Let me check it again.

😊 你多找我錢。

迷你句 The change is too much.

完整句 You gave me too much change.

🎧 感謝您的提醒。
Thanks for noticing.

😊 這東西應該有特價才對。

迷你句 Isn't it on sale?

完整句 This item is supposed to be on sale.

🎧 抱歉，這個東西並沒有特價。
Sorry, this item is not on sale.

😊 你還沒有找我零錢。

迷你句 Where is my change?

完整句 I didn't get my change back yet.

🎧 這是您的零錢和收據。
Here is your change and receipt.

我已經付了 20 美元的訂金。

迷你句 I've paid a $20 deposit to you.

完整句 I've paid you a 20 deposit.

請問您有帶收據來嗎？
Do you have your receipt?

我剛剛才刷過這張卡不可能不能用。

迷你句 I just used the card.

完整句 That can't be! I just used this card.

或許您已經刷超過限額了。
Maybe you have gone over your limit.

你還沒有給我信用卡。

迷你句 Where is my credit card?

完整句 You didn't give my card back.

不，我已經給您了。
I gave it to you already.

[Vocabulary] 生字不用另外查字典！

01 算錯 miscalculate

02 犯錯 make a mistake

03 提醒 remind

04 特價 on sale

05 標籤 tag

06 正確的 correct

07 訂金 deposit

08 限額 limit

09 收據 receipt

10 使用 use

11 信用卡 credit card

12 已經 already

旅遊常用句型＋超多替換字，套入馬上用！

買化妝品

● 我可以試試這款 _____ 嗎？
Can I try this _____?

01 唇膏 **lipstick**	02 睫毛膏 **mascara**
03 眼影 **eye shadow**	04 粉底霜 **foundation**
05 指甲油 **nail polish**	06 眼線筆 **eyeliner**

買首飾珠寶

● 我想要看看那 _____。
I would like to take a look at that _____.

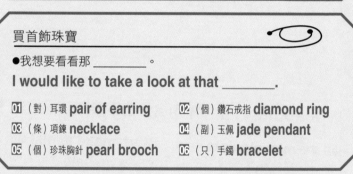

01 （對）耳環 **pair of earring**	02 （個）鑽石戒指 **diamond ring**
03 （條）項鍊 **necklace**	04 （副）玉佩 **jade pendant**
05 （個）珍珠胸針 **pearl brooch**	06 （只）手鐲 **bracelet**

買電器用品

● 我想為我的新廚房買個 _____。
I'm trying to find a _____ for my new kitchen.

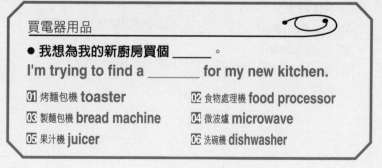

01 烤麵包機 **toaster**	02 食物處理機 **food processor**
03 製麵包機 **bread machine**	04 微波爐 **microwave**
05 果汁機 **juicer**	06 洗碗機 **dishwasher**

要找這個顏色

● 這件洋裝有 _____ 的嗎？
Do you have this dress in _____?

01 白色 white
02 深藍色 dark blue
03 黑色 black
04 卡其色 khaki
05 淺褐色 light brown
06 米色 beige

要求試穿

● 我可以在哪裡試穿這件 _____？
Where can I try on the _____?

01 洋裝 dress
02 短褲 shorts
03 上衣 blouse
04 裙子 skirt
05 長褲 trousers
06 襯衫 shirt

退貨相關

● _____ 是不能退貨的。
_____ are non-returnable.

01 特價商品 Sale items
02 （男）內褲 Underpants
03 貼身衣物 Undergarments
04 （女）內褲 Knickers
05 食物及飲料 Food and beverages
06 書籍雜誌 Books and magazines

海外購物禮節

旅途中購物是最讓人最開心的一個環節！但到文化風俗不同的國家購物時，必然也有些禮節習慣要知道，才能快樂購物。

01【店面不二價】

一般來說，西方國家商店中的商品均為不二價，因此不應隨便殺價，路邊小攤販除外；外國人付款時也偏好以信用卡取代現金付款。

02【購物稅率】

在美國購物時，除了商品本身的訂價外，還要再外加上各州的購物稅（各州州稅率百分比不同），因此商品最後的價格應是售價＋州稅。所以就算同一樣商品，在不同地方購買，價格會應州稅不同而有差別。

加拿大與美國情況類似，在加國購物時，要付聯邦稅和省稅（各省稅率百分比不同）。

紐澳跟台灣相似，商品本身已內含購物稅或加值營業稅。紐西蘭的商品售價，已包含 12.5%的營業稅；澳洲的消費稅率則為 10%。

英國地區購物稅率為 17.5%，同樣也是包含在商品的售價中。

03【退換貨＆退稅】

商品的退換貨在西方國家是習以為常的，但必須要有完整的購物收據。通常在購物之日起，7 到 60 天內，都可以做退換貨的服務，但依各店家標準不同。外國的稅率普遍比台灣高，但是遊客退稅措施完善，記得妥善保留購物收據，即可在機場退稅。

PART 09
交朋友

😊：你要會說的一句話　🔊：你會聽到的問／答　**MP3** Track ▶ 091

[Must be...] 這個時候最需要的一句話！

👄 請問你是這裡的居民嗎？
　迷你句 Do you live here?
　完整句 Are you local people?

🔊 是的，有什麼需要幫忙的嗎？
　Yes, how can I help you?

👄 我真的很喜歡這裡。
　迷你句 It is a nice place.
　完整句 I really like it here.

🔊 很高興聽到您這麼説。
　I am glad to hear that.

👄 這是我第一次來到洛杉磯。
　迷你句 It is my first time here.
　完整句 I have never been to Los Angeles before.

🔊 這會是個難忘的經驗。
　It will be a great experience for you.

👄 抱歉，我想要問一下。
　迷你句 Excuse me.
　完整句 Pardon, I have some questions.

🔊 有什麼疑問嗎？
　Yes?

👄 可以請你幫我個忙嗎？
　迷你句 Can you do me a favor?
　完整句 Can I ask you for a favor?

🔊 好的，什麼事呢？
　Yes, what is it?

😮 不好意思，可以借過一下嗎？
迷你句 Excuse me.
完整句 Can I go through?

👂 抱歉，請過。
Sorry, go right ahead.

😮 不好意思我搞錯了。
迷你句 Oops, my mistake.
完整句 I'm sorry I made a mistake.

👂 沒關係。
That is okay.

😮 你還好嗎？
迷你句 Are you okay?
完整句 Are you all right?

👂 是的，謝謝您。
Yes, thank you.

😮 謝謝你的提醒。
迷你句 Thanks for telling me.
完整句 Thanks for warning me.

👂 不客氣。
You are welcome.

[Vocabulary] 生字不用另外查字典！

01 居民 local people

02 幫忙 help

03 高興 glad

04 經驗 experience

05 問題 question

06 幫我一個忙 do me a favor

07 借過 go through

08 搞錯了 make a mistake

09 提醒 warn

10 居住 live

11 聽到 hear

12 不客氣 You are welcome

👄：你要會說的一句話　🗣：你會聽到的問／答

[**Must be...**] **這個時候**最需要的一句話！

👄 很高興認識你。
　迷你句 Nice to meet you.
　完整句 I am so glad to meet you.

👂 我也是。
　Nice to meet you, too.

👄 請問你是從哪裡來的？
　迷你句 Where are you from?
　完整句 Where do you come from?

👂 我從台灣來的。
　I am from Taiwan.

👄 請問您在哪裡高就？
　迷你句 What is your job?
　完整句 What do you do to make a living?

👂 我是一個工程師。
　I am an engineer.

👄 請問你住哪裡？
　迷你句 Where do you live?
　完整句 Where do you reside?

👂 我住在台北。
　I live in Taipei.

👄 你要一起來嗎？
　迷你句 Do you want to join us?
　完整句 Why don't you come along?

👂 好啊。
　Why not?

😮 請問你接下來要去哪裡？
(迷你句) Where will you visit next?
(完整句) Where are you going to visit next?

👂 我下個禮拜要去日本。
I am going to Japan next week.

😮 請問你願意跟我跳支舞嗎？
(迷你句) Shall we?
(完整句) Would you like to dance with me?

👂 我跳得不好。
I can't dance well.

😮 請問你的興趣是什麼？
(迷你句) What is your hobby?
(完整句) What are you interested in?

👂 我喜歡看電影。
I like to watch movies.

😮 請問你休閒時間都做什麼呢？
(迷你句) What do you do in your free time?
(完整句) What do you like to do in your leisure time?

👂 我喜歡聽音樂。
I enjoy listening to music.

[Vocabulary] 生字不用另外查字典！

01 高興 nice
02 認識 meet
03 來自 come from
04 工程師 engineer
05 居住 reside
06 一起來 come along
07 拜訪 visit
08 跳舞 dance
09 興趣 hobby
10 看電影 watch movie
11 休閒時間 leisure time
12 喜歡 enjoy

259

：你要會說的一句話　　：你會聽到的問／答　 **MP3** Track ▶ 093

[Must be...] 這個時候最需要的一句話！

我叫做王安妮。　**迷你句** I am Annie Wang.
　　　　　　　　完整句 My name is Annie Wang

很高興認識你。
Nice meeting you.

我今年30歲。　**迷你句** I am 30.
　　　　　　　完整句 I am 30 years old.

我也是。
Me, too.

我喜歡聽流行音　**迷你句** I like pop music.
樂。　　　　　　**完整句** I enjoy pop music.

我喜歡爵士樂。
I like jazz.

我還是大學生。　**迷你句** I am a student.
　　　　　　　　完整句 I am still a student in college.

你幾年級？
What year are you?

我是台灣人。　**迷你句** I am Taiwanese.
　　　　　　　完整句 I come from Taiwan.

我是西班牙人。
I am Spanish.

這是我第一次出國。

迷你句 It is my fist time.

完整句 It is my fist time to go aboard.

您一定感到很興奮。
You must be very excited.

我喜歡旅遊。

迷你句 I love traveling.

完整句 I like to go traveling.

您去過幾個國家？
How many countries have you been to?

我的專長是跳舞。

迷你句 I am good at dancing.

完整句 I can dance very well.

或許您改天可以教我。
Maybe you can teach me someday.

我早上都會慢跑。

迷你句 I jog in the morning.

完整句 I usually go jogging in the morning.

這真是個好習慣。
That is a good hobby.

[Vocabulary] 生字不用另外查字典！

01 名字 name
02 流行音樂 pop music
03 爵士樂 jazz
04 台灣人 Taiwanese
05 西班牙人 Spanish
06 出國 go abroad
07 興奮 exciting
08 旅遊 travel
09 國家 country
10 跳舞 dance
11 慢跑 jog
12 習慣 hobby

👄 ：你要會説的一句話　　👂 ：你會聽到的問／答　　**MP3** Track ▶ 094

[Must be...] 這個時候最需要的一句話！

👄 這位是李小姐。　　**迷你句** This is Miss Lee.
　　　　　　　　　　完整句 This one is Miss Lee.

👂 嗨，您好嗎？
Hello, how are you?

👄 請問那個人是誰
啊？　　　　　　　**迷你句** Who is he?
　　　　　　　　　　完整句 Who is that guy?

👂 您是指哪一個？
Which one do you mean?

👄 請問那位穿著白色　**迷你句** Who is that girl?
衣服的女孩是誰？　**完整句** Who is that girl in white dress?

👂 她是黃小姐。
She is Miss Huang.

👄 可以把我介紹給那　**迷你句** Can you introduce me?
位女士嗎？　　　　**完整句** Can you introduce me to that lady?

👂 沒問題，請跟我來。
Of course, please come with me.

👄 請問那是麥可夫婦　**迷你句** Are they Mr. and Mrs. Michaels?
嗎？　　　　　　　**完整句** Is the couple over there Mr. and Mrs.
　　　　　　　　　　　　　　Michaels?

👂 沒錯，您認識他們嗎？
Yes, do you know them?

請問他叫什麼名字？
迷你句 His name?
完整句 What is his name?

他是鮑伯·史密斯。
He is Bob Smith.

請問他還是單身嗎？
迷你句 Is he married?
完整句 Is he still single?

不，他上個月才剛結婚。
He just got married last month.

可以介紹一下你的家人嗎？
迷你句 I would like to meet your family.
完整句 Can you introduce your family to me?

當然，她們是我的女兒。
Sure, these are my daughters.

我想要認識那邊那個女孩。
迷你句 I want to meet that girl.
完整句 I would like to know that girl.

好的，我可以幫您介紹。
Ok, I can introduce you to her.

[Vocabulary] 生字**不用另外查字典**！

01 穿著 **dress in**

02 介紹 **introduce**

03 女士 **lady**

04 夫婦 **couple**

05 單身 **single**

06 結婚 **marry**

07 家人 **family**

08 女兒 **daughter**

09 跟我來 **come with me**

10 在那邊 **over there**

11 認識 **know**

12 熟悉 **be acquainted with**

[Must be...] 這個時候最需要的一句話！

可以給我一張名片嗎？
迷你句 Can I have your name card?
完整句 May I have your name card?

沒問題，這是我的名片。
Of course, here it is.

可以給你你的連絡方式嗎？
迷你句 How can I contact you?
完整句 Can I have you personal information?

可以啊，你需要我的名片嗎？
Do you need my name card?

請問我要怎麼連絡你？
迷你句 How can I reach you?
完整句 How can I contact you?

我可以給您我的手機號碼。
I can give you my cell phone number.

可以給你你的電子郵件信箱嗎？
迷你句 May I have your email?
完整句 Can you give me your email address?

我可以寫下來給您。
I can write it down for you.

請問你住在哪裡？
迷你句 Where do you live?
完整句 Would you tell me where do you live?

我的房子就在這附近而已。
My house is just nearby here.

請問你家地址是？　　**迷你句** Your address?

　　　　　　　　　　完整句 Can I have your address?

我的名片上就有了。
It is on my name card.

請問你有臉書嗎？　　**迷你句** Do you have facebook?

　　　　　　　　　　完整句 Do you use facebook?

有，我女兒幫我辦了一個。
Yes, my daughter set it up for me.

可以給我你的
MSN 帳號嗎？　　　**迷你句** May I have your MSN account?

　　　　　　　　　　完整句 Can you give me your MSN account?

沒問題，在這裡。
Yes, here you are.

請問你有在使用推
特嗎？　　　　　　**迷你句** Do you have Twitter?

　　　　　　　　　　完整句 Do you use Twitter?

不，我不知道那是什麼東西。
No, I don't know what that is.

[Vocabulary] 生字不用另外查字典！

01 名片 name card　　　　　　**02** 個人資訊 personal information

03 連絡 contact　　　　　　　　**04** 手機號碼 cell phone number

05 電子郵件 email address　　　**06** 寫下來 write down

07 房子 house　　　　　　　　　**08** 附近 nearby

09 地址 address　　　　　　　　**10** 臉書 facebook

11 MSN帳號 MSN account　　　**12** 推特 Twitter

：你要會説的一句話　⑨：你會聽到的問／答　　**MP3** Track ▶ 096

[**Must be...**] 這個時候最需要的一句話！

要不要一起去哪裡
玩呢？

迷你句 Want to go somewhere?

完整句 Do you want to go somewhere with me?

⑨ 好啊，我可以開車。
Sure, I can drive.

這是個適合出遊的
天氣。

迷你句 What a nice day.

完整句 It is a great day to go out.

⑨ 説得沒錯，你想要去哪裡玩？
That is right. Where do you want to go?

你願意跟我去約會
嗎？

迷你句 Would you like to go out?

完整句 Would you like to hang out with me?

⑨ 我得考慮一下。
I have to think about it.

要不要去看電影？

迷你句 Let's go to see a movie.

完整句 Would you like to see a movie?

⑨ 好啊，你喜歡哪種類型的電影？
Ok, what kind of movie do you like?

約幾點比較好？

迷你句 When will be better?

完整句 What time is okay for you?

⑨ 我們可以約在早上10點鐘。
We can meet at 10 in the morning.

你想去哪裡？　　　**迷你句** Where do you like?
　　　　　　　　　完整句 Where do you like to go?

我想在公園野餐是個不錯的選擇。
I think the park is a great place for a picnic.

我可以請你喝咖啡嗎？　**迷你句** Can I buy you a coffee?
　　　　　　　　　　完整句 Do you want to have some coffee?

謝謝，你人真好。
Thank you, you are really nice.

我可以開車去載你。　　**迷你句** I will drive.
　　　　　　　　　　完整句 I can go to pick you up.

太好了。
That will be great.

你今晚有空嗎？　　　**迷你句** Are you free tonight?
　　　　　　　　　完整句 Are you available tonight?

抱歉，我得完成我的工作才行。
Sorry, I have to finish my work.

[Words to Use] 替換字放空格，一句多用!!

● 你願意跟我_____嗎？
Would you like to _____ with me?

01 約會 hang out

02 看電影 see a movie

03 喝咖啡 have some coffee

04 出遊 go out

05 吃晚餐 have dinner

06 參觀博物館 visit the museum

267

[**Must be...**] 這個**時候**最需要的一句話！

👄 抱歉，我辦不到。　**迷你句** I can't do it.

　　完整句 Sorry, but I don't think I can do it.

👂 請再考慮一下我的請求。
Please re-consider my request.

👄 我幫不了你。　**迷你句** I can't help with that.

　　完整句 I am afraid that I won't be able to help you.

👂 我了解您的處境。
I understand your situation.

👄 我不能答應你。　**迷你句** No promises.

　　完整句 I can't promise you.

👂 如果真的不行也沒關係。
It is okay if you have to say no.

👄 我管不了了。　**迷你句** It is out of my control.

　　完整句 I cannot control over it.

👂 請告訴我這裡誰可以做決定。
Please let me know who has the authority to make the decision here.

👄 我無法決定。　**迷你句** Not my call.

　　完整句 I can't make the decision.

👂 謝謝您盡力了。
Thank you for trying your best.

😊 抱歉,我得走了。 **迷你句** Sorry, I have to go.

完整句 Sorry, I don't have time.

👂 好的,祝您有個愉快的一天。
Ok, have a great day.

😊 我不需要,謝謝。 **迷你句** No, thanks.

完整句 I honestly don't need it, thanks.

👂 您確定真的不需要嗎?
Are you sure you really don't need it?

😊 別跟著我。 **迷你句** Don't follow me.

完整句 Stop stalking me.

👂 抱歉讓您感到不愉快。
Sorry to make you feel unpleasant.

😊 你不是我喜歡的
型。 **迷你句** Sorry, you are not my type.

完整句 No offense, but you are not my type.

👂 我沒有要搭訕你。
I'm not hitting on you.

[Vocabulary] 生字**不用另外查字典!**

01 考慮 **consider**

02 請求 **request**

03 處境 **situation**

04 答應 **promise**

05 決定 **make the decision**

06 控制 **control**

07 盡力 **try your best**

08 愉快的 **great**

09 跟著我 **follow me**

10 型 **type**

11 不愉快 **unpleasant**

12 權力 **authority**

08 到別人家裡作客

👄 : 你要會說的一句話　　🔊 : 你會聽到的問／答

[Must be...] 這個時候最需要的一句話！

👄 謝謝您的邀請。　　**迷你句** Thanks for having me over.
　　　　　　　　　　完整句 Thank you for inviting me over.

🔊 真高興您來了。
I am glad you are here.

👄 這是給您的。　　**迷你句** This is for you.
　　　　　　　　　完整句 Here is something for you.

🔊 謝謝，你真是太好了。
Thank you, it is very nice of you.

👄 這真好吃。　　**迷你句** Yummy!
　　　　　　　　完整句 This is really delicious.

🔊 您要再多吃一點嗎？
Would you like some more?

👄 你真是個好廚子。　　**迷你句** You are a good cook.
　　　　　　　　　　　完整句 Your cooking is wonderful.

🔊 謝謝您的誇獎。
Thanks for your compliment.

👄 我吃飽了。　　**迷你句** I am full.
　　　　　　　　完整句 I have had enough.

🔊 甜點在這裡。
Here are some desserts.

可以用一下洗手間嗎？
迷你句 Can I use the restroom?
完整句 I need to use the bathroom.

好的，請便。
Sure, help yourself.

請問洗手間在哪裡？
迷你句 Where is the restroom?
完整句 Where the bathroom is?

就在那邊。
It is over there.

我一定得走了。
迷你句 I gotta go.
完整句 I must be going now.

我幫您叫計程車。
I will go get you a taxi.

謝謝你的酒。
迷你句 Thanks for your wine.
完整句 I appreciate the drink.

很高興可以跟您聊聊。
It is really nice to talk with you.

[Things to Know] 一定要知道的**旅行常識**

　　在國外，如果要到別人家裡做客，需要注意當地的拜訪禮節，切勿未經約定就擅自登門。外國人強調個人生活至上，對不期而至的造訪不甚歡迎。所以首先要向主人提出拜訪的意向，然後按對方提議或同意的時間準時抵達，早到或遲到都是不禮貌的。多數情況下，禮節性拜訪的時間安排在上午 10 點或下午 4 點左右。

👄：你要會說的一句話　👂：你會聽到的問／答　 **MP3** Track ▶ 099

[**Must be...**] 這個時候最需要的一句話！

👄 吃東西時發出聲音不禮貌。

迷你句 It is impolite to slurp.

完整句 It is not polite to slurp when your're eating.

👂 我感到很抱歉。
I am very sorry about that.

👄 西裝和領帶是必要的。

迷你句 A jacket and a tie are required.

完整句 You have to wear a jacket and a tie.

👂 好，我會穿的。
Ok, I will wear them.

👄 請問我要穿著正式服裝嗎？

迷你句 Do I need to be formal?

完整句 Do I need to dress formally?

👂 是的，我們有服裝規定。
Yes, we have a dress code.

👄 請問可以拍照嗎？

迷你句 Can I take a photo?

完整句 Is it ok to take a picture?

👂 抱歉，這裡禁止拍照。
Sorry, taking pictures here is forbidden.

👄 請把音樂轉小聲一點。

迷你句 Please turn it down.

完整句 Could you please turn down the music a little bit?

👂 好吧，這樣可以嗎？
All right, is this ok?

請別插隊。　　　(迷你句) Please line up.

　　　　　　　　(完整句) Please don't cut in line.

抱歉，我不知道要排隊。
Sorry, I didn't know there was a line.

別去那裡。　　　(迷你句) Don't go there.

　　　　　　　　(完整句) I think you should stay out of there.

怎麼了嗎？
What is the problem?

請問這裡可以吃東　(迷你句) Can I eat here?
西嗎？
　　　　　　　　(完整句) Is it ok to have food here?

抱歉，這裡禁止飲食。
Sorry, eating here is not allowed.

請安靜一點。　　(迷你句) Be quiet.

　　　　　　　　(完整句) Keep your voice down.

抱歉，我沒有注意到。
Sorry, I was unaware of that.

[Vocabulary] 生字**不用另外查字典**！

01 不禮貌 impolite

02 抱歉 sorry

03 西裝 jacket

04 領帶 tie

05 注意 careful

06 正式服裝 dress formally

07 服裝規定 dress code

08 拍照 take a photo

09 關小聲 turn down

10 插隊 cut in line

11 安靜 quiet

12 沒有注意 unaware

10 抱怨

😊 ：你要會說的一句話　　🦻 ：你會聽到的問／答　　**MP3** Track ▶ 100

[Must be...] 這個時候最需要的一句話！

😊 真沒禮貌。　　**迷你句** How rude!
　　　　　　　完整句 That is rude.
🦻 沒關係啦。
It is not a big deal.

😊 真無禮。　　**迷你句** So impolite.
　　　　　　完整句 That is not polite.
🦻 您太緊繃了。
You are too uptight.

😊 我受夠了。　　**迷你句** I have reached my limit.
　　　　　　　完整句 I have almost had enough.
🦻 別理他了。
You should just let it go.

😊 我得發洩一下怒氣。　　**迷你句** I need to vent.
　　　　　　　　　　完整句 I need to let out of my anger.
🦻 放輕鬆。
Chill out.

😊 你把我惹毛了。　　**迷你句** You make me mad.
　　　　　　　　完整句 You really pissed me off.
🦻 請冷靜。
Please calm down.

274

我無法再忍受他了。
迷你句 I can't do it anymore.
完整句 I can't stand him anymore.

發生什麼事了?
What is wrong?

你說過你會幫我處理的!
迷你句 You said you would do it for me!
完整句 You promised you would do it for me!

很抱歉我忘記了。
I am very sorry that I forgot it.

你答應過我的!
迷你句 You said it!
完整句 You promised!

抱歉,我已經盡力了。
Sorry, I have tried my best.

我已經忍無可忍了。
迷你句 I've really had enough.
完整句 I really can't stand it anymore.

深呼吸。
Take a deep breath.

[Vocabulary] 生字不用另外查字典!

01 粗魯的 rude
02 無禮 impolite
03 緊繃 uptight
04 限制 limit
05 發洩 let out
06 怒氣 anger
07 惹毛 piss off
08 冷靜 calm down
09 忍受 stand
10 答應 promise
11 盡力 try one's best
12 忍無可忍 lost patience

275

：你要會說的一句話　：你會聽到的問／答　**MP3** Track ▶ 101

[Must be...] 這個時候最需要的一句話！

我不這麼認為。　**迷你句** I don't think so.

完整句 I don't think it is right.

您有什麼意見？
What is your opinion?

我不同意你的說法。　**迷你句** I don't agree.

完整句 I don't agree with you.

為什麼呢？
Why is that?

我不確定我明白你的意思。　**迷你句** I don't understand.

完整句 I am not sure that I follow you.

我可以再教您一遍。
I can show you again.

我腦子裡搞不太清楚。　**迷你句** I am confused.

完整句 I don't have it clear in my head.

我用別種方法說明。
I will try to put it another way.

我一定有什麼東西漏掉了。　**迷你句** I don't get it.

完整句 There must be something that I am missing.

我來幫您簡化一下。
I will make it simple for you.

可以再說一次嗎？　迷你句 Can you repeat that?

完整句 Can you say it again?

如果您不懂沒關係。
It is okay if you don't understand it.

這好像比我想像中
的還多。　迷你句 Sounds complicated.

完整句 There seems to be a lot more to it than I thought.

這應該沒有那麼複雜。
It shouldn't be so complicated.

我有不同的看法。　迷你句 I have a different thought.

完整句 I have different thought from you.

好的，請告訴我您的意見。
Ok, please tell me about your thought.

我反對。　迷你句 I object.

完整句 I am against it.

您有任何的建議嗎？
Do you have any suggestions?

[Vocabulary] 生字**不用另外查字典**！

01 認為 **think**

02 意見 **oplnion**

03 同意 **agree**

04 明白 **understand**

05 跟上思緒 **follow**

06 顯示 **show**

07 困惑的 **confused**

08 方式 **way**

09 漏掉 **missing**

10 簡化 **simple**

11 聽起來 **sound**

12 複雜 **complicated**

旅遊常用句型 + 超多替換字，套入馬上用！

自我介紹

● 我來自 ＿＿＿＿。你是哪裡人？

I am from ＿＿＿＿. Where are you from?

01 台灣 **Taiwan**
02 南韓 **South Korea**
03 日本 **Japan**
04 馬來西亞 **Malaysia**
05 新加坡 **Singapore**
06 泰國 **Thailand**

聊聊嗜好

● 你最喜歡的 ＿＿＿＿ 是什麼？

What's your favorite ＿＿＿＿?

01 戶外活動 **outdoor activity**
02 電影類型 **type of movie**
03 休閒活動 **leisure activity**
04 旅遊形式 **form of travel**
05 音樂類型 **type of music**
06 西班牙食物 **food in Spanish**

引薦他人

● 讓我為您介紹我的 ＿＿＿＿ 傑米。

Let me introduce you my ＿＿＿＿, Jamie.

01 朋友 **friend**
02 丈夫 **husband**
03 哥哥／弟弟 **brother**
04 姪子 **nephew**
05 表／堂哥（弟）**cousin**
06 叔叔 **uncle**

詢問聯絡方式

● 你介意給我你的 ＿＿＿？
Do you mind giving me your ＿＿＿？

01 電話號碼 phone number　　02 LINE 帳號 LINE ID
03 手機號碼 mobile number　　04 臉書帳號 Facebook ID
05 電郵地址 e-mail address　　06 聯絡資訊 contact information

邀約出遊

● 我們何不找一天一起去 ＿＿＿？
Why don't we go ＿＿＿ together sometime?

01 逛街 shopping　　　　　　02 爬山 mountain climbing
03 健行 hiking　　　　　　　04 高空彈跳 bungee jumping
05 野餐 picnicking　　　　　 06 潛水 scuba diving

婉拒別人

● 我很想，但我 ＿＿＿。
I'd love to, but I ＿＿＿.

01 有宵禁 have a curfew　　02 得讀書 nccd to study
03 必須加班 have to work late
04 照顧我弟弟 have to look after my brother
05 已經有其他計劃 already have other plans
06 已經有約了 have a prior engagement

到別人家裡作客

● 謝謝你邀請我參加你的 ＿＿＿ 派對。

Thanks for inviting me to your ＿＿＿＿＿ party.

01 生日 **birthday**　　　　　　　　**02** 變裝 **costume**

03 喬遷 **housewarming**　　　　　**04** 雞尾酒 **cocktail**

05 週年紀念 **anniversary**　　　　**06** 百樂（自帶餐點）**potluck**

禮節進退

● 我帶了 ＿＿＿ 給你。希望你喜歡。

I brought you ＿＿＿＿＿. Hope you like it

01 一些自己做的餅乾 **some homemade cookies**　**02** 一瓶酒 **a bottle of wine**

03 一些花 **some flowers**　　　　　　　　**04** 一個蛋糕 **a cake**

05 一份小東西 **a little something**　　　**06** 一份禮物 **a gift**

抱怨

● 你那麼做 / 說實在是非常 ＿＿＿＿。

It is very ＿＿＿ of you to do/say that.

01 自私 **selfish**　　　　　　　　**02** 失禮 **discourteous**

03 不得體 **inappropriate**　　　　**04** 幼稚 **childish**

05 無禮 **rude**　　　　　　　　　**06** 不成熟 **immature**

與英語系國家的人交朋友

英、美、加、紐、澳這些英語國家的種族多元，要注意禮貌和尊重。與朋友們碰面時要記得互相問候，即使他們心情不好，也會回 Fine 或 Good，但因為聲音的不同，你可以從中感覺他是好或不好。另外他們都非常注重隱私，舉凡年齡、宗教、婚姻、薪水等話題都盡量不要觸及。

01【英國、美國】

身為民族大熔爐，種族議題在英、美國相當敏感，不要隨意拿膚色來開玩笑。美國人也不喜歡冷場，並習慣在社交場合侃侃而談，如果相處時話少或面無表情，會被認為沒禮貌或太難相處。美國喝酒的合法年齡是21歲，而且嚴格實行，店家幾乎都會要求檢查證件。

02【加拿大】

十分注重環境衛生，亂丟垃圾會罰到 500 加幣；同時他們也喜歡在周末從事戶外活動。就外型來說，他們覺得有點肉才是健康的，所以有時候你跟人家說「你變瘦了！」他們還會不高興呢。除此之外，加拿大的年輕人們慶祝生日通常都會有個不成文的規定，就是必須讓朋友們照你的歲數狠狠地揍上你幾拳，所以將在加拿大過生日的朋友，請繃緊你的皮囉！

03【紐西蘭、澳洲】

進海關的時候，一定要清楚載明要攜帶入境的東西，並且注意禁止攜帶的物品。因為他們對於海關入境的檢查非常嚴格，一不小心可能就會馬上被拘捕或遣返出境。和美國一樣，他們對於飲酒年齡的限制很嚴，一定要出示證件。到澳洲朋友家裡作客的時候，沒有所謂主客之分，有禮貌的客人是要能夠幫主人分擔幫忙一切事情。除此之外，澳洲見面基本禮儀是握手，但是有時候也會有人碰臉頰。

各國禁忌看似繁瑣，但要記得微笑是國際共通的語言，保持友善笑臉迎人，就是最棒的旅行工具喔！

PART 10
通訊聯繫

[Must be...] 這個時候最需要的一句話！

請問哪裡有公共電話？
迷你句 I need a public phone.
完整句 Where can I find a public phone?

那個便利商店有公共電話。
That convenience store has a public phone.

請問附近有付費電話嗎？
迷你句 Where is the pay phone?
完整句 Is there a payphone around?

沒有，這棟大樓裡沒有付費電話。
There are no payphones in this building.

請問公共電話亭在哪裡？
迷你句 Is there a phone booth?
完整句 Where is the phone booth?

入口處旁邊有公共電話亭。
There is a phone booth near the entrance.

請問這個電話可以打長途電話嗎？
迷你句 Can I make a long-distance call?
完整句 Can I use this phone to make a long-distance call?

可以，但是您必須要有電話卡。
Yes, but you need a calling card.

請問可以幫我打個電話嗎？
迷你句 Could you help me make a call?
完整句 Would you assist me with a phone call?

當然，請問您身上有銅板嗎？
Sure, do you have some coins on you?

請問我要去哪裡買電話卡？
迷你句 Where can I buy a calling card?
完整句 Where can I purchase a calling card?

您可以到那間雜貨店買。
You can get one at that grocery store.

請問我要投多少錢？
迷你句 How much do I need to put in?
完整句 What is the amount I need to deposit?

至少要投五分錢。
At least 5 cents.

請問我可以用這個電話撥到台灣嗎？
迷你句 Can I make a call to Taiwan?
完整句 Can I use this phone to call to Taiwan?

不行，這個電話不能撥國際電話。
No, you can't call internationally on this phone.

請問我可以跟您借電話嗎？
迷你句 Can I use your phone?
完整句 May I borrow your phone?

沒問題，我的電話在這裡。
No problem, here is my phone.

[Vocabulary] 生字不用另外查字典！

01 公共電話 public phone
02 便利商店 convenient store
03 付費電話 pay phone
04 大樓 building
05 公共電話亭 phone booth
06 入口 entrance
07 長途電話 long-distance call
08 電話卡 calling card
09 銅板 coin
10 雜貨店 grocery store
11 存款 deposit
12 國際電話 international call

👄：你要會説的一句話　👂：你會聽到的問／答　**MP3** Track ▶ 103

[Must be...] 這個時候最需要的一句話！

👄 請問我要怎麼打國際電話？
迷你句 How to call internationally?
完整句 How do I make an international call?

👂 照著電話卡後面的指示來操作。
Follow the instructions on the back of the calling card.

👄 請問國際電話代碼是？
迷你句 Is there an international code?
完整句 What is the international dialing code?

👂 國際電話代碼是 002。
The international code is 002.

👄 請問我可以用這張電話卡打國際電話嗎？
迷你句 Does this work for international calls?
完整句 Can I use this calling card to make international calls?

👂 可以，這是張國際電話卡。
Yes, this is an international calling card.

👄 請問台灣的國家碼是多少？
迷你句 How do I dial to Taiwan?
完整句 What is the country code for Taiwan?

👂 台灣的國家碼是 886。
The country code for Taiwan is 886.

👄 我要買一張電話卡。
迷你句 I need a calling card.
完整句 I would like to buy a calling card.

👂 最便宜的一張要 5 美元。
The cheapest one is $5.

請問這個電話是不是故障了？
迷你句 Is it broken?
完整句 Is this telephone out of order?

是的，我去叫工人來修。
Yes, I will call the workmen.

請問我要怎麼打回台灣？
迷你句 How to dial to Taiwan?
完整句 What should I do to call to Taiwan?

您需要一張國際電話卡。
You need to get an international calling card.

我要打一通對方付費的電話到台灣。
迷你句 I need to call Taiwan collect.
完整句 I need to make a collect call to Taiwan.

好的，讓我來幫您。
Ok, let me help you.

請問中華航空的電話號碼是多少？
迷你句 What is the number for China Airlines?
完整句 Do you have the number of China Airlines?

我不確定，但是我可以幫您查詢。
I am not sure, but I can find out for you.

[Vocabulary] 生字不用另外查字典！

01 指示 instruction
02 後面 back
11 中華航空 China Airline
04 國家碼 country code
05 電話卡 calling card
06 故障 broken
07 工人 workmen
08 號碼 number
09 找到 find out
12 按照 follow
03 國際電話代碼 international dialing code

 **03 郵寄**

:你要會說的一句話　　:你會聽到的問／答　　 **MP3** Track ▶ 104

[Must be...] 這個時候最需要的一句話！

請問用平信寄的話
要多久才會到？

迷你句 How long will it take?

完整句 How long will that take to send it with
regular mail?

通常要花 5 到 7 天的時間才會到。
It usually takes 5 to 7 days to arrive for regular mail service.

這封信我要寄掛
號。

迷你句 Please send this registered.

完整句 Please add registered mail service to
this letter.

好的，掛號信有包含在快遞郵件內。
Ok, registered mail service is included in express mail service.

我需要寄這張明信
片到台灣。

迷你句 To Taiwan.

完整句 I need to send this postcard to
Taiwan.

好的，您想要怎麼寄？
Ok, how would you like to send it?

請問如果用空運寄
要多久？

迷你句 How long will it take?

完整句 How long it will take if I send them
via air service?

會花大概 3 天的時間。
It will take about three days.

我要寄這兩個包裹
到紐西蘭。

迷你句 These are going to New Zealand.

完整句 I need to send these two parcels to
New Zealand.

請問您想要怎麼寄這個包裹？
How would you like to send your parcel?

請問小包裹有任何的限制嗎？
(迷你句) Any rules for small parcels?
(完整句) A there any rules for small parcels?

小包裹的重量限制是 3 公斤。
The weight limit for small parcel service is 3 kilograms.

我要領我的包裹。
(迷你句) I am here for pick up.
(完整句) I want to picking up my parcel.

抱歉，我們還沒有收到這個包裹。
Sorry, we don't have this parcel here yet.

請問寄空運要多少錢？
(迷你句) How much is airmail?
(完整句) How much will it cost if I send them via air?

要花 20 美元。
It will cost $20.

包裹裡面只是一些個人物品。
(迷你句) It is just personal effects.
(完整句) There are just some personal items in this package.

好的，請填寫這張表格。
Ok, please fill out this form.

[Vocabulary] 生字不用另外查字典！

01 平信寄 regular mail
02 寄掛號 registered mail
03 包含 include
04 快遞郵件 express mail
05 明信片 postcard
06 郵寄 send
07 包裹 parcel
08 重量限制 limited weight
09 公斤 kilogram
10 撿起 pick up
11 寄空運 airmail
12 個人物品 personal item

旅遊常用句型＋超多替換字，套入馬上用！

尋找公共電話

● 這附近有 ＿＿＿＿ 嗎？

Is there a ＿＿＿＿ around here?

01 付費電話 **pay phone**　　02 投幣式公共電話 **coin-operated public telephone**

03 公共電話 **public phone**　　04 投幣式電話 **coin telephone**

05 電話亭 **phone booth**　　06 插卡式電話亭 **card phone booth**

使用公共電話

● 這台公共電話可以用 ＿＿＿＿ 嗎？

Does this public phone take ＿＿＿＿?

01 信用卡 **credit cards**　　02 硬幣 **coins**

03 電話卡 **phone cards**　　04 一分硬幣（一便士） **pennies**

05 電話卡 **calling cards**　　06 紙鈔 **banknotes**

打國際電話

● ＿＿＿＿ 的國際電話代碼是什麼？

What's the international dialing code for ＿＿＿＿?

01 美國 **the USA**　　02 英國 **the UK**

03 法國 **France**　　04 台灣 **Taiwan**

05 德國 **Germany**　　06 中國大陸 **the Mainland China**

從飯店打電話

● 我可以用飯店房間電話撥打 ＿＿＿ 嗎？
Can I make ＿＿＿ from the hotel room phone?

01 市內電話 a local call　　　02 國際電話 an international call
03 長途電話 a toll call（收費）　04 到另一個房間的電話 a call to another room
05 長途電話 a long-distance call 06 到台灣的電話 a call to Taiwan

郵寄時間

● 這個以 ＿＿＿ 的方式寄送要多久？
How long would it take if I send this by ＿＿＿?

01 海運 surface　　　　02 空運 air
03 船運 ship　　　　　04 空運平信 regular air
05 快遞 express　　　　06 聯邦快遞 FedEx

郵寄內容

● 包裹裡裝的是 ＿＿＿。
There are ＿＿＿ in the package.

01 衣服 clothes　　　　02 易碎物品 fragile item
03 書本 books　　　　　04 個人物品 personal items
05 飾品 accessories　　　06 電腦零件 computer components

常用電話用語

電話裡的常用句，跟日常生活中常用的英文句子有一些不一樣，尤其當沒有手勢、表情的輔助時，想要流利地對話，就一定要先知道一些基本的電話用語。

01 喂，是蘇珊嗎？
   Hello. Is Susan there?

02 你一定打錯電話了。
   You must have the wrong number.

03 請問您是哪位？
   Who is this?

04 我可以和莉莉講話嗎？
   May I please speak to Lily?

05 對不起，我打錯電話了。
   I'm sorry. I have the wrong number.

06 請問您貴姓？
   May I have your name, sir?

07 這裡是521－8864嗎？
   Is this five-two-one double eight six-four?

08 不，這裡是521－8835。
   No. This is five-two-one double eight three-five.

09 沒有這個人。
   No one lives here by that name.

10 請問你是誰？
   May I ask who I am talking to?

11 我是代表A公司打電話來的。
   I am calling for the A company.

12 你要留話嗎？
   Do you want to leave a message?

PART 11
緊急狀況

01 身體不舒服

🗨 : 你要會說的一句話　　🔊 : 你會聽到的問／答

[Must be...] 這個時候最需要的一句話！

👄 我覺得不舒服。　　**迷你句** I feel sick.

　　　　　　　　　　完整句 I am not feeling well.

👂 怎麼了嗎？
What is wrong?

👄 我感冒了。　　**迷你句** It's the flu.

　　　　　　　　完整句 I have the flu.

👂 您需要多喝水然後休息。
You need to drink lots of water and rest.

👄 我發燒了。　　**迷你句** I am hot.

　　　　　　　　完整句 I have a fever.

👂 您的體溫多少？
What is your body temperature?

👄 我的鼻水流不停。　　**迷你句** My nose is running.

　　　　　　　　　　　完整句 I have a runny nose.

👂 您覺得還好嗎？
Are you feeling okay?

👄 我覺得頭暈。　　**迷你句** I am dizzy.

　　　　　　　　　完整句 I am feeling dizzy.

👂 或許止痛藥會有幫助。
Maybe pain killers will help.

我覺得胃不舒服。　(迷你句) My stomach is not right.
(完整句) My stomach is not feeling well.

您有帶藥嗎？
Do you have medicine?

我有一點想吐。　(迷你句) I want to vomit.
(完整句) I feel a bit nauseous.

您可能是食物中毒。
It might be food poisoning.

我的手臂都是疹子。　(迷你句) The rash covers my arms.
(完整句) I have rashes all over my arms.

您有什麼樣的症狀呢？
What symptoms do you have?

我抽筋。　(迷你句) I am cramping.
(完整句) I am having a cramp.

您是哪裡抽筋？
Could you tell me exactly where the cramp is?

[Vocabulary] 生字不用另外查字典！

01 病 **sick**　　　　　　02 感冒 **flu**

03 休息 **rest**　　　　　04 發燒 **fever**

05 體溫 **body temperature**　06 頭暈 **dizzy**

07 止痛藥 **pain killer**　08 胃 **stomach**

09 藥 **medicine**　　　　10 吐 **vomit**

11 食物中毒 **food poisoning**　12 疹子 **rash**

出門在外，一定要學會怎麼說自己的身體部位，還要表達痛的方式。把下面的生字還有說法記下來，別人才知道怎麼幫你！

【常見生字】

頭	head	脖子	neck
喉嚨	throat	手	hand
手臂	arm	手指	finger
肩	shoulder	胃	stomach
肚子	belly	腿	leg
腳	foot	腳趾	toe
腳踝	ankle	膝蓋	knee
腰	waist	胸	chest
臉	face		

【最常用的旅行句】

01 我的腳痛到我快受不了。

My leg is killing me.

02 我的胸腔很不舒服。

I felt a great deal of pain in my chest.

03 我左腳膝蓋很痛。

My left knee hurts a lot.

痛覺說明

傷口癢癢的怎麼説？傷口很刺痛，又要怎麼講？這些精確的描述記下來，醫生和藥師更能對症下藥！

【常見生字】

頭痛	headache	胃痛	stomachache
牙痛	toothache	腹痛	tummy ache
心痛	heartache	耳朵痛	earache
喉嚨痛	sore throat	抽筋	cramp
疼痛	pain	刺痛的	stinging
火燒感的	burning	發癢的	itching

【最常用的旅行句】

01 我頭痛。

I have a headache.

02 我喉嚨痛，是不是感冒了？

I have a sore throat now. Does it mean I got a cold?

03 我的傷口好癢。這樣正常嗎？

The wound is itching. Is this normal?

04 我的傷口很刺痛，我覺得很不舒服。

The stinging wound is hurting me.

：你要會說的一句話　　：你會聽到的問／答　　 **MP3** Track ▶ 106

[Must be...] 這個時候最需要的一句話！

我覺得手臂斷了。　　**迷你句** I broke something.

　　　　　　　　　　完整句 I think I broke my arms.

我們得送您去醫院。
We have to get you to the hospital.

我的肩膀脫臼了。　　**迷你句** My shoulder is out.

　　　　　　　　　　完整句 I dislocated my shoulder.

我去叫救護車。
I will call the ambulance.

我只是擦傷。　　　　**迷你句** Only some scratches.

　　　　　　　　　　完整句 I just have some scratches.

我有一些OK繃。
I have some band-aids.

我不小心切到手
指。　　　　　　　　**迷你句** I accidentally cut it.

　　　　　　　　　　完整句 I cut my finger accidentally.

我想我們得先止血。
I think we need to stop the bleeding first.

我踩空樓梯撞到
頭。　　　　　　　　**迷你句** I bumped my head on the stairs.

　　　　　　　　　　完整句 I fell off the stairs and bumped my
　　　　　　　　　　　　　　 head.

您有受傷嗎？
Are you injured?

😮 他昏過去了。　　　**迷你句** He passed out.

　　　　　　　　　　完整句 I think he passed out.

👂 有人知道怎麼做CPR嗎？
Does anyone know how to perform CPR?

😮 她的雙腿嚴重受傷。　**迷你句** She has seriously hurt her legs.

　　　　　　　　　　完整句 She suffered serious injuries to the legs.

👂 我去找人來幫忙。
I will get someone to help.

😮 請快叫救護車。　　　**迷你句** Call 911.

　　　　　　　　　　完整句 Can anyone call the ambulance?

👂 我用手機打了。
I called on my cell phone.

😮 我跌倒把腳踝扭傷了。　**迷你句** I twisted my ankle.

　　　　　　　　　　完整句 I fell and twisted my ankles.

👂 我可以讓你搭便車到醫院去。
I can give you a ride to the hospital.

[Vocabulary] 生字不用另外查字典！

01 手臂 arm

02 斷 break

03 醫院 hospital

04 肩膀 shoulder

05 脫臼 dislocate

06 救護車 ambulance

07 擦傷 scratch

08 OK繃 band-aid

09 手指 finger

10 止血 stop the blood

11 撞到頭 bump the head

12 受傷 injure

各種外傷説明

出門在外，難免會遇到小狀況，身體也可能會受傷。萬一不小心有了皮肉傷，記得趕快到藥局買藥或找藥師盡快處理，以防傷口加劇。把下面的常見傷痛記下來，尋找藥品、找醫生處理就可以最快、最輕鬆！

【常見生字】

手臂斷了	break one's arm	肩膀脱臼	dislocate one's shoulder
擦傷	graze	切到手指	cut the finger
撞到頭	bump the head	燙傷	scald
燒傷	burn	割傷	cut
瘀青	bruise	肌肉拉傷	hot pepper

【最常用的旅行句】

01 從樓梯上摔下來，手臂摔斷了。

I broke my arm when I fell down the stairs.

02 我洗菜刀的時候切到手指。

I cut my finger when I was washing the kitchen knife.

03 今天早上喝茶時燙到舌頭。

I burned my tongue when I was drinking hot this morning.

各種常見症狀

 逛地球旅遊專欄

【常見生字】

嘔吐	vomit	失眠	insomnia
便秘	constipation	腹瀉	diarrhea
耳鳴	ringing in ears	胃潰瘍	gastric ulcer
腸胃炎	enterogastritis	偏頭痛	migraine
蕁麻疹	urticaria	水痘	chicken pox
流感	flu	咽炎	pharyngitis
砂眼	trachoma	中耳炎	tympanitis
口腔潰瘍	dental ulcer	肺炎	pneumonia
肝炎	hepatitis	中風	stroke
高血壓	hypertension	心臟病	heart disease

【最常用的旅行句】

01 我一直耳鳴，很不舒服。

I've got ringing in ears for a while. It don't feel very good.

02 這會不會是中風的症狀？

Would it be a stroke symptom?

03 妳有拉肚子的藥嗎？

Do you have medicine for diarrhea?

03 去醫院

🗣️：你要會說的一句話　👂：你會聽到的問／答　 **MP3** Track ▶ 107

[Must be...] 這個時候最需要的一句話！

🗣️ 我得去看醫生。　　　**迷你句** I need a doctor.
　　　　　　　　　　　完整句 I need to see a doctor.

👂 發生什麼事了。
What happened?

🗣️ 我有旅遊保健。　　　**迷你句** I have insurance.
　　　　　　　　　　　完整句 I have travel health insurance.

👂 您的健保編號是？
What is your health insurance number?

🗣️ 我對阿斯匹靈過敏。　**迷你句** I am allergic.
　　　　　　　　　　　完整句 I am allergic to Aspirin.

👂 好的，還有什麼嗎？
Ok, anything else?

🗣️ 請問我要去哪裡領藥？　**迷你句** Where to get the medication?
　　　　　　　　　　　　完整句 Where can I pick up my medication?

👂 您要到藥局去。
You have to go to the pharmacy.

🗣️ 請問我要去哪裡拿處方籤？　**迷你句** I want to get the prescription.
　　　　　　　　　　　　　完整句 Where can I get the prescription?

👂 您可以到那個窗口去領處方籤。
You can get your prescription at that window.

302

請問我的保險有涵蓋醫療嗎？
迷你句 Is medication covered?
完整句 Does my insurance policy cover the medication?

是的，您的觀光包含在保險內。
Yes, your visit is covered by your insurance policy.

我需要會講中文的醫生。
迷你句 I need a Chinese doctor.
完整句 I need a doctor who can speak Chinese.

林醫生會說中文。
Doctor Lin can speak Chinese.

請問我需要動手術嗎？
迷你句 Do I need surgery?
完整句 Do I need an operation?

我們得先照張X光。
We have to take an X-ray first.

我想我需要掛急診。
迷你句 I need an emergency appointment.
完整句 I think I need an emergency appointment.

可以告訴我您的病情嗎？
Can you tell me what is wrong with you?

[Vocabulary] 生字不用另外查字典！

01 醫生 doctor
02 發生 happen
05 阿斯匹林 Aspirin
06 對......過敏 be allergic to
07 領藥 pick up my medication
08 藥局 pharmacy
09 處方籤 prescription
10 手術 surgery
11 X光 X-ray
12 急診 emergency appointment
03 旅遊保險 travel health insurance

問診常用問答

先知道醫生會怎麼說，要怎麼詢問醫護人員，就算身體不舒服，也不會再緊張！

【醫生最常説】

· 你怎麼了？
  What's wrong with you?
· 你感覺怎麼樣？
  How do you feel?
· 感覺還好嗎？
  Do you feel well?
· 你沒事吧？
  Are you OK?
· 感覺好點了嗎？
  Do you feel better?

【旅人跟醫生説】

· 我的手臂很痛。
  My arm hurts so bad.
· 我頭很暈。
  I feel quite dizzy.
· 我最近沒有胃口。
  I've had no appetite recently.

· 我該吃什麼藥？
  What medicine should I take?
· 我覺得有一天天好轉。
  I feel much better day by day.

【旅人問醫護人員】

· 請問在哪裡掛號？
  Where can I register?
· 急診室怎麼走？
  How to get the emergency room?
· 請問這裡是小兒科診所嗎？
  Is this the Pediatric clinic?
· 我找不到手術室。
  I can't find the operating room.
· 請問拿藥的地方是在二樓嗎？
  Is the medicine room on the second floor?

如果在國外不舒服，又還不需要去看醫生，那可以到當地藥房買一些成藥。以下是常見成藥的藥品名稱。

【常見生字】

止痛藥	pain killer	解酒藥	anti-alcoholic drug
阿司匹靈	aspirin	維他命C	vitamin C
咳嗽糖漿	cough syrup	痘痘軟膏	acne ointment
眼藥水	eye drop	止瀉藥	anti-diarrheal
止癢藥	anti-pruritic	消炎藥	anti-inflammatory

【最常用的旅行句】

01 滴完眼藥水後，請閉眼一分鐘。

Keep your eyes closed after using the eye drop.

02 你吃幾顆維他命C，應該就會比較好了。

You would feel better after taking a few Vitamin C.

03 我有點不舒服。我覺得我需要咳嗽糖漿。

I don't feel very good. I think I need some cough syrup.

👄：你要會説的一句話　🔊：你會聽到的問／答　**MP3** Track ▶ 108

[Must be...] 這個時候最需要的一句話！

👄 請問藥劑部在哪裡？

迷你句 Where is the pharmacy?

完整句 Where is the pharmacy department?

🔊 就在轉角處。
It is right at the corner.

👄 我需要一些止痛藥。

迷你句 I need pain killers.

完整句 We have to get some pain killers.

🔊 這種止痛藥是非處方藥。
This pain killer is non-prescription medicine.

👄 請問你有咳嗽糖漿嗎？

迷你句 Cough syrup?

完整句 Do you carry any cough syrup?

🔊 您想要哪種口味？
Which flavor do you want?

👄 我正在找感冒發炎藥。

迷你句 Something for cold sores.

完整句 I am looking for a cold sore medicine.

🔊 請小心，這藥不適合6歲以下的小孩。
Be careful, this is not good for children under 6.

👄 我需要抗生素藥膏。

迷你句 An antibiotic cream, please.

完整句 I need some antibiotic ointment.

🔊 在這裡，用之前請先閱讀用藥説明。
Here you are, read the drug description before use.

請問我要在哪裡買止痛藥？

迷你句 Where to buy pain killers?

完整句 Where could I buy the pain killer?

在櫃檯那邊可以買。
It is over the counter.

請問有沒有解酒藥？

迷你句 Is there something that can alleviate a hangover?

完整句 Do you have anything to alleviate a hangover?

有，您需要多少？
Yes, how many do you need?

請問維他命C多少錢？

迷你句 How much is it?

完整句 How much is vitamin C?

一罐35美元。
It is $35 a bottle.

可以幫我包紮傷口嗎？

迷你句 Could you bandage it?

完整句 Can you bandage the wound?

沒問題，請跟我來。
Sure, please follow me.

[Words to Use] 替換字放空格，一句多用!!

● 請問我要在哪裡買_____？
Where can I buy some _____?

01 止痛藥 **pain killers**

02 解酒藥 **anti-alcoholic drugs**

03 阿斯匹靈 **aspirin**

04 抗生素藥膏 **antibiotic ointments**

05 咳嗽糖漿 **coughing syrup**

06 維他命C **vitamin C**

05 失竊與搶劫

👄：你要會說的一句話　👂：你會聽到的問／答

[Must be...] 這個時候最需要的一句話！

👄 我的袋子被偷了。　　**迷你句** It was stolen.
　　　　　　　　　　　完整句 My bag is stolen.

👂 袋子裡有任何重要物品嗎？
Are there any expensive things in your bag?

👄 有人偷了我的手機。　**迷你句** My cell phone was stolen.
　　　　　　　　　　　完整句 Someone stole my cell phone.

👂 您確定手機真的被偷了嗎？
Are you sure your phone was stolen?

👄 我的車子被破門而入。　**迷你句** They broke in.
　　　　　　　　　　　　完整句 My car got broken into.

👂 車子裡有什麼東西不見了嗎？
Is there anything missing from your car?

👄 我的自行車本來在這裡，現在卻不見了。
　迷你句 It was right here before.
　完整句 My bike was here but now it is gone.

👂 你應該到警局報案。
You should report it to the police.

👄 我的筆電不見了。　**迷你句** My laptop is missing.
　　　　　　　　　　完整句 I can't find my notebook.

👂 你有發現是誰拿走了筆電嗎？
Did you find out who took your laptop?

他向我勒索1000美金。
迷你句 He extorted me.
完整句 He extorted $1000 form me.

他長什麼樣子？
What does he looks like?

他騎車從背後搶走我的皮包。
迷你句 He took my bag from my back.
完整句 He was riding a motorcycle and took my bag form the back.

有任何證人嗎？
Are there any witnesses?

我的錢包被扒走了。
迷你句 A pickpocket stole my wallet.
完整句 My wallet was taken by a pickpocket.

你有看到他的臉嗎？
Did you see his face?

我的手錶差一點被偷走。
迷你句 It was almost stolen.
完整句 That thief almost steal my watch.

請小心您的隨身物品。
Be careful with your personal belongings.

[Vocabulary] 生字不用另外查字典！

01 袋子 bag
02 重要物品 expensive things
03 偷盜 steal
04 手機 phone
05 破門而入 break into
06 車子 car
07 自行車 bike
08 警局 police station
09 筆電 laptop
10 勒索 extort
11 摩托車 motorcycle
12 證人 witness

06 遺失物品

：你要會説的一句話　　：你會聽到的問／答

[Must be...] 這個時候最需要的一句話！

我找不到我的皮夾。
迷你句 I have lost my wallet.
完整句 I can't find my wallet.

您所有的證件都遺失了嗎？
Did you lose all your IDs?

請問你有看到我的背包嗎？
迷你句 Where is my backpack?
完整句 Have you seen my backpack?

您可能把背包遺忘在某處了。
You might have forgotten your bag somewhere.

我的相機不見了。
迷你句 My camera is gone.
完整句 My camera is missing.

我在那邊的長椅上找到這台相機。
I found this camera on the bench over there.

我想我把手機留在餐廳裡了。
迷你句 I left my cell phone in the restaurant.
完整句 I think I left my camera in the restaurant.

那麼你最好快點回去拿。
Then you better hurry back to get it.

我的信用卡掉了。
迷你句 My card is missing.
完整句 I lost my credit card.

仔細找找您的皮夾吧。
Look in your wallet closely.

請馬上幫我把信用卡作廢。
迷你句 Please cancel it now.
完整句 Please cancel my credit card immediately.

我會馬上處理。
I will take care of it right away.

請問哪裡有失物招領處？
迷你句 Where is the lost and found office?
完整句 Is there a lost and found office nearby?

在旅客服務中心裡有。
There is one at the Passenger Service Center.

我需要填寫財物遺失單。
迷你句 I need a Lost Property Form.
完整句 I need to fill out the Lost Property Form.

您掉了什麼東西？
What did you lose?

這是我的個人連絡資料。
迷你句 This is my name card.
完整句 Here is my personal information.

我們一找到就會馬上通知您。
We will contact you as soon as we find it.

[Words to Use] 替換字放空格，一句多用!!

● 請問你有看到我的_____嗎？
Have you seen my _____?

01 背包 **backpack**

02 皮夾 **wallet**

03 相機 **camera**

04 手機 **cell phone**

05 信用卡 **credit card**

06 皮包 **purse**

👄：你要會說的一句話　🔊：你會聽到的問／答　　**MP3** Track ▶ 111

[Must be...] 這個時候最需要的一句話！

👄 我的護照掉了。
　　迷你句 I lost my passport.
　　完整句 My passport is missing.

🔊 您應該馬上到警察局去。
　　You should go to the police station immediately.

👄 請問我可以馬上拿到新護照嗎？
　　迷你句 Can I get a new one right away?
　　完整句 Can I get another passport immediately?

🔊 恐怕沒有這麼簡單。
　　I am afraid it won't be too easy.

👄 請問補發的時間需要多久？
　　迷你句 When will I be able to get another one?
　　完整句 How long will it take to get it reissued?

🔊 我不確定。
　　I am not sure.

👄 請問台灣辦事處在哪裡？
　　迷你句 Where is the Taiwan Representative Office?
　　完整句 I can't find the Taiwan Representative Office.

🔊 請問您有地圖嗎？
　　Do you have map?

👄 我找不到我的護照。
　　迷你句 I can't find it.
　　完整句 I have no idea where my passport is.

🔊 您最後一次看到它是什麼時候？
　　When did you last see it?

😮 請問我應該通知誰？

迷你句 Who should I find?

完整句 Who should I inform?

👂 您應該帶著警局筆錄到台灣辦事處去。
You should take the police report to the Taiwan Representive Office.

😮 請問有人撿到我的護照嗎？

迷你句 Anyone find my passport?

完整句 Has anyone turned in my passport?

👂 抱歉，我們還是沒找到您的護照。
Sorry, we still can find your passport.

😮 我不確定我是在哪裡掉的。

迷你句 I don't know where I lost it.

完整句 I am not sure where I lost it.

👂 您今天早上去了哪些地方？
Where did you go this morning?

😮 有人搶走了我的護照。

迷你句 My passport was stolen.

完整句 Someone robbed my passport.

👂 您有看到他的臉嗎？
Did you see his face?

[Things to Know] 一定要知道的**旅行常識**

　　出國前一定要留一份護照影本，護照與錢物最好分開放。如果護照遺失，首先應該向當地警方報警，報案資料可以作為日後補辦護照、證明遊客在該國合法入境居留的憑證之一。報案後，要立即向我國在當地辦事處報告，並提供護照影本，方便補辦。其間使館會發給短期旅行者一個臨時的旅行證件，方便旅客回國。

[Must be...] 這個時候最需要的一句話！

👄 我的兒子不見了。　**迷你句** My son is missing.
　　　　　　　　　　完整句 I can't find my son.

👂 您最後一次在哪裡什麼時候看到他的？
When and where did you last see him?

👄 我應該要去警局報　**迷你句** Should I call the police?
　　案嗎？　　　　　**完整句** Should I report to the police?

👂 請冷靜一點。
Please calm down.

👄 他從市區回來的途　**迷你句** He was missing when we got back
　　中不見了。　　　　　　　　from downtown.
　　　　　　　　　　完整句 He was missing on the way home
　　　　　　　　　　　　　　from downtown.

👂 他長什麼樣子？
What does he looks like?

👄 我的小孩被綁架　**迷你句** He was kidnapped.
　　了。　　　　　　**完整句** My kid was kidnapped.

👂 您確定嗎？
Are you sure about that?

👄 她穿著一件紅色洋　**迷你句** She's in a red dress with a ponytail.
　　裝，綁著馬尾。　　**完整句** She is wearing a red dress with a
　　　　　　　　　　　　　　ponytail.

👂 我們會幫您找到她的。
We will help you to find her.

請問最近的警局在哪裡？
迷你句 Where is the police station?
完整句 Where is the nearest police station?

直走到最底就會看到了。
Go straight to the end of the road and you will find it.

請問你有看到我的女兒嗎？
迷你句 Did you see a little girl?
完整句 Did you see my daughter?

抱歉，我沒有看到。
Sorry, I didn't see any little girls.

我的小孩走失了。
迷你句 My child is lost.
完整句 My child went missing.

他就在那邊。
He is right over there.

我不知道該怎麼辦。
迷你句 What should I do?
完整句 I don't know what to do.

別擔心，我幫您報警。
Don't worry, I will call the police.

[Vocabulary] 生字不用另外查字典！

01 兒子 son
02 警局 police
03 冷靜 calm down
04 市區 downtown
05 途中 on the way
06 綁架 kidnap
07 紅色洋裝 red dress
08 女兒 daughter
09 走失 lost
10 報警 call the police
11 最近的 nearest
12 馬尾 ponytail

 **09** 天災

🗣：你要會說的一句話 🗨：你會聽到的問／答 **MP3** Track ▶ 113

[Must be...] 這個時候最需要的一句話！

🗣 大樓好像失火了。　**迷你句** Is that a fire?

完整句 It looks like there is a fire in that building.

🗨 我來報警。
I will call 911.

🗣 有地震。　**迷你句** Earthquake!

完整句 It is an earthquake.

🗨 請保持鎮定。
Please remain calm.

🗣 街道都被水淹了。　**迷你句** The streets are underwater.

完整句 The major street are all flooded.

🗨 我們必須等待救援。
We will have to wait for the rescue team.

🗣 請幫我們打911。　**迷你句** Call 911!

完整句 Please call 911 for us.

🗨 有人受傷嗎？
Is anyone hurt?

🗣 天氣預報說會有龍捲風。　**迷你句** A tornado is coming.

完整句 The weather report says that there is going to be a tornado.

🗨 進一步指示前請勿亂跑。
Please don't go anywhere until further instructions.

我的房間著火了！

迷你句 There is a fire!

完整句 My room is on fire.

還有人在裡面嗎？
Is anyone still inside?

我被困在電梯裡了。

迷你句 I am stuck.

完整句 I am stuck in the elevator.

好的，我把門鋸開。
Ok, I will saw the door open.

我的房子被水沖走了。

迷你句 It was washed away.

完整句 My house was washed away by the flood.

大家都還好嗎？
Is everybody okay?

氣象預報員說明天會颳大風。

迷你句 There will be strong winds tomorrow.

完整句 The weatherman said that there will be a strong wind tomorrow.

您明天最好不要出門。
You'd better not go out tomorrow.

[Vocabulary] 生字不用另外查字典！

01 失火 on fire

02 地震 earthquake

03 報警 call 911

04 鎮定 calm

05 街道 street

06 水災 flood

07 救援 rescue

08 等待 wait for

09 受傷 hurt

10 龍捲風 tornado

11 電梯 elevator

12 颱大風 a strong wind

旅遊常用句型 + 超多替換字，套入馬上用！

身體不舒服

●我已經 _____ 兩天了。

I've got a/an _____ for two days.

01 頭痛 headache 　　　　　02 胃痛 stomachache
03 牙痛 toothache 　　　　　04 背痛 backache
05 喉嚨痛 sore throat 　　　　06 胸口痛 chest ache

受傷

●我不小心 _____ 我的手臂了。

I accidentally _____ my arm.

01 (刀)割傷 cut 　　　　　02 (火)燒傷 burned
03 (沸水)燙傷 scalded 　　　04 扭傷 twisted
05 拉傷 strained 　　　　　06 擦傷、刮破 scraped

去醫院

● 我的 _____ 最近越來越嚴重。

My _____ is getting worse these days.

01 咳嗽 cough 　　　　　02 胃灼熱 heartburn
03 流鼻水 runny nose 　　　04 皮膚過敏 skin allergy
05 鼻塞 stuffy nose 　　　　06 偏頭痛 migraine

天災

● 因為 _____，我們必須中斷行程。

We have to break off our trip because of the _____.

01 暴風雨 storm
02 洪水 flood
03 地震 earthquake
04 海嘯 tsunami
05 颶風 hurricane
06 颱風 typhoon

被搶劫

● 那男子攻擊我，並拿走我的 _____。

The man attacked me and took my _____.

01 項鍊 necklace
02 手提包 handbag
03 手錶 wallet
04 現金 cash
05 皮包 purse
06 手機 cellphone

去藥房

● 可以推薦我一款 _____ 嗎？

Can you recommend me a/an _____?

01 消炎止痛藥膏 anti-inflammatory pain relief cream
02 止癢藥膏 anti-itch cream
03 防曬油 suntan lotion
04 護手霜 hand cream
05 燒燙傷藥膏 ointment for scalds and burns
06 痠痛貼布 pain relief patch

緊急狀況時的應變方法

如果在外遇到搶劫，要記得對方通常只要錢或值錢的商品，請務必鎮定把錢財交出，以保自身安全。要去治安較差的國家，也可以在口袋裡放小額的金錢，不要身上沒有半毛錢，這樣遇劫時可能會惹搶匪生氣。若要就醫，也一定要先知道自己對哪些藥物過敏，事先告訴醫生，也可以在出發前先請醫生開證明，好在國外快速告訴當地醫生自己的情況。在國外遇到緊急狀況，因為身處異地，請更加小心謹慎。以下是遇到緊急情況時，你可以找的人或單位：

01【警察】

大多數國家的警察都有責任幫助你，所以請大力地向警察求助。但是有些國家的警察會對旅人敲詐賺外快，所以在尋求協助時，要記得不要太快把護照正本或影本交到對方手中，因為護照就像我們在國外的身分證，如果身分證出了問題，後續處理非常麻煩。

02【醫院】

在許多國家，看醫生是非常昂貴的事情。記得要先在台灣辦理保險，假如出國時身體不舒服或受傷了，就不會因為高額的醫藥費而遲遲不在國外就醫，壞了身體。

03【駐地外交人員】

在國外遇到緊急狀況，不管是簽證、受傷或是任何意外，都可以詢問駐在當地的外交人員，他們會樂意幫忙，政府機關也會幫忙通知你的家人。出發前應先上網查詢目的地國家的台灣辦事處，好在狀況發生時，第一時間可以找到援手。

附錄
不可不看的
旅遊資訊！

01 買機票

【購買機票】

訂購機票時，較少直接向航空公司購買，反而選擇旅行社或票務中心，因為往往可以拿到較便宜的價格。購買機票時最好避開價格較高的寒、暑假旺季。若一定要在旺季出發，建議提早三至四個月訂購。

【機票使用時間】

機票使用期限，普遍為半年、3個月、1個月，有的甚至不滿一個月。時間越短通常越便宜。另一種則為長達一年的年票。年票的價格往往較貴，也較無折扣，但是機票的更改彈性較大，可隨時更改起程回程時間及日期。越便宜的機票，通常限制越多，需注意。

【購買機票考慮事項】

長程旅行勞心又勞神，飛行時間會影響機票票價。直航飛行時間短，但票價較貴。非直航之班機雖然票價便宜，但通常時間點較差，且要注意轉機的時間是否充裕，並避免轉機次數過多的班機，以減少行李遺失之風險。機票訂購完成後，應先檢查機票上的姓名，是否與護照上的英文拼音姓名完全符合，機票上的護照號碼、班機時間和目的地也應正確無誤。在搭機前三天記得再向航空公司確認，確保行程無誤。

【電子簽證國家或地區】

前往下列國家前，只要事先通過上網申請等方式，即可以電子簽證出入境。詳細申請辦法與須知請逕自前往外交部網站查詢。

國家	可停留天數
澳大利亞、加彭	3個月
象牙海岸	90天
印度、菲律賓、卡達、土耳其	30天
巴林	14天

02 落地簽證國家／地區

持台灣護照至這些地方旅遊，不需事前申請簽證，可以在入境時辦理落地簽證、即時生效，入境旅遊。各國申請落地簽證所需的資料、金額、標準各有不同，請逕自前往外交部網站查詢，公告內容以各國法律為準。

01【亞太地區】

國家	可停留天數
索羅門群島	90天
巴布亞紐幾內亞	60天
孟加拉、柬埔寨、馬爾地夫、馬紹爾群島、尼泊爾、帛琉、東帝汶、吐瓦魯、萬那杜	30天
泰國	15天
汶萊	14天
寮國	14-30天

02【亞西地區】

國家	可停留天數
亞美尼亞	120天
塔吉克	45天
約旦、哈薩克、黎巴嫩、阿曼	30天
伊朗、吉爾吉斯	15-30天

03【美洲地區】

國家	可停留天數
巴拉圭	90天

04【非洲地區】

國家／地區	可停留天數
坦尚尼亞、聖海蓮娜、烏干達	90天
吉布地	1個月以上
維德角、埃及、衣索比亞、馬達加斯加、馬拉威、茅利塔尼亞、莫三比克、喀麥隆、聖多美普林西比、塞席爾	30天
布吉納法索、賴比瑞亞	7-30天
多哥	7天

＊以上簽證資料來源：外交部網站 http://www.boca.gov.tw

03 免簽證國家／地區

現在免簽證的國家有很多，以下是外交部 2016 年公布的免簽證國家列表。以下名單僅供參考，實際簽證待遇狀況、入境各國應備文件及條件，可參考領事事務局網站查詢，惟仍以各該國之法令為準。

01【亞太地區】

國家／地區	可停留天數
斐濟	120天
日本、韓國、紐西蘭、新喀里多尼亞、法屬玻里尼西亞、瓦利斯群島和富圖納群島	90天
關島	90天/45天
北馬里安納群島	45天
庫克群島	31天
印尼、吉里巴斯、澳門、馬來西亞、密克羅尼西亞聯邦、諾魯、紐埃、薩摩亞、新加坡	30天

02【亞西地區】

國家	可停留天數
以色列	90天

03【美洲地區】

國家／地區	可停留天數
福克蘭群島	連續24個月期間內至多可獲核累計停留12個月
蒙哲臘	6個月

國家／地區	可停留天數
加拿大、巴拿馬、祕魯	180天
多米尼克	3個月
美國、貝里斯、百慕達、波奈、智利、哥倫比亞、厄瓜多、薩爾瓦多、格瑞那達、瓜地洛普、圭亞那、海地、宏都拉斯、馬丁尼克、尼加拉瓜、沙巴、聖巴瑟米、聖佑達修斯、聖克里斯多福及尼維斯、聖馬丁、聖皮埃與密克隆群島	90天
聖露西亞	42天
安奎拉、維京群島	1個月
阿魯巴、開曼群島、古巴、古拉索、多明尼加、聖文森、土克凱可群島	30天
瓜地馬拉	30－90天

04【歐洲地區】

國家／地區	可停留天數
申根區：安道爾、奧地利、比利時、捷克、丹麥、愛沙尼亞、丹麥法羅群島、芬蘭、法國、德國、希臘、丹麥格陵蘭島、教廷、匈牙利、冰島、義大利、拉脫維亞、列支敦斯登、立陶宛、盧森堡、馬爾他、摩納哥、荷蘭、挪威、波蘭、葡萄牙、聖馬利諾、斯洛伐克、斯洛維尼亞、西班牙、瑞典、瑞士	左列國家/地區之停留日數合併計算，6個月期間內總計可留至多90天
英國	180天
阿爾巴尼亞、波士尼亞與赫塞哥維納、保加利亞、克羅埃西亞、賽浦勒斯、直布羅陀、愛爾蘭、科索沃、馬其頓、蒙特內哥羅、羅馬尼亞	90天

05【非洲地區】

國家／地區	可停留天數
甘比亞、留尼旺島、索馬利蘭、史瓦濟蘭	90天

＊以上簽證資料來源：外交部網站 http://www.boca.gov.tw

04 英、美、加、紐、澳的簽證

購買機票時,要注意即將前往的國家,是否需要簽證才能入境。雖然現在已有許多國家開放免簽證優惠待遇,但建議出發前應先查詢各國簽證及法規是否有異動,及對以免簽方式入境有無規定。一般國家會要求旅客所持護照要有六個月以上效期,因此也要特別注意個人護照的效期。作廢後的舊護照上的簽證仍未過期,若想與新版護照合併使用,相關規定各國不盡相同,因此出發前應上外交部領事事務局的官方網站查詢。

目前主要英語系國家的旅遊簽證規定如下:

【英國】

免簽可以停留 180 天

【紐西蘭】

免簽可以停留 90 天

【加拿大】

免簽可以停留 180 天

【澳洲】

台灣護照持有人(有國民身分證統一編號),可透過指定旅行社代為申辦,並當場取得一年多次電子簽證,每次可停留3個月。

【美國】

台灣已成為美國免簽證計畫第37個參與國,因此前往美國觀光,不須再耗費大量金錢及時間申請簽證。未來在台灣設籍之中華民國國民,凡持新版晶片護照赴美從事90日以下之商務或觀光旅行,並事先上網申請「旅行授權電子系統(Electronic System for Travel Authorization, ESTA)」取得授權許可,且無其他特殊限制而無法適用者,即可免除預先申請美國B1/B2簽證而直接赴美。

詳細ESTA申請辦法可上美國在台協會官網查詢:http://www.ait.org.tw/

資料來源:
外交部:http://www.mofa.gov.tw/
外交部領事處http://www.boca.gov.tw/

05 長度單位換算

台灣習慣用公分來計算,但外國人則換算成英呎(foot)跟英吋(inch)來計算。在與外國朋友或購物時,若是不清楚對方說的尺寸,就會發生買錯東西,或是會錯意的窘境。

【常用尺碼簡單對照法】

1 英呎(foot)=12英寸(inch)=30.48公分(cm)

1 英呎(foot)=12 英吋〔inch〕

1 英吋〔inch〕=2.54 公分〔cm〕

例如:某人身高 5 呎 3 吋,換算成我們習慣的說法,為 160.02 公分。

【常用尺碼速查表】

公分 (cm)	0.1	1	100	2.54	30.479
英吋 (inch)	0.044	0.394	39.371	1	12
英呎 (foot)	0.003	0.033	3.281	0.083	1

06 重量／體積單位換算

重量攸關郵寄包裹、行李總重量,因此非常重要,對於歐美常用的重量單位不可不知。以下列舉幾種。由於各單位換算後,皆有小數點,在此取四捨五入至小數點第二位。

【常用重量／容量單位簡單對照法】

1 磅 = 0.45 公斤
1 公斤＝2.2 磅
1 盎司＝28.3 公克
1 公克
1 加侖＝8 品脫＝ 4.55 公升

例如:某人體重為 100 磅,那換算成台灣常用説法,就是 45.4 公斤。

【常用重量單位速查表】

公斤	25.00	50.00	75.00	100.00
磅	55.12	110.23	165.34	220.46

07 華氏／攝氏溫度換算

天氣是影響旅行的重要因素之一，若是無法判斷華式溫度，就會誤判天氣，也可能造成形成不愉快。至今只有美國仍主要使用華氏溫標，多數國家使用攝氏溫標。華式的標示為 ℉，攝氏為 ℃。

【華氏－攝氏簡易對照法】

0 ℃（水的冰點）為 32 ℉
100 ℃（水的沸點）為 212 ℉
37 ℃（人體常溫）為 98.6 ℉

例如：美國費城在 12 月 29 號的氣溫為 26.6 ℉，就是約為 -3 ℃。

【華氏－攝氏簡易換算法】

$$℉ = \frac{9}{5}℃ + 32$$

$$℃ = \frac{5}{9}(℉ - 32)$$

【華氏－攝氏換算速查表】

華氏	0	20	32	50	70
攝氏	-17.8	-6.7	0	10	21.1
100	120	150	170	190	212
37.8	48.9	65.6	76.7	87.8	100

08 尺碼換算

各國在鞋子衣物上的測量尺寸及表示方法有所不同，在購買時要多多注意，以免尺寸不合，買回國無法退換。鞋子購買前記得試穿。至於服飾方面，西方人的身材都較東方人來得高大，所以衣服的版型也稍大了一點，可以選擇比自己平常穿的再小一號。

女鞋尺碼表						
歐碼	36	37	38	39	40	41	42
英碼	3.5	4.5	5.5	6.5	7.5	8.5	9.5
美碼	6.5	7.5	8.5	10.5	10.5	11.5	12.5

男鞋尺碼表								
歐碼	39	40	41	42	43	44	45	46	47
英碼	5.5	6.5	7	8	8.5	9.5	10.5	11.5	12
美碼	6	7	7.5	8.5	9	10	11	12	12.5

男服飾尺碼表					
統一碼	XS	S	M	L	XL
歐碼	44	46	48-50	52-54	56-58
英／美碼	34	36	38-40	42-44	46-48

女服飾尺碼表				
統一碼	S	M	L	XL
歐碼	36	38	40	42
英碼	10	12	14	16
美碼	4-6	8-10	12-14	16-18

09 國際證件介紹

出門在外,有些證件不可少,當出國旅遊或唸書時,一定要具備的有:

【國際學生證】

國際學生證(ISIC)即International Student Identity Card,接受申請對象為學生身分,是受聯合國教科文組織(UNESCO)唯一認可的世界唯一國際通用學生證件;此證件有許多的幫助與優惠,如:24小時免費的全球緊急救援和諮詢服務、購買交通票券及租車享有優惠、多數的博物館也可享有優惠。

【國際青年卡】

國際青年卡(IYTC)即International Youth Travel Card。若為非學生身分、未滿 26 歲之青年,皆可辦理。全球有 50 多個國家、共 200 多處的服務機構,一樣可享有在購買交通票券、觀光風景區門票上的折扣。

【YH國際青年旅舍卡】

全球國際青年旅舍採會員制,僅提供持有 YH 卡會員入住,以服務全球各地自助旅行背包客及提供一個清潔安全的住宿環境為目的。此卡在購買機票、搭乘巴士或租車享有更多的優惠;在購買如博物館的文化票券、異國美食餐廳、購買旅遊保險、旅遊用品、參加當地的旅遊行程等,也都可享有折扣。申辦資格無年齡限制,是一張只要擁有旅遊熱情的心,皆可申請的卡片。

【國際駕照】

要在異國開車旅遊,需先申請國際駕照。國際駕照手續簡便,申請當日即可取照,效期與國內駕照相同。只要備齊相關證件,到各地監理所及填寫申請表格,即可當場領取國際駕照。申辦國際駕照時,要注意欲前往之國家是否承認台灣國際駕照。國際駕照有效期限最長三年,若台灣的駕照有效期限低於三年,則以台灣駕照的有效期限為準。

10 旅遊行前安全須知

出門旅遊，安全至上！行前多花點時間做好功課，避免不必要的麻煩，才可以玩得開心、玩得安心。

【行前準備】

· 複印旅遊行程：留給台灣親友，必要時可聯絡。

· 查閱出國旅遊資訊＆旅外急難救助網頁：至外交部網站，瞭解目的地旅遊安全資訊。另可下載「中華民國駐外館通訊錄」，內有各駐外館處之急難救助電話。外交部緊急聯絡中心的免付費專線：**800-0885-0885**。

· 海外保險不可少：在先進國家，通常外國人的醫療費用都極為昂貴，此時若有海外醫療險就可幫助不少；另外也有旅遊不便險，針對旅行中班機延誤及行李延誤、遺失所作的理賠。

· 複印兩份護照、電子機票、駕照、信用卡資料：一份可隨身攜帶，一份可留給台灣的親友。

【行李裡該有的東西】

· 簡便行李：行李應簡便為主，以利行動方便；在每件行李上都寫上名字、地址、電話避免遺失。

· 國際電話卡：你需要一張國際電話卡，並事先查詢如何從外國撥打電話回台灣

· 證件照2～3張＆護照基本資料頁影本：以便護照不見或被偷時，可迅速申請補發。

· 常用藥包：可至家庭診所拿取基本的出國常用藥，以備不時之需，若有醫生開立的處方箋或證明也應隨身攜帶，減少通關時遭遇的麻煩。

資料來源：外交部領事事務局
http://www.boca.gov.tw

11 交各國朋友的禁忌

跟不同國家的人交朋友，是旅行中的一大樂事。每個國家文化不同，我們雖然不需要完全迎合別人的文化風俗，但是若在事前先注意到不同朋友的喜好，貼心的你就可以讓旅途更開心。

【説話時要注意】

在不同國籍、不同語言的朋友面前，説話請盡量以大家都聽得懂的語言為主，盡量不要在大家面前，用中文與自己的朋友聊天。各國國情不同，台灣對宗教非常包容，但是出了國門，就盡量不要提及宗教，因為可能引起兩位不同宗教信仰的朋友的爭端。喜歡旅遊是不分年齡的，在旅途中你可能會遇到許多不同年紀的朋友，但還不是很熟的時候，為了他人隱私，盡量不要詢問年齡。

【飲食上要注意】

遇到不喜歡的食物時，請不要面露嫌惡，只要不吃即可。太劇烈的討厭反應，就像我們看見外國人討厭豬血糕、臭豆腐還有雞腳時嚇到一樣，對當地人來說的確是某種程度的不禮貌。在吃東西時，盡量不要浪費食物，要盡量把東西吃完，或是依自己的食量點餐。在去到珍惜食物的國家時，浪費食物也是對當地人的不尊重。

【購物時要注意】

在台灣，我們喜歡在買完東西後，跟身邊的朋友比價錢，看誰買得最划算，算是一種消遣；但是在國外，跟朋友比價錢可能被認為是一種競爭，會被認為很好勝、難相處，所以如果跟還不熟的朋友購物後，也不要太積極地跟對方詢價，才是尊重別人。

訂了機票，就出發！
旅行不能忘記帶的英語百寶袋（暢銷增訂版）

旅遊英文≠考試，英文不合文法也沒關係，老外聽得懂最重要！

作　　者	黃文姝、溫志暉
顧　　問	曾文旭
總 編 輯	黃若璇
編輯總監	耿文國
特約編輯	蔡文宜
美術編輯	李澤恩
文字校對	黃姿瑋
法律顧問	北辰著作權事務所

再版 **3** 刷	2018 年 4 月
出　　版	凱信企業集團 - 凱信企業管理顧問有限公司
電　　話	（02）2752-5618
傳　　真	（02）2752-5619
地　　址	106 台北市大安區忠孝東路四段 250 號 11 樓之 1

定　　價	新台幣 299 元 / 港幣 100 元
產品內容	1 書 +1 旅遊情境句 MP3

總 經 銷	商流文化事業有限公司
地　　址	235 新北市中和區中正路 752 號 8 樓
電　　話	（02）2228-8841
傳　　真	（02）2228-6939

港澳地區總經銷	和平圖書有限公司
地　　址	香港柴灣嘉業街 12 號百樂門大廈 17 樓
電　　話	（852）2804-6687
傳　　真	（852）2804-6409

國家圖書館出版品預行編目資料

訂了機票，就出發！旅行不能忘記帶的英語百寶袋
/ 黃文姝、溫志暉合著 . -- 再版 .
－ 台北市 : 凱信 , 2016.06
面 ; 公分
ISBN 978-986-5916-81-7（平裝附光碟片）

1. 英語 2. 旅遊 3. 會話

805.188　　　　　　　　　　　105009487

凱信企管

用對的方法充實自己，
讓人生變得更美好！

凱信企管

用對的方法充實自己，
讓人生變得更美好！